Foul Weather

Mary Ann Farron

Enjoy the novel!

Foul Weather

Mary Anne Larson

Copyright © 2000 by Mary Anne Larson.

Library of Congress Number:		00-193523
ISBN #:	Hardcover	0-7388-5856-0
	Softcover	0-7388-5855-2

All rights reserved. No part of this book may be reproduced or transmitted in any form or by any means, electronic or mechanical, including photocopying, recording, or by any information storage and retrieval system, without permission in writing from the copyright owner.

This is a work of fiction. Names, characters, places and incidents either are the product of the author's imagination or are used fictitiously, and any resemblance to any actual persons, living or dead, events, or locales is entirely coincidental.

This book was printed in the United States of America.

To order additional copies of this book, contact:
Xlibris Corporation
1-888-7-XLIBRIS
www.Xlibris.com
Orders@Xlibris.com

The author lives on the Oregon coast with her husband, Robert, two dogs and a cat, in an area very like the village in her story.

She is currently at work on the sequel to Foul Weather. And sometimes when she writes, if it is that stormy time of year, the wind rattles the windows and fog creeps cold and silent down from the cape. Then, from the corner of her eye, she catches a glimpse of someone standing in the ancient woods, ready to be included in the next scene.

DEDICATION

*To my much cherished family near and far,
especially Erick and Freda who live forever in our hearts.*

*To the Lemonade Ladies, old friends,
I lift my glass to you.*

*To the real-life Spinner,
my beloved husband who's always there for me.*

And, of course, to my friend in the swing

ACKNOWLEDGMENTS

I AM GRATEFUL to the following individuals for sharing their special knowledge with me:

My writing friends in Newport and Lincoln City, especially, those wise teachers, Chantall Van Wey and Julie Reynolds-Otrugman. All of you, your encouragement and enthusiasm sustained me through this lengthy endeavor.

Barbara Coyle, the first to edit the finished manuscript, your input was invaluable. As I rewrote, I knew you were right on.

My copy readers for picking up those numerous mistakes, God love 'em. Kudos to Elaine and David Boerger, Bill and Marilyn Durst, Bernetta Hanson, and Sweetjack Fallin.

Marilyn Durst, the artist among us and my creative consultant.

Penultimately, to Betty Jane Andersen, who was to write the most inspirational last chapter of them all.

And, to Robert Gerke, Milwaukee's best kept secret, my special guy who likes movies, for all the help on those action scenes and his superb photography.

AUTHOR'S NOTE

ON THE OREGON coast, there are places called by the names used in this book, but certain geographical and historical liberties have been taken by the author. And, although the author does have a group of friends called the Lemonade Ladies, all of the characters and events in this novel are purely fiction.

Thunder and lightning. Enter three witches

Fair is foul, and foul is fair:
Hover through the fog and filthy air.

Macbeth by Wm. Shakespeare
(1. 1. 11-12)

FOUL WEATHER

Early March of 1778.

Off the cape, a British galleon plunged and rolled in the stormy seas while the explorer, Captain James Cook, tried to steady himself on the slippery deck.

The ship had been attempting land for several days, but the captain's spy glass could not penetrate the heavy fog that hid the shore.

"This is a place of foul weather," the captain growled. "We shall call it Cape Foulweather and the land beyond, New Albion."

They were anchored just off the site of our story.

This story begins and ends in the village of New Albion, just two miles north of Cape Foulweather.

In this place, spirits walk the paths of ancient forests, roam the cliffs above the cape and haunt the sheltered cove.

People live and die here.

Some, before their time.

PROLOGUE

January, 1988
The Northwest Woods
Washington State

IT RAINED A lot that January.
It rained on the body of a dead girl in the deserted state park. She was far off the trail, effectively hidden by the wild growth of salal.

The girl had been there, on the forest floor, for two days but nature had been kind to her. The banquet had not yet begun.

She was eighteen years of age and had been very pretty. Long brown hair, wet with rain, framed an oval face. Dark lashes enhanced crystal blue eyes. Wide-open, they stared unseeing at the magnificent towering trees.

She lay slightly to one side, long legs twisted beneath her, her upper body an atrocity of rent fabric and congealed black blood. One hand, its nails well shaped and polished, displayed a high school class ring with a ruby at its center.

It had been the girl's senior year.

CHAPTER 1

January, 1998, 5:00 P.M.

THE WEATHER WAS dismal, the first days of January and already a record rainfall. Even for the central Oregon coast, it was a wet one.
Darkness fell early but Cape Foulweather could still be discerned in the distance, its high cliffs pummeled by wind and swelling seas. Two miles north of the cape on the small harbor, the village of New Albion suffered an incessant avalanche of rain.

This late afternoon, few cars traveled scenic Highway 101. The main street of town was deserted. Even the tourists had abandoned the little shopping strip with its restaurants and novelty stores.

On the bridge, a single car crossed, its lights shining on the slick pavement, wheels leaving fans of rain in their wake. The old stone structure seemed to sway and rock with the force of the waves sweeping under its pilings, battering at its ramparts, churning fragments of earth and gravel out to sea.

A solitary figure appeared on the bridge, walking like a shore bird through the deepening water.

* * *

High on the hill overlooking the harbor, a lone light shone from a window on the south side of the high school.

Inside, the halls were empty and deserted. The offices off the vast atrium closed and locked for the weekend.

No students waited in the outer reception room of the counseling center, but inside one office, a girl sat in front of a large old desk weeping into her hands. Across from her the counselor sat waiting patiently while the rain fell.

* * *

"The police are so mean! Nate's been in jail for *three* weeks and he didn't do anything. He swore to me he didn't."

Susanne was a senior, a gorgeous girl with creamy skin and an extraordinary tumble of streaky blonde hair. Her big blue eyes were brimming with tears and she opened her mouth and began to wail.

"Now my parents won't let me see him at all. I'm eighteen years old but they treat me like a baby. It's not fairrrr!"

"Whoa, Susanne. Slow down, honey."

The woman pushed a box of tissues across the desk toward the weeping girl. This problem would take a half-box, maybe more, the counselor thought. It was apparent, from the moment Susanne walked in, she was carrying a weight of worry in her backpack.

"They hate Nate. I have to lie and sneak around to see him!"

Susanne's tears were reaching tsunami level. She was inconsolable.

The listening woman was tired. It was five o'clock on

FOUL WEATHER

Friday. The school was deserted for the weekend and a torrential rain was pounding the windows of the counseling center.

Anneka Ericsson was a counselor at Captain Cook High. Her day had been a particularly strenuous one. She'd been about to clear her desk and leave when she'd been broadsided by this hysterical teenager.

The usually so patient Anneka was sorely tempted to tell Susanne to mop up the tears, sic the dogs on the felonious Nate, and cross her legs tightly for the next five years, or at least, until Monday. This much baggage was going to take hours to unravel.

The counselor studied Susanne carefully. She looked impossibly young and vulnerable, even with streaks of makeup making a blotchy mess of her face. She wore the standard teen-age uniform: a little white blouse that almost, but not quite, covered her navel, the ubiquitous jeans with huge tears on each knee, and a large army jacket that lay discarded on the floor with her backpack.

Anneka lowered her voice to a comforting pitch and plunged ahead.

"Susanne, take a deep breath and try to relax. I'm here to listen, okay?"

"Ms. Ericsson, I don't know where to turn. My parents would come unglued if they knew I was seeing Nate at all. They'd *kill* me if they thought I was having *sex*.

"I can talk to you because you're young so you understand, but they're so old. They just don't have a cluuuuuue!"

Susanne grabbed a handful of tissues and buried her face. Her sobbing increased and her shoulders shook.

Anneka digested this information. Susanne's parents would be upset, all right. His Honor, the venerable mayor of the town, and the equally honorable Mrs. Slocum, president of the Junior League, wouldn't care for their only daughter being seen in the company of Nate Dupray, the infamous Nate

23

Dupray who should have been drowned at birth or left in the rushes in hopes no one would find him. The young man was very good-looking and emanated that combination of sex and danger that teenage girls found so irresistible. For the parents of a young girl, he was their worst nightmare.

"I know, Susanne. Sometimes, it's hard to talk to our parents, even if they are the people who love us most in the world."

That damned Nate. Somebody better stop the little shit before he impregnates every girl in the county.

To punctuate Anneka's thoughts, a burst of thunder sounded mightily, and a fresh onslaught of rain drummed against the windows.

It took a good fifteen minutes to calm Susanne down. Her mascara had tracked down her cheeks, her eyes were swollen and red; but she had stopped crying and was responding to Anneka's soothing words of encouragement.

"Susanne, it's late and this storm's getting worse. Let's make an appointment for Monday at three. Put off any decisions for the time being. The sun will come up tomorrow, betcha bottom dollar. Well, this being the coast, maybe not, but things will look brighter, honest. And tomorrow's Saturday. You can go shopping. Maybe even get some new jeans that aren't all ripped up, huh? Just kidding, just kidding. I know, those are probably your favorites."

Anneka draped the old army jacket over Susanne's shoulders and with an effort heaved the bulging backpack off the floor. "What are you carrying in here, girl, the public library?"

She continued her gentle patter, guiding the girl to the door at the same time.

"Go right home, have dinner and a warm bath. Crawl in bed with your teddy bear. Okay? Here . . . let's mop up some of this mascara. You're scaring me."

Having managed to solicit a little hiccup of a giggle from Susanne, Anneka hugged her warmly. Teenagers with problems were like little children. Susanne was no exception. She thanked Anneka profusely and closed the door behind her.

Anneka breathed a sigh of relief and sank back in her chair.

There was still her desktop to clear and reports to be filed. She hated to come back on Monday morning to a messy desk.

She paused to listen to the silence, the strange quiet in a school after everyone's gone home. She shook her head, trying to clear it of anxiety over Susanne. Nate was a felon. Susanne had such a promising future. What could she see in him? Anneka hoped they'd keep him in jail for a long time.

Well, the girl was safe, at least for now. Organizing her desk would help clear her mind and she set to work.

* * *

Susanne closed the outer door to the counseling center and hurried through the deserted atrium.

Quiet out here . . . spooky almost. I've got to get home. Dad's probably already out looking for me—

Hey! What happened to the lights?

"Hello? We need the lights back on. Anybody there?"

Gawd! It's pitch black out here. Like I've gone blind. I better go back to the counseling center. No, that's dumb, gotta get home. As it is, we won't have any time to—

"Oof—damn!"

Can't see a thing out here. I hate the way they put furniture in the middle of the floor. Okay . . . this is right. I'm going right. I'll just hold my arms in front of me till I find my way out. No, I'll keep one arm on the wall and just walk straight. This is the door to the attendance office. Just a short distance now to the corner. Seems a mile in the dark . . . but this is the hall to the back, I'm positive.

What's that light? A flashlight? Must be the janitor . . .

"Hello? Hel-lo? Could you give me some help getting out of here?

I've got to get to the back parking lot. Excuse me?

"I can't see with the light shining in my eyes. Would you mind pointing it away?

"Oh, it's you! Whoa, you scared me to death. I was expecting the custodian . . .

"Lucky you had a flashlight with you. Now, we can find our way out together. Ah, no . . . I've got to go out the back way to the back parking lot. Would you mind helping me? Wow, that thunder sounded close, huh?

"No. I've really got to get home . My parents will be having a—What are you doing? Let go of my hair! That hurts! Stop pulling me! Stopit—stopit!

"WHAT—"

The girl screamed in terror at the first plunge of the knife. It ripped through her soft abdomen and plunged again, this time below her belted waist. She screamed again with the pain of it. Wet warmth soaked her blouse, her jeans.

She was still on her feet. She tried to run, to break free, but she couldn't. Her arms and legs moved like puppet parts on strings. Her mouth cried for help but there was no sound.

An awful realization hit Susanne. She was in terrible danger, here. She might even be dying.

She tried to pull air into her lungs, to breathe. She struggled feebly but her body wouldn't work. It was broken. Couldn't breathe.

Susanne fell and the ocean's roar filled her ears.

Still, she heard her killer's whispered words quite clearly.

"Nothing personal, honey. You were just in the wrong place at the wrong time."

*　*　*

Anneka finished the filing and looked contentedly around the spacious office, a large corner office with a view that swept down to the Pacific. Most days the view was spectacular but tonight the sea was raging, the storm worsening, as darkness claimed the world outside.

With the encroaching night, a feeling of utter aloneness crept over Anneka. She jumped when the phone rang. The pattern of rings indicated a call from inside the school which surprised her. Somebody else was working overtime.

"Counseling center. This is Anneka." No sound. Only the rain. "This is Anneka Eriksson. May I help you?" The silence on the line was charged, alive. Then, the sound of someone's ragged breathing.

"Doggone kids. Probably fooling with the phones out in the gym."

Anneka spoke out loud to relieve her tension. She was surprised to feel her hand quivering when she replaced the receiver.

Time to leave. She locked the office door and proceeded through the waiting room where she turned off the lights in the counseling center and opened the door to the immense atrium that doubled as a lobby.

She stepped into a black void.

All the lights were off.

"What the hell—I can't see a damn thing! Hello? Anybody out here?"

All the offices opened to the atrium, the center of the administrative building. The custodian always left the lights on until everyone had left.

Anneka stepped tentatively into the blackness, when the phone in her office began to ring.

"Oh yeah, right. I'm falling for that a second time, kids. Guess again." She took a moment to orient herself, then began to feel her way carefully through assorted tables and chairs in the lobby to the main entrance on the other side. Her car was parked in the staff parking lot in front of the building. *C'mon, Anneka, you've walked this way a million times. Just follow your nose. Monday, for sure, I'm checking out where the light switches are. This scene is playing like a remake of Friday the Thirteenth.*

A bit of light came from the outside through the window of the faculty mail room. Anneka hesitated. It would take only a second to check her mailbox. She hadn't picked up her messages all day. It was just inside, second box on the right. She started to feel her way through the door when a crackling bolt of lightning turned the world white.

Shadows lunged. Anneka shrieked and fled—through the main exit into the stormy night.

* * *

The crashing metal doors sent bullets of sound echoing and reechoing against the walls and high ceiling.

A crouching figure in the corner of the mailroom erupted in rage. Its elongated shadow leaped from wall to wall in the lightning's flash. Curses ripped the black silence.

CHAPTER 2

ANNEKA'S WAS THE only vehicle in the faculty lot. She ran for it, muddy water splashing into her shoes. The damn umbrella was in the truck again. Without her hooded raincoat, she'd have been completely drenched.

Hitting the remote, Anneka threw herself into the front seat and sank back in the soft leather. She was out of there for a whole blessed weekend. She could do whatever she wanted for two whole days. She breathed in deeply and expelled a long sigh of satisfaction. There was a lot to be said for being single again.

Anneka turned the key and listened appreciatively to the engine's purr. Her new Durango was perfect for the coast and bright red, just what she'd wanted. From the CD Kevin Mahogany wrapped his velvet voice around her like a verbal massage. Checking the time, she followed the long winding drive from the high school and turned onto the coast highway. She was late for her date with the Lemonade Ladies, an affectionate term for her close group of friends. They got together every Friday for happy hour gossip, drinks (never, lemonade), and dinner.

Anneka felt her muscles relaxing. She put her whole body into overdrive and coasted down Highway 101.

The Lemonade Ladies had come to her rescue when she'd first arrived in New Albion from the Midwest, newly divorced, needing friends and a change of scene. She'd spent five tumultuous years married to a possessive Italian who should have been buried to the neck in linguine and hot olive oil and left to die.

The River Road House was a short turn off Highway 101 on the old river road. The restaurant boasted a scenic overlook of the Siletz River, sizzling steaks, generous drinks and the coziest bar around. It laid claim to fame in the sixties when it was the setting for the movie *Sometimes a Great Notion* starring Paul Newman. Nothing much about it had changed. The river and the old dwellings clinging to its shores remained the same. On a nice day, you could sit on the verandah, watch the fishing boats glide by and imagine yourself back in a kinder, more peaceful time.

The parking lot was full but Anneka found a place next to the black truck belonging to Maggie Ramirez. Maggie was the principal of Captain Cook High School and one of the Lemonade Ladies.

Anneka flipped down the lighted cosmetic mirror, patted her blonde tousled hair into place, and applied some fresh lipstick.

"Gawd, I look as tired as I feel. Time to have some fun."

Laughter, smoke and the warm rush of relaxed, happy people greeted Anneka as she entered the bar. Lainey waved to her over a sea of heads and signaled the waitress. Lainey was the unofficial social director for the group.

Anneka ordered her favorite drink. "Give me a vodka martini, straight up with a couple of olives, please." She could handle two, tops.

"Give everybody a refill," Lainey said. "That's a glass of the house champagne for me."

Lainey could drink more cheap champagne than anyone this side of the Continental Divide. Her friends suspected this was in part due to a rather shaky marriage. Her good-looking, successful husband had a wandering eye. But now, troubles cast aside, Lainey was bubbling like the champagne, shaking her shiny cap of black hair, her dark eyes shining.

Anneka made a mental note. She was sure she'd be driving Lainey home, but she didn't mind, Lainey was the other counselor at Cook High and Anneka was extremely fond of her.

Next to Lainey was Skye Bellingham, a counselor from Toledo, a small town about twelve miles east on the Siletz River. Skye was a Native American, tall and regal. She was looking like a fashion plate, even in this howling storm.

"How! Paleface. What took you so long?"

"Skye, your hair looks fabulous slicked back like that. I'd kill for those cheekbones, damn it."

"You're staying later and later these days, Anneka." Maggie sat at the head of the table, in a no-nonsense suit and crisp white blouse. "Your car was the only one in the lot when I left. Couldn't get rid of John Clayton's father. You know, your favorite parent?"

"What's his problem now?" Anneka asked.

"He's determined to get John's physics grade changed so he'll keep his perfect four point. Kept telling me over and over John's an honors student and he's never earned less than an A in anything."

"Mr. Clayton is a plain pain in the ass," Lainey said. "He always gives me that John-is-an-honors-student crap. Someday, I'm going to tell him, Sir, your son may be a genius, but *you* are a perfect idiot!"

"You can think it, but you can't say it, Lainey," Maggie

said. "Clayton's about to slap the district with a law suit as it is."

"Because of that last special ed. meeting for his daughter?" Anneka asked.

"Yeah, he can't accept the fact that Jamie's not an honors student like her brother and never will be. Her behavior's getting more bizarre, too. I'm calling in the new school psychologist to help with the next meeting."

"I'm having a counseling session with Jamie on Monday," Anneka said. "Maybe that will shed some light— Oh, here comes Nogood. Hey, N.G.! Over here."

Nogood, whose real name was Nancy-George Geoffreys was the assistant principal at Captain Cook High, in charge of discipline. The initials N.G. had translated into Nogood over time because her behavior in her personal life was often outrageous but she was a complete professional in her job. She lived alone in a small house in town next to the fire station. Dirty Harry, a fifteen-year-old parrot, was her only companion. The Lemonade Ladies despised Harry. He was an odious foul-mouthed bird. They joked about boiling him up and serving him on a covered platter, like the scene in *Whatever Happened To Baby Jane?*

"Does everybody have a head start on me? Do I need a drink! Lainey, get that barmaid over here," Nogood demanded.

"All right, but stop ordering me around. We're out of school now."

Skye leaned over to address the table. "Yeah, you're acquiring quite a reputation, Nogood. I had a transfer student today who said the assistant principal at Cook High was so mean, she'd scare the shit out of Ted Bundy. That's a direct quote and I'm passing on the compliment."

"Well, I'm glad to have made a lasting impression on somebody. Maybe they won't end up in the holding tank for juvies, which is where I just came from."

"Who do we have there, now ?" Anneka asked. The juvenile holding facility under the New Albion police station housed offenders from areas around the coast. Some of the young people had already established records for major crimes, including sex offenses and murder.

"Well, I was supposed to sit in on an interrogation of Nate Dupray, but when I got there, somebody had bailed the little bastard out," Nogood said.

"They let him go? Damn it!" Anneka's first thought was of Susanne. "That's crazy. How could they let him go?"

"You're not the only one who was surprised, Anneka. There was a little girl there looking for him. She claimed to be his wife and she was sporting two of the worst shiners I've ever seen."

"Nate Dupray is married?"

"That's what this girl said. She looked about thirteen and I'd say she's about two months away from the maternity ward. She was bawling like Nate was really worth a rat's ass. Said he hasn't come back to the trailer where they're living and nobody has seen him. Apparently, he's been holing up with her family and she's got a couple of brothers who are fighting mad he's taken a powder."

Anneka was fuming. There'd be a heavy session with Susanne on Monday. Nate being married, was going to be a *big* surprise.

"How could they just let him go? He was arrested for armed robbery, for Gawd's sake!" Maggie said.

"I don't know all the details. Apparently, some pretty pricey lawyer showed up with his bail, but let's talk about something else. I'm really tired of dealing with that little shit." Nogood lifted her glass and said, "To Friday night, the Lemonade Ladies, happy hour, and my new boyfriend, Manny."

"Your new boyfriend, Manny? Isn't that the guy you picked up at the Lazy Dog last Friday?" Lainey asked.

"Yup, I spent the whole weekend with him. We had a blast. He thinks I look like Shirley Maclain. I'm in love."

33

"Nogood, you're insane. That guy was a real dirt bag and he stayed for the weekend? Holy Shit! You need a keeper," Lainey slapped her forehead dramatically and fell back in her chair.

"Oh, come on, he's really sweet."

"What's his last name, Nogood?" Anneka watched as a sheepish look swept over the other woman's face. "You forgot to ask him, didn't you? You took him home, spent the whole weekend with him and didn't even get his last name."

"Well . . . the subject didn't come up, Come on, you guys, I've got good instincts. Manny's okay."

"Nogood, instinct's got nothing to do with it. You'd be attracted to Jack the Ripper, if he had a nice tush and you'd had enough to drink," Skye said. "You need to be more discriminate. Maybe even start dating inside your own species."

"You should be on Letterman, Skye, you're so hilarious," Nogood said and adroitly changed the subject.

"Hey, you know what Dirty Harry says now? He says, 'A girl, can't be *too* careful.' And, he pauses after a girl. You know, a girl, pause, can't be too careful. Isn't that darling?"

"First of all, Nogood, there's nothing that bird could say that would be darling. Second, you should heed his advice, you think it's so darling," said Lainey.

It might be good advice but Anneka knew Nogood wasn't likely to take it. She liked to walk on the wild side.

Anneka stood up to be heard. "Hey, ladies. Listen to this one. "What do you call the insensitive bit at the base of the penis?"

"I give," said Skye. "What do you call it?"

"The man."

They burst out laughing.

"I'll drink to that," hooted Lainey.

"Hell, you'd drink to anything," said Maggie.

In the midst of the toast that followed, Anneka glimpsed the very bald but very handsome head of Dr. Rutger

Hartmann, the new psychologist. She had seen him at meetings but had never spoken with him personally. He hesitated, then began to weave his way toward their table.

"Holy Shit, it's Hartmann, that new guy from Wisconsin. He's cute. Who could we hook him up with? He's not married, you know," Lainey whispered, way too loudly.

"Jeez, Lainey, can we just let the guy have five minutes before you marry him off?" Anneka hissed back.

The man in question leaned over their table and smiled engagingly.

"Ladies, if this is an all-girl party, I'll go away. Otherwise, I'd like to buy you a drink. I'm a stranger to these parts."

"Sit down, please, Rutger. We'd love to have you join us," Maggie said.

"Rutger, here, take my place. I've got to head back to Toledo or I'll never get back. The Siletz was already about to crest on my way in," Skye said.

Anneka watched her friend's tall figure make her way through the crowd. Skye always left early, Anneka thought, even when the weather was nice. It was like she handled a social situation for just so long and then she split.

"Maybe it's time we ordered dinner," Anneka said, but allowed Rutger to include her in another round of drinks. She relaxed and pushed all thoughts of school, Susanne and voiceless telephone calls from her mind. Lifting her second martini, Anneka toasted the new arrival.

"Hey, how great is this?" Dr. Hartmann said.

CHAPTER 3

IT WAS STILL raining. Anneka had taken both Lainey and Nogood home, so it was past one a.m. when she turned into the gates of Spirit Cove.

Too small to appear on most maps, Spirit Cove was one mile north of Cape Foulweather, where Captain Cook first sighted the American Coast. The small community was adjacent to a larger cove called Whale Cove, the two separated by high cliffs covered with scrub pine and salal.

Spirit Cove was beautiful, a place where thunderous waves crashed on rugged basalt cliffs and gray whales fed in kelp beds just off shore. Paths wound along the cliffs down to the secluded fresh water cove that kissed the sea. A wooden walk ran through acres of ancient cedar forest and in the summer, the meadows filled with wild flowers and the songs of birds.

The area was steeped in history and Indian lore. Anneka loved to hear Skye talk about her tribe's legends and the stories she'd heard growing up on the reservation. Skye had frequently entertained the Lemonade Ladies with tales of the haunting of Spirit Cove and the surrounding forest.

One legend spoke of a young Indian girl who lived during the time Sir Frances Drake had explored the cove and the surrounding coastal areas. The girl was killed by her tribe for giving birth to an illegitimate baby. The tribe's elders said her ghost still roamed the seawalk and the cove.

Skye's great-grandmother, Lawelatha, claimed to have once seen the ghost of an Indian woman said to have committed suicide by throwing herself from the cliffs.

One day, the young Lawelatha was fishing off the cove's rocks when she was swamped by a wave and washed out to sea. She swore the spirit of a woman carried her back to the beach, to safety. Legend said this same spirit had come to the aid of other people in danger, especially young women. Tribal elders believed many such ancient spirits inhabited the rain forest and sometimes appeared on the steep bluffs reaching out to sea.

Anneka had wanted to hear more, but Nogood had heard enough. "Oh, sure, it gets so damn crowded up there, the ghosts start pushing each other off the rocks. I've seen this, personally."

That had terminated the conversation. The spell was broken.

But Anneka knew the cove had a sacred feel to it. It was easy to imagine the ancient trees whispering secrets of years gone by and singing haunted melodies in the wind. Walking along the cliffs, easier still, to imagine a spirit presence in the thick fog.

Anneka's house sat on a high cliff that sloped down to the cove. The house was sheltered by towering trees and had a crows-nest where she could sit and watch the sea. If she saw things through her window that made her wonder, she never spoke of them. They were too quickly gone.

A tall totem of a Siletz chieftain stood as sentry at the

FOUL WEATHER

entrance to Spirit Cove. Anneka saluted the chief, hit the remote for the security gate and drove through. She passed the outdoor tennis courts and the recreation center, turned into Breakers Scarp, cruised between the dense trees and into her garage. The wind quieted as the garage door closed behind her.

She walked through the house quickly, turning on soft lights and music, and calling for her cat. She felt guilty. He'd be protesting his late supper

"Kitty Shameless? Here, kitty, kitty."

She entered the kitchen where the cat sat forlornly beside the cupboard that housed his food.

"Uh oh, I know you're mad at me, Shameless. But look here, I saved you some filet from my dinner."

Anneka cut the steak in kitty pieces and threw in a handful of dry kibbles. Shameless stretched mightily, showing his backside, but then began to eat with his usual gusto, purring in appreciation.

"Whew! Saved from his majesty's wrath by a bit of choice beef."

That night, the view from the wall of windows was dark and foreboding . Rain drummed on the glass. Anneka felt lonely and exposed. She had never covered the windows because they looked out on a wooded expanse shielded from the neighbor's view or any passers-by.

She thought of the voiceless telephone call and shivered. Suddenly, wary of the stormy night beyond the window, she swept up the cat and headed for her more private bedroom area in the loft.

Large enough for a bed and bath, the loft had a wrought-iron circular staircase in the far corner that led to the crow's nest, her lofty perch at the top of the house.

She donned a warm robe and soft slippers before climbing the stairs to her favorite spot. It was her habit to spend a few moments before bedtime gazing out the windows at the dramatic view. But tonight, she saw only torrents of rain, a black curtain hiding a pounding sea.

The crow's nest also served as Anneka's office for her computer, answering machine and an additional phone. She loved to work, read or just relax, there on top of the trees.

A light was flashing on the answering machine and she pressed the message button.

A voice, whispery and raspy, coiled into the small space and turned Anneka to stone.

"BITCH! I was waiting for you, Anneka . . . I was wa-a-ai-ting in the mail room."

"Who is this? What do you want?"

The voice came back like wire tapping on metal.

"What I wan-n-n-nt is you-u-u-u. Dea-e-e-e-e-ed. Die-ie-ie-ie.

* * *

Anneka remained motionless for a long time, not able to move, to act. When she regained some control and could think with some logic, she decided notifying the police could wait till morning. Nothing could be done about the situation at this hour.

She poured a large shot of brandy, gulped it down and went to bed.

But the brandy did not bring sleep. She tossed and beat at her pillow, her body agitated, her mind racing.

It was clear, the threatening caller had been the real thing. The reference to the mail room proved that. Someone had been waiting there for her. A student? She thought not, the voice hadn't sounded young, but it had been disguised, of course. It could have been anyone.

Remembering the whispering voice made her stomach lurch and her heart stop for a second too long. She took deep breaths and tried to push away the fear.

FOUL WEATHER

The buoy sounded off shore, that lonesome bell sound . . .
When sleep came, it brought dreams. Dreams of a lurking shadow, breathing, anticipating, concealed in the shadows of the mailroom. Dreams that went swirling to the sea walk a short distance away where a figure appeared in the fog. Fog that obscured and then cleared like little puffs of smoke. A dark cloak waved and billowed in the wind . . . The cloth scratched on the jagged rock . . . scraped . . .

* * *

She came instantly awake, sitting up in bed, all senses alert.
What was that? A scraping sound—a sound that shouldn't be there. It was coming from downstairs. From the back of the house.
Another furtive scraping sound. What *was* that?
This was no dream. This was no ghost.
Anneka grabbed her robe at the foot of the bed and crept to the edge of the loft. She peered down into darkness, straining to see, to hear through the wind. The rain had stopped and a bit of watery moonlight filtered through the skylight overhead.
. . . *Scraaaaaaape* . . . The kitchen doors, the French doors to the back deck.
Oh, my God!
The phone. Hurry! Anneka scrambled back to the bedside phone, hit "security" on her speed dial. Three rings and Ed answered.
"Ed! It's Anneka. Someone's trying to break in!"
"Turn on the lights. Call your neighbor. I'll be right there!"
The phone slammed in her ear. She hit the next number on her speed dial; the number that alerted the next link in the neighborhood emergency watch.
"Answer! C'mon, answer!"

41

"Keith, this is Anneka— I have a prowler."

"On my way. Be careful!"

Anneka switched on the bedside light and went for the gun in the nightstand. With shaking hands she checked the chamber. She'd practiced with the magnum a few times. She thought she could fire it.

Taking a deep quivering breath, she headed for the stairs.

The tinkle of falling glass. They were coming in!

Anneka felt a wave of white hot rage. It propelled her forward, gave her strength.

No way!

No-fucking-way was anybody coming into her house!

She moved rapidly down the stairs and crept along the wall to the kitchen entrance, holding the magnum in front of her, just as she remembered from her defense class.

* * *

Weak moonlight outlined a tall figure against the French doors. Anneka watched in horror as a gloved hand slithered through the broken pane of glass.

"Get out of here! I've got a gun! *Get out!*"

The shadowy figure raised long arms and flapped, like a demented bird. She heard a low laugh, a stifled giggle.

Then, the hand came through the glass once more and turned the knob.

Anneka raised the heavy gun and fired, somewhere in the vicinity of the door. The gun's blast knocked her back a foot or more. She struggled to raise the weapon again. Her hands were shaking violently and her arms felt like lead.

But the black shape was suddenly gone.

Loud shouts came from outside and a bright spotlight hit the back deck.

"That was a shot!"

"Someone's running back there!"

FOUL WEATHER

More shouts. Some from the deck. Some farther away.

"He's headed towards the boardwalk!"

Anneka heard the shouts, the chase. She collapsed to the floor like a ragdoll, still clutching the magnum.

"Watch out for a gun! I heard a shot!"

"Somebody find Anneka! Where's Anneka?"

With heroic effort, she struggled to her feet and switched on the deck lights. She walked out on the deck, shaking violently, her voice a hoarse whisper.

"I'm all right. All right."

But her knees gave way and she sank to the top step of the deck.

Ed Johnson, the security guard lowered himself beside her. Anneka threw her arms around his bulky figure and held on.

"Okay, Okay. Let loose of that gun, gal. You're making me nervous!"

Anneka released Ed but kept the weapon clutched to her chest.

"I shot him. Did I hit him?"

"No, but you've got a dead flowerpot and a hell of a hole in the door. "C'mon, give me the gun. We'll save it for the next elephant stampede."

"He got away, Anneka," a neighbor said. "There's no way we could catch him, once he hit the trees. Probably went through the Coast Guard cottages and out that way."

"Or he could have gone down the cliff to the cove and then climbed the path over to Big Whale Cove beach," another neighbor suggested.

Whoever the intruder was, he was gone.

"Probably just some damn kid who thought your house was unoccupied for the winter, Anneka. But you scared him good. He won't be back."

This reassurance came from her nearest neighbor, Keith Gray. His usual perfectly groomed silver hair stood straight

43

up. He wore red-striped pajamas and only one slipper. He leaned over and patted Anneka's shoulder awkwardly.

"Nothing to worry about now," Keith said. "In fact, you're spending the rest of the night with me and Thea. You'll have to get that door fixed tomorrow. C'mon, get your toothbrush. Everything's okay."

Anneka nodded, but she didn't feel at all okay, even in the protective embrace of her little neighborhood posse.

Anneka knew, she was absolutely certain, the voice on the phone, the shadow in the mail room and the gloved hand that crept through the broken pane were one and the same.

* * *

I never meant to kill the girl. If she hadn't seen me in the hall, I wouldn't have killed her. Hey, I love kids.

Who'd have thought that whining do-gooder would have a gun? Damn lucky she can't hit the side of a barn or I'd be dead.

Well, there won't be any warning the next time. I'll be in the house already or hiding in the trees when she takes her walk.

She didn't even notice me at the Road House last night. Too busy eye-fucking that psychologist. Like a couple dogs in heat. Disgusting.

Whew, I'm exhausted. Climbing over Big Whale Cove and then having to run from those idiots. Good thing I'm in such great shape.

That's twice I've missed her now. Still, it's been fun, all the spying and stalking. Like a game.

Sleepy, so sleepy . . . Nothing like a great bed and a downy pillow when you're tired.

Thanks, Mom.

And with a light touch, the lamp went dark.

CHAPTER 4

Memo: Jan. 15, 1998
From: Nancy George Geoffreys

We have had several complaints about teachers and staff receiving troublesome or obscene phone calls from within the building.
Please monitor student use of all phones and lock your classrooms and offices when you leave.
Thank you for your cooperation.

MONDAY MORNING AND Anneka was digging out a pile of memos and paper work crammed tightly into her mail box.
In the light of day, with bright sun streaming through the window, it was hard to imagine the mail room as a menacing place, a place where someone had waited for her in the dark.
She shook the feeling off and hurried to her office. Jamie Clayton's meeting was coming up first thing. This time,

Anneka was determined to hold her own with Jamie's father. Having Maggie and Dr. Hartmann there would be a big help.

She'd been sorely tempted to stay home today. But home no longer seemed the safe haven it had once been and that sickened her. The broken pane had been replaced in her French doors and she'd ordered blinds for them as well. The view out her back deck wasn't as enchanting anymore, either.

She couldn't hide from the world, though. Too much to get done. Today she had several letters of recommendation to write, letters that would play an important role in getting her seniors into their dream colleges.

The door to Lainey's office was still closed. She must have been delayed this morning. That was happening more and more frequently.

Anneka entered her office, switched on the lights and the computer and checked her desk calendar for the day.

She had that conference with Susanne Slocum at three o'clock. No matter what, she had to be finished in time for that. With Nate Dupray out of jail, it was vital that Susanne break off their relationship. He was dangerous. Anneka intended to tell Susanne about the young girl Nogood had seen at the juvenile facility, the girl who purported to be Nate's wife. That ought to be fun.

Maybe Nate had left town with the girl's brothers in hot pursuit. Still, Anneka was thinking seriously of alerting the Slocums. Of course, Susanne was eighteen but she was definitely at risk if she continued to see Nate.

With so much to get done, Anneka's heart sank when Lou Wagoner charged into the office. Her body language signaled trouble.

The history teacher threw herself into the chair in front of the desk and stuck out her prominent chin.

Anneka cringed. The woman looked very angry, not to mention bizarre, in the outfit she was wearing, far too youthful for a woman in her late forties. And her hair, formerly steel gray and short-cropped had grown long and was dyed a brassy yellow. Lou had been a history teacher for over twenty years. In a constant pique over one thing or another, she was burned out, big time.

"I'm telling you, Anneka. I'm sick of the caliber of student I'm getting in my classes. The teachers that you like get the honors classes. I only have one honors and the rest of the day I'm stuck with the dregs and I'm sick sick sick of it!"

Anneka sighed. There wasn't much point telling Lou the computer scheduled the students at the beginning of each semester and the head of the department scheduled the honors classes. This woman needed to be pacified.

"Lou, you look ready to explode. Is there a student in particular you're having problems with?"

Lou tugged at an unruly hank of dyed hair and adjusted the red flower she had tucked behind one ear. She wore a tweed skirt that was much too short. It kept riding up on her thighs and she pulled at it impatiently. Her face was flushed and her breathing was rapid, as though she had been running.

"Yeah, I've got a particular student I'm having problems with, all right, and he's just one too damn many! Nate Dupray's got to go. I'm not putting up with that little creep one more day!"

"Nate is back in school? You've seen Nate?"

"I saw him in the hall this morning and when he comes to class, I'm sending him down here. I don't want the little bastard one more day, Anneka. I mean it!"

Anneka thought furiously. If Nate had shown up today, did he really mean to start attending classes again? Everyone knew he came to school just to keep his drug connections flowing but so far, he hadn't been caught with anything. If he was in school, she needed to get to Susanne earlier than this afternoon. Damn, if only they had just kept him in jail.

"Lou, you know I can't just take him out of class unless

he's committed some serious infraction. I know he's difficult but we all have to deal with him."

"Would this be considered an *infraction*, Anneka? The last time he showed up for class, he raises his hand in the middle of my lecture and he says, "Did you know I had sex with your mother, Ms. Wagoner?" I was stunned. I said, "Nate, my mother is dead." And he says, "Yeah, she wasn't that good.""

Lou's face had gotten redder and now she pounded on Anneka's desk with a clenched fist.

"Is that a big enough infraction for you? When I told him to get the hell out of my class, he called me a dried-up old bag. Right in front of the other students. And some of them even laughed at that sick joke about my mother."

"God! I'm sorry, Lou. That's terrible."

Anneka was watching Lou with alarm. She looked apopleptic.

"Nate is totally out of control. You don't have to put up with that behavior. But I can't remove him from class, Lou. I don't have the authority. Ms. Ramirez or Ms. Geoffreys will have to deal with him. If he shows up today, send him to the office and write up what you've just told me."

"I knew you'd pass the buck. You sit here in your cushy office and the rest of us on the front lines doing the real work can just go to hell, huh, Anneka?"

Lou Wagoner stormed out of the office, almost knocking over Rutger Hartmann as he struggled to gain control of several testing kits and a briefcase.

"Um, is this your flower?"

Lou snatched the artificial red rose from his hand and ran out, slamming the outside door of the counseling center behind her.

"Whoaaa! That's one mad lady."

"She's gone postal all right. Just what I needed to start my day. Call me Anneka, please."

"Okay and you can call me Spinner."

"Spinner?"

"A name I inherited from my dad when I was a little kid. He said I was a regular whirling dervish. When you've got a name like Rutger Hartmann, you ask your friends to call you something less formal."

He laughed and eased himself into the chair Lou Wagoner had just vacated.

"I wanted to tell you I had a great time with the Lemonade Ladies Friday night. Thanks for letting me join you."

"Wasn't it fun? We like to unwind on Friday nights. Sorry, I had to leave, but I was concerned about Lainey and Nogood getting home."

Anneka thought the psychologist looked very attractive this morning. Distinguished with the silver sideburns and beard. Nice blue eyes, too, or were they just so blue because of the blue sweater he was wearing? And he smelled like soap. She loved men who smelled like soap...

On the other side of the desk, the psychologist was thinking he loved this woman's smile and the rest of her wasn't bad either. He liked the way her hair curled behind her ears and was that a dimple in her cheek?

"I realized you had appointed yourself the designated driver," Spinner said. "But you left before I could ask you to go to dinner with me some night."

While Anneka was absorbing this new development, the phone rang. It was Lainey calling from the next office. She was talking in an excited whisper.

"Hey, I see you've got Dr. Hartmann in your office! I think he's dishey *and* he's single! Maybe we could fix him up with Jenny? You know she's been real down since she broke up with that—"

"Um, maybe we won't do that, Lainey. I'll talk to you later." Anneka hung up. Lainey, the little matchmaker. Why did she just naturally assume Anneka wouldn't be interested?

Like she'd suddenly catapulted into menopause or something? Anneka liked this man. She felt a little fluttery, even.

"Okay Spinner, that sounds great but right now, let me fill you in on this upcoming meeting from hell. We really need your help."

"Gonna be that bad, huh?"

"Trust me on this one, Spinner. I'd rather spend the morning coughing up blood."

CHAPTER 5

As SPINNER AND Anneka walked through the hall to the staff conference room where the meeting was being held, the intercom crackled.

    Susanne Slocum, please report to the main office. Susanne Slocum, if you are in the building, please report to the office immediately.

"Spinner, would you wait just a second? I need to check on a student."

Anneka ducked into the attendance office in time to see Nogood put down the microphone at the switchboard and turn away with a worried frown. A large group of students waited at the long counter. Anneka pushed past them to reach the switchboard.

She bent to speak in Nogood's ear.

"What's that all about? I have an appointment with Susanne today. Isn't she here?"

"Not only isn't she here, she hasn't been home all weekend. The mayor and his wife are frantic. They haven't seen her since she left for school on Friday. Some of her friends think she may have taken off with Nate Dupray."

"Oh, my God!" Under her breath, Anneka whispered, "Lou Wagoner said she saw Nate in the hall this morning. Have you asked him about it?"

"Nate didn't report for first period. I checked with his teacher. If Lou saw him, it's news to me.

"I've questioned all of Susanne's friends, Anneka. Even her best friend, Miranda, doesn't know where she is. The mayor's alerted the police and the sheriff's department. Everybody's looking for her."

Nogood pushed a lock of auburn hair off her forehead and sighed. She looked exhausted and the day was just beginning.

"I was hoping there might be a chance she's hiding somewhere in the building because she's afraid to go home. But I'm certain none of her friends know where she is. They're all too worried. Susanne had plans with some of them for the weekend and she never showed up."

"Damn it, Nogood, I feel terrible about this. Susanne was with me late Friday afternoon. It was after five when she left. She was upset about not being allowed to see Nate. We made another appointment for today. I never dreamed they'd let Nate out of jail. I feel like this is my fault."

"Anneka, if she was going to run off with Nate, she'd have done it, no matter what any of us said. We all thought they'd hold Nate longer at juvenile, then send him to the county jail. He just turned eighteen, you know. But somebody got him sprung. They posted his bail and he was out of there."

The students gathered at the counter were becoming impatient. Nogood turned and motioned for them to quiet down.

"You kids better have a good reason for being out of class.

FOUL WEATHER

The attendance clerk will be here in a second. So line up and wait for her."

Just like magic the students arranged themselves in an orderly manner and lowered their voices to a whisper. Nobody messed with Ms. Geoffreys.

"Don't you have a meeting for Jamie Clayton, Anneka? You'd better go. I promise I'll let you know the minute I hear something— Hey, isn't that Hartmann out there? He's rather attractive."

Nogood leaned over and murmured in Anneka's ear.

"I think he's got the hots for you, kid."

"Jeez. I hardly know the man."

* * *

"I'm sorry if we've kept you waiting," Anneka said to the people around the large conference table. "This is Dr. Hartmann."

"It's okay, Anneka. Mr. Clayton's not here yet. Good morning, Dr. Hartmann." Maggie was already at her place, looking over the minutes of the last meeting.

Anneka was dismayed to see Lou Wagoner. "When's this meeting going to start anyway? I've got better things to do than wait here while a substitute baby-sits my class," Lou said.

Dwight Ridout, a physical education teacher and coach, sat next to Lou in a pair of designer sweats and a California haircut. He was always tan, whatever the weather. He looked like a surfer. Privately, the Lemonade Ladies referred to him as a "Himbo."

Jamie Clayton's special education teacher, Sandra Barkowski, was restless, nervously shuffling the papers in front of her. Mr. Clayton often took his personal agenda out on the teachers.

"We'll wait awhile longer, Ms. Wagoner," Maggie answered.

Anneka took advantage of the lull, to lean across to Maggie and tell her about the break-in. It would probably hit the local papers on Wednesday and she hadn't had a chance to tell her friends about the incident.

"You actually had to shoot at someone?" Maggie whispered back. "Anneka, this is frightening. Was it an attempted burglary, do you think?"

Anneka told Maggie about the late phone call and the threatening reference to the mail room by the caller.

Spinner leaned over and said, "Anneka, this sounds like it's all related. Did you tell the police?"

"I thought it was related too, but the police don't think so. They wrote it off as a burglary attempt. Said it was probably some kid who came in through the Coast Guard cottages and over the boardwalk by the cove. I didn't tell them about the phone call I had before I left school Friday. I think it was this same person calling from somewhere in the building to see if I was still in my office."

"Anneka, I don't like this," Maggie said. I don't like it at all. I talked to Fred about all the lights being off when you left on Friday night. He said they were on when he left the building. If the custodian didn't turn the lights off, who did? This gives me the creeps. Your house's so isolated from your neighbors and you live alone. What if this person comes back?"

"Well, there's always my trusty Magnum. I shot it once. I'll be more accurate the second time."

Roger Clayton marched into the room flanked by his attorney and a child advocate from the Adults and Children With Learning Disabilities Association, the ACLD.

He settled himself importantly at the head of the table with one of his supporting cast on either side. He pulled a tape recorder from his brief case and placed it in front of him. The attorney and advocate burrowed into their respective attaches and sifted through myriad legal-looking documents.

FOUL WEATHER

Holy shit, Anneka thought. *We're in for a real dog fight..*
Maggie adopted her full battle stance.

"Mr. Clayton, before we make introductions, your daughter has the right to be in attendance at this meeting," Maggie said.

The attorney cut in. "Perhaps later, Mrs. Ramirez. We would prefer Jamie not be present if there are dissenting viewpoints and contentious discussion."

"That's fine. But, for the record, Jamie's of legal age and has a legal right to make decisions on her own behalf."

Brava, Maggie ! Anneka thought.

Ms. Ericsson, I know you counsel with Jamie on a regular basis. What are your thoughts on this?" Maggie asked.

"I feel Jamie can handle discussions that relate to her and her future. If she's delegating her father to act in her behalf, all right. But I think the committee should ask her if she wants to attend the meeting or not."

Mr. Clayton exploded from his seat. "You are fully entitled to your opinion, Ms. Ericcson, but I am Jamie's father. I have already discussed this with her and I don't want her here while we debate these issues!"

> Will the head custodian please report immediately to the faculty lounge off the cafeteria. I repeat, Fred Nordstrom, please report immediately to the faculty lounge off the cafeteria.

It was Nogood on the school intercom. Her voice was shaking.

Maggie pushed her chair back. This announcement was a pre-planned signal to all administrative personnel in the building. It indicated an emergency that needed to be dealt with immediately without alarming the student body.

Lainey burst through the door and gestured wildly at Maggie.

55

"I'm sorry, this meeting will have to be rescheduled." Maggie said.

"What do you mean, rescheduled?" Mr. Clayton shouted, outraged. "My daughter's needs have to be addressed. I've taken time from my business and I'm paying for an attorney's time!"

"Ms. Ericsson, Dr. Hartmann, come with me, please," Maggie said.

"Mr. Clayton, call my secretary for another meeting time. Or if you wish, call the president of the school board and register your complaint."

The three of them rushed from the room.

CHAPTER 6

"WE'RE SUPPOSED TO meet Nogood in the custodian's office. She's there with Fred."

Lainey tried to catch her breath as they raced toward the west side of the building.

"What's happened?" Maggie asked.

"She called on the radio, said to get you right away—a real emergency— maybe Fred's found a bomb or something."

The custodian's office was down at the end of the main hall where it intersected with B wing. Spinner reached it first and stepped aside for the women to enter. Students passed through the hall engaged in their usual banter, in a hurry to get to their respective classes. It was just an ordinary Monday.

Spinner closed the door as they entered the larger of the maintenance storage rooms and headquarters for Fred Gervey, head custodian for the high school.

Fred stood in the middle of buckets and brooms, a dazed expression on his face.

Nogood was slumped in a chair. Her head rested on a small table. She was inhaling and exhaling deeply through her mouth. Behind her a door opened to a room with closets and wall to wall shelves filled with cleaning materials and stacked boxes.

"What's happened? What's wrong?" Anneka cried.

Nogood took a long shuddering breath. "We found Susanne Slocum."

Maggie shook her shoulder. "What do you mean? Where's Susanne? Fred, what's going on?"

"I was working in the autoshop building, Ms. Ramirez, so I didn't get to my office until after classes started. When I went to unlock the door, it was already open and I found... this." He gestured at the stains that trailed into the next room. "I thought someone had dropped paint or something till I realized it was—"

"Fred, what is it? *Where's Susanne? Where is she!*"

Fred pointed a shaking finger. "In there, Ms. Ramirez. In the closet. There was a chair propped under the door knob. Had an old army jacket hanging from it. I couldn't understand why there'd be a chair... and there was blood... a whole lot of blood was—" Fred broke off with a choked sob.

* * *

Susanne lay sprawled on the closet floor.

An opened backpack covered with colorful decals and pins was beside her. Scattered books and papers were soaked in blood. Blood was everywhere.

A fly crawled from the corner of a wide blue eye. Startled, it flew from the closet buzzing furiously.

Susanne's eyes stared at them, fixed and vacant.

Anneka stared back, feet frozen to the spot where she stood. Time stopped. Her mind refused to register what she saw. She was aware of a putrid odor mingled with the pun-

FOUL WEATHER

gency of disinfectants... From far away she heard Maggie urging her to step back, step back. Maggie crying for Spinner to call the police.

It was the same Susanne she had seen Friday, just two days ago.

Except Susanne had stopped crying.

Her cheeks still bore mascara tracks, though, and she wore that same little white blouse that didn't quite cover her belly button.

But everything else was different.

The pretty blouse was soaked with blackish blood around hideous holes. Susanne's lips formed a surprised O around the filthy rag stuffed in her mouth. Her hands had bloody broken nails.

A knife protruded from the torn place where her navel should have been.

Susanne hadn't left the building on Friday after all. Susanne had stayed after school.

* * *

As Anneka and the others stared at the dead girl, the Captain Cook High School band marched past the window, their instruments blaring a rousing rendition of Cook High's fight song. Young voices sang boisterously over the sound of blasting horns.

"Fight, Cook Captains! Fight right down that field! Pass the ball around the foe, men. A touchdown every time! Rah Rah Rah!"

Anneka fainted. The band played on.

CHAPTER 7

THE AFTERMATH OF Susanne's murder was a blur. Anneka walked through the days on automatic pilot, dealt with police, dealt with the media, questions from reporters, television and newspaper people from the area and from out of state. She dealt with the daily routine of her office and the grieving students who shuffled into the counseling center in an unending stream.

What she found most difficult to deal with were her feelings of guilt. She felt an immense responsibility for Susanne's death. If she had kept her in the office longer. If she had walked with her to her car. If she had only known what was waiting for Susanne in the blackness outside the counseling center.

All these things swept through Anneka's mind in an unending litany of remorse.

Memories of the funeral still ran in slow motion through her mind. She remembered her friends in a protective circle and Spinner's strong arm as he stood by her side. She remembered Susanne's best friend, Miranda. Miranda had to be helped to the grave site where she shook off the solicitous hands and placed a single white rose on the casket before her knees collapsed and she fell to the wet ground and began to sob. This last memory remained the keenest, accompanied by the scent of flowers and fresh earth as a gentle mist wept softly over the mourners.

Anneka was surprised the sheriff and the special investigative team from Portland had only questioned her one time. They were concentrating on the search for Nate Dupray who had not been seen since the Monday after Susanne's murder. Anneka had told them about the phone calls and the break-in at her home. The men listened attentively and politely but it was clear they thought the phone calls and the intruder were completely unrelated to the murder. They were convinced Nate had been waiting for Susanne, the two had quarreled and he had killed her. They assumed he was on drugs at the time and lost control. The boy was known to be involved with drugs, to be highly volatile and violent.

Anneka had last seen Nate when a student reported he was harassing her, and making derogatory and obscene comments. She remembered the pregnant girl at the juvenile detention center who claimed to be Nate's wife. Anneka made a mental note to find her and talk to her.

If Nate was responsible for killing Susanne, Anneka wanted to help put him away forever. She wanted to be in the court room when he was convicted, she wanted to watch when they led him away, knowing he'd be locked up for the rest of his miserable life.

* * *

One week later

It was early evening on a Wednesday. Dusk had already fallen and Anneka was in the kitchen, chopping up vegetables

FOUL WEATHER

and preparing crab and spinach dip for the Lemonade Ladies and Spinner. She poured chips into two bowls, hurriedly tidied up the kitchen and carried the big tray into the living room where she placed it on the low table by the fire. She plumped the pillows on the huge, floppy couch and looked around in satisfaction. Everything was ready. The living room looked warm and comfortable. Firelight danced on the high ceiling and quiet music played through the speakers mounted on the walls. There was the added ambiance of a pale moon shining through the tall windows. It darted in and out of swiftly moving clouds. The night was cold and windy but no rain had fallen.

They needed a chance to talk, to hash over the events of the last week and to give each other some much needed support. Their usual haunts would be too public, too noisy and crowded. The media was still a constant presence. Reporters and television crews were everywhere

Anneka needed to finish bringing the rest of the food from the kitchen and then she could sit down and relax. Where was Kitty Shameless, she wondered. He was usually in front of the fire. She glanced out the window. Shameless wasn't on the deck railing, his regular perch. She'd never spot that cat if he didn't want to be found. He'd come in when he got hungry.

* * *

Through the telephoto lens, the killer could stand a good distance from the house and see Anneka in her living room.

It was just like being there. Anneka was wearing a soft flowing caftan and her blonde hair was tucked behind her ears. The killer watched as she placed a tray of food on the table and walked back through the door to the kitchen.

Lights shone from the living room and illuminated a small patch of the cedar and tall spruce that lined the house. But the killer's hiding place was well back from the house, dark and secret, the moon shielded by clouds. *"Even if the bitch looks out the window, she'll only see trees. This is the perfect hiding place. Like being at the movies."*

The killer shuddered in excitement.

* * *

They were all there, the Lemonade Ladies and Spinner, gathered in Anneka's living room, trying to kick back and relax after the hell they'd lived through all week. The little village of New Albion and Captain Cook High School had achieved fame in a way they could never have imagined.

Maggie had been inundated with reporters, police and the members of the school board who were a constant presence as she tried to deal with the horror of the mayor's daughter being murdered and found on campus.

Nogood had spent the week interviewing students in the hope that someone would know something that would aid the police.

Lainey and Anneka had worked with students, grieving the loss of one of their own. Children never think of dying. They look at their own life as something that will go on forever. With Susanne's brutal murder, it was doubtful any of the students would look at life the same way again.

Skye was there to lend support. She was the only Lemonade Lady who hadn't seen the monstrous sight of Susanne Slocum, gagged and dead in the janitor's closet. But Toledo High school was just a short distance away and many of her students had known the dead girl. Skye's days had also been filled with students who needed comforting or just needed to talk.

Spinner sat quietly in the comfortable recliner in the corner. His Lab, Ollie, lounging beside him, his chin on Spinner's loafer.

"Don't you ever wear socks, Spinner? It's the dead of winter. Loafers with no socks is so Miami Vice, don't you think?" Nogood drawled from her perch on the downy sofa in front of the fire.

"Shut up, Nogood. Don't start picking on Spinner," Skye said.

"I can't think with my socks on," Spinner said. " My feet have got to breathe."

"Yeah, Nogood. If that Texas cowboy you picked up last weekend isn't working out, don't take it out on the innocent people around you," Lainey said and poured herself another glass of wine.

"My boyfriend is perfectly fine and working out beautifully, thank you, and he happens to be from Arizona, not Texas," Nogood said.

"Spinner, I heard through the grape vine that Lou Wagoner asked you over for dinner," said Lainey. "Is that true? What's it like being the most eligible bachelor on the central Oregon coast?"

"Lainey, where do you hear all this gossip? I think we should get to the business at hand and stop embarrassing the only man in the group," Anneka said. The suggestion that other women were taking an interest in Spinner wasn't a surprise but Anneka found the thought disquieting. Spinner had been a real comfort during the funeral and the events since. Anneka was getting accustomed to having him around.

"Nogood, how come Fred didn't find Susanne sooner?" Skye asked.

"Because he started out that morning cleaning the auto shop and he finished in there before going to his office. He saw the . . . blood right away and there was . . . an odor." Nogood slumped back in her chair and shook her head.

Anneka sickened as she remembered the smell not quite masked by the odor of ammonia and cleansers scattered around the body. "Did Fred keep that closet locked?"

"Apparently not," said Nogood. "Fred didn't see the need to lock it , since he keeps the door to the hallway locked but

65

that door was unlocked as well. He swears he locked it before he left on Friday."

"Was there any sign the door was forced? How would the killer have gotten in there?" Spinner asked.

"Fred's office can be opened by any of the keys the teachers have," Maggie answered. "It wouldn't be too difficult to get one and have a copy made, I guess. The teachers leave their keys in their mailboxes when they leave the building. Kids are in the mailroom all the time, picking up mail for the teachers, putting in notices, that kind of thing. I think we're going to have to change all of the locks." said Maggie. She sighed heavily, the strain visible on her face.

"When I think of that monster waiting in the mailroom for Anneka, it scares my pants off!" Lainey wailed.

"Could you tell it was Nate who called you Friday night, Anneka?" Skye asked.

"No, the voice was more like a croak. It had no age or sex. It was like something... dead. It was hideous. And the phone call to my office after Susanne left, well, that was totally anonymous but I knew someone was there, waiting on the other end of the line."

"How much time elapsed from the time Susanne left your office until you received that phone call? " Spinner asked.

"I don't know. I guess it took me about forty-five minutes to clear up the work on my desk."

"Plenty of time to kill the girl and get back to the mailroom and wait for you," Spinner said.

"From now on, we leave the counseling center together and we don't stay after hours." Lainey took another long gulp of her wine and reached for more.

"From now on, there won't be anyone working alone after hours," Maggie said. "Not until the police have apprehended Nate or we know who did this. That's an order."

The room turned quiet. The fire crackled. The low music was accompanied by Ollie's faint snore.

"Nogood, where can I find this girl who claims to be Nate's wife?" Anneka asked.

"You might try the woman's shelter. I advised her to go there. I don't think the poor kid even had a place to stay."

"Before you go doing any detective work on your own, call me first," Spinner said. "I know some of the counselors and they might be more inclined to give me information. They're real stringent about confidentiality."

Skye had been quietly sipping her wine, deep in thought. Now, she sat up in her armchair and addressed Anneka.

"Where's the ghost my grandmother Lawelatha told me about, I wonder? You needed her here that night. She's supposed to help women in distress."

"Yeah, a ghost. That would be a big help," Nogood said. "Maybe she's got a gun and hopefully she's a better shot than Anneka."

Skye glared at Nogood and turned back to Anneka. "Tell us about the break-in. Do you remember anything in particular about the intruder?"

"I was so terrified, I don't remember much except that gloved hand coming through my door before I shot at him. All I saw was a black shape through the glass. I guess he was fairly tall. The neighbors saw him running toward the trees but they couldn't tell much. It was too dark."

"He had to have been on foot or he couldn't have gotten in the gate," Spinner said. That means he probably left a car parked somewhere off 101. Are the police looking into that, Anneka?" Spinner asked.

"They're convinced my prowler was unrelated to the murder so they're not taking the time to do much of an investigation. I think it all ties in, though. The phone calls at school, the call here, Susanne's murder, and a break-in all within a twenty four hour period? I don't believe in coincidences like that."

"Anneka. Nate's violent," said Maggie. "We know that.

Maybe he was waiting for Susanne, they quarreled and he blames it on you. Maybe he thought you were advising her not to see him anymore. So, after he killed her, he decided to get revenge on you."

"Maybe, but it seems pretty far-fetched."

"I don't think murderers are real logical, Anneka," Skye said. "You need to be very careful until the police find Nate."

"Were there any cars in the parking lot when you left school?" Spinner asked.

"No. And Maggie left before me and she said the parking lot was empty. But that doesn't mean somebody couldn't have parked in one of the other lots or behind the library or even the gym."

They continued to rehash events and sort through details, but it brought no satisfaction. Still, Anneka felt better with her friends surrounding her. The fear she had lived with all week was lessening.

Spinner lingered awhile after the others, checking windows and doors. " How about I leave Ollie tonight? He's a great watchdog and good company."

"Oh, I'll be fine, really. Please don't worry."

But she felt a chill of trepidation as she slid the dead bolt on the front door and climbed the stairs to the loft. Even her cat had pulled a disappearing act. Once again, she was alone with her demons and her dreams.

* * *

That night she dreamed of a watcher in the fog. Standing on the very edge of the rocks that plunge sharply down to the cove. A dark hooded figure, looking out to sea... There was no sense of malice. It seemed to belong there, a spirit melting into the mist...

The spirit of Mourning Ann

Mourning Ann stood on the bluffs of the small cove and watched the spume on the horizon. She saw the whale breach in a mighty heave, then plunge to the ocean's depths.

Last night, as she camped with her husband and children by the fresh water cove, she could hear the whales' sound. She imagined it had been the same for thousands of years.

Today, the Boones would fish. They always snagged a plentiful catch. Enough food to feed the children for weeks to come. The berries were plentiful too. She sent the children to pick. Along with the berries, the children gathered shell fragments. Fragments from ancient middens that the ocean had revealed, but whose secret remained buried.

Mourning Ann seldom smiled. She was a silent woman, aptly named by her tribe, for she was most often sad. From a distance, her body appeared old and stooped, near, her face looked young. She had borne thirteen children, the same number of the years she had lived, when she became the bride of Boone.

Mourning Ann sometimes left for hours wandering the cliffs and staring out at the sea. It made her husband and children wonder. There was something mysterious in Mourning Ann.

Once her husband asked what she was thinking as she sat for hours, never moving. She told him she did not belong to this time, that her heart yearned for something that had gone before. He never questioned her again. She had gone slightly mad, he thought.

In her faded cloak, she bent against the wind and drew the cloth close around her head, protection from the mist and the people around her.

CHAPTER 8

THE YOUNG GIRL behind the scarred and battered table was painfully thin, except for the hard round belly where her hands rested protectively. Her face bore bruises, some a purplish blue, others fading to yellow. She had long dark hair and pale sallow skin. The dress she wore was handmade and it hung on her small frame like a sack, except where it strained over her stomach.

She looked about twelve years old.

"Have you seen Nate? He never came home after he got out of jail," she said. Her mouth quivered revealing the remains of a broken tooth. The girl had unusual eyes, dark, deep and huge in her thin face. They shimmered with unshed tears.

The small room in the women's shelter was dark and damp. A place where there was no sun.

"Destry, you're shaking."

"Miss, my brothers are looking for Nate because he beat me up. If they find him, they'll kill him. They can be really mean."

"It looks like Nate can be pretty mean, too. Isn't that who gave you those bruises and that broken tooth?"

"He was drunk. Nate's usually nice to me. We're going to have a baby."

The young girl smiled tentatively, for the first time.

"Destry, are you aware the police are looking for Nate? They want to question him about one of my students. She was murdered."

The girl's chair crashed back from the table and she faced Anneka defiantly, like a small cornered animal.

"No! Nate didn't have anything to do with that girl. He told me she was always bothering him at school, leaving him notes and calling him all the time. He *told* her he was married and we were going to have a baby. Nate didn't have anything to do with that girl. No."

Her anger left as quickly as it had appeared and was replaced with despair. Destry sank back in her chair and covered her face with her hands. The nails were bitten to the quick.

"Do you know where Nate is, Destry? If he didn't have anything to do with the murder, he should turn himself in. That way he can clear himself."

"I don't know where he is! If he doesn't come back for me, what am I going to do? I'm not going back to that trailer with my brothers! I can't go back there!"

Destry was crying in earnest now. Tears ran from her swollen blackened eyes and mucous streamed from her nose. Anneka handed her some wadded tissue from her purse.

She thought how ironic it was, ironic and terrible to be mopping up tears from another of Nate Dupray's victims. These two girls couldn't have been more different. The mayor's daughter, born with everything and this poor unfortunate girl, with nothing.

"Destry, how old are you, honey?"

"I was fifteen last week. We had a birthday party in the

trailer and Nate started drinking. Then my brothers started fighting with Nate and some neighbor called the police. I think they were already looking for Nate, though, because he said he was in bad trouble.

"Now he's gone. We were going to get a place of our own, just us and the baby. Nate promised me."

Anneka took the weeping girl in her arms. Her thin body was shaking violently.

"Destry. You can stay here in the shelter. You need to see a doctor. The counselors will help you decide what to do next."

"But I don't *want* to stay here. I just want Nate to come for me. If you see him, please tell him I'm here, *please.* "

Anneka tried to comfort her but the girl was beyond that. She was still crying hopelessly, her face buried in her hands when Anneka left.

* * *

Anneka headed back to school in a black mood, a sharp contrast to the unusually sunny day. At least, Highway 101 was free of tourist traffic. As she sped along the ocean's edge, she scarcely noticed the sun on the water. In the distance, a lighthouse stood alone on the edge of a high cliff and sea birds soared and dipped to the shining sea.

Anneka wished she could set sail on that bright blue sea until she reached some sunny island, somewhere far, far from here. But bright visions of tropic isles eluded her, lost to persistent images of the face of a murdered girl . . . and the face of the beaten girl she had left in the shelter.

Anneka believed Destry when she said she didn't know where Nate was hiding. She wasn't capable of deception. Were the brothers really as violent as Destry said they were? If they were looking for Nate, had they found him? Who had bailed Nate out of jail?

Her mind spun a thousand mysteries, as she manipulated the Durango into the staff parking lot. She thought wearily of all the things still left to do this afternoon. There was Jamie Clayton's special ed meeting to reschedule for one thing. Mr. Clayton was raising hell about the delay. She dashed up the incline to the main entrance, dodging students all the way. A group of the more radical student contingent was lounging against the bronze sculpture of Captain James Cook, cigarettes dangling from their fingers. They did make an attempt to hide them from her but smoke escaped from their noses and the corners of their mouths as she pushed through the group.

"Yo! Ms. Ericsson! How ya doin?"

"Thanks for asking but I wish you wouldn't smoke in front of Captain Cook," Anneka commented in passing.

"We've got all these bad habits, Ms. Ericsson! We need counseling! Call us in!"

"Yeah, preferably during Ms. Wagoner's history class. Borrrrring!" hooted another student with green hair.

"In your dreams!" Anneka retorted. "Your vices are your own business. So are your black lungs and yellow teeth. You little snots better pay attention in Ms. Wagoner's class. You could accidentally even learn something."

"We're not little snots, Ms. Ericsson. We're out here trying to be role models for the rest of the student body!"

"Yeah, and Ms. Wagoner *is* boring! We think she needs a man in her life!"

"Take me out of that class!" another student wailed, his hair an astonishing shade of purple. If I wasn't so bored, I might even get a passing grade in history!"

"It's my daily prayer," Anneka shot back. She loved these kids, even the ones with purple hair.

Their comments about Lou Wagoner puzzled her. More and more students were reluctant to take Lou's classes these days. She used to be popular with the students . . . Well, even

FOUL WEATHER

the best of teachers went into a burn-out phase from time to time. Teaching was a real energy drainer. Anneka made a mental note to see what could be done to help Lou out.

Waving at Lainey, Anneka unlocked the door to her office. The students were still at lunch and several were draped over tables in the waiting room, searching through college catalogs and scholarship files.

Anneka checked out her voice mail messages and switched on her computer.

"Ms. Ericsson, I've been waiting to talk to you. Can I come in?"

It was Jamie Clayton. Her face wore its habitual look of anxiety.

"Of course, Jamie. I was wanting to talk with you, too. We need to reschedule your meeting."

"Well, then, could we call my dad? He forgot to give me my lunch money this morning and I'm really hungry."

Anneka tried to suppress her annoyance. Jamie was nineteen years old and still coming in to call her father about everything she had forgotten or needed.

"Jamie, your dad didn't forget your lunch money. *You* forgot to get your lunch money. It's your responsibility, don't you think?"

"No, he forgot it, Ms. Ericsson. He gives me my lunch money every day and he forgot to give it to me today."

Save your breath, Anneka, she thought. *The girl just doesn't get it.*

"We were real late getting up. Daddy wakes me up every morning and this morning he didn't wake up. I wouldn't have woke up, either, but he was on my side of the bed and he rolled over on me."

"Excuse me, Jamie? Did you say your father rolled over on you?"

"OOOPs, I wasn't supposed to tell anybody that!" Jamie

75

clamped a hand over her mouth. "Don't tell him I told you that, Ms. Ericsson. I promised I'd keep it a secret."

Jamie, I don't understand. Why was your father sleeping in your bed?"

"Well, we've been remodeling my parents' upstairs bedroom, so Mom's just sleeping on the couch in the living room but Daddy wanted to be comfortable."

"When did this remodeling project start, Jamie?"

"A couple of months ago. Please, Ms. Ericsson, don't tell Dad I told you. He made me promise. He said nobody would understand how close a family we are. Don't say I told you? Do you promise?"

CHAPTER 9

THE MAJOR CRIME team had cordoned off the hall leading to the custodian's office. Both ends of the hall were blocked as the outer perimeters of the crime. Fred's office and the closet where the body had been found made up the inner perimeter. No one but members of the crime team could enter.

Along with detectives from Toledo, Lincoln City and Newport, the crime team included the Oregon State Police, the sheriff's department, the Lincoln County medical examiner and the district attorney. It was the latter Anneka recognized now as she circumvented the hall and walked around the building to reach the main administrative offices.

"Sorry, for the inconvenience, Ms. Ericsson," George Riley called out to Anneka as he entered the building. The young district attorney looked exhausted.

"No problem, George. Whatever we can do . . . Any news of Nate Dupray?"

"None at all. It's like he's vanished off the face of the earth. We've got a wide net out for him. He'll surface sooner or later. If you hear anything from the students— rumors, ideas, anything, please let us know."

"Oh, I will, I will."

"Umm, George, I wondered if you've questioned the brothers of Destry Murphy. Destry told me they've been looking for Nate because he beat her up. She's about to have Nate's baby and she claims to be his wife.

"That's good information to have. Thanks. I'll be sure to let the detectives know."

"Destry's at the women's shelter and she's badly depressed, so tell them to go gentle with her, okay?"

"You bet. They'll send a woman officer. We've called the Oregon state crime lab to help us process this murder scene. Hopefully, that will free a detective to do some more checking around."

Anneka waved and continued around the building to the main entrance and then to Maggie's office. Nogood was with her. Anneka needed to tell them about Jamie Clayton's revelation.

"Hi, Anneka. We were just getting ready to call you. We need to get the team together and finish up the Clayton meeting. His attorney just called and he was very insistent," Maggie said.

"Ironic. I came to talk to you about Jamie. She was just in my office, and she inadvertently spilled the beans about Daddy. It seems they slept late this morning and she didn't wake up until Daddy rolled over on her."

"What!" Maggie gasped.

"She was very upset that she slipped and told me she and her father have been sleeping together. She wasn't supposed to tell anyone because, and get this, no one would understand what a *close* family they are!"

"Good God, I'm calling child protective services about this! That bastard!" Maggie fumed.

"I already talked to the CPS people, Maggie. There's no

law broken here. Although we know that Jamie is socially a child, she is chronologically, nineteen years old. There's nothing social services can do."

"Bureaucracy sucks!" Nogood exploded. "We have to sit and listen to that jerk pontificate about Jamie's emotional needs and how the school has done nothing to help her and he's sleeping with her! And we can't do anything about it?"

"It's sick, all right," Anneka said.

"Oh, Clayton called about another thing, Anneka. He wants John out of Lou Wagoner's honors class and Jamie out of her general U.S. history class," Maggie said through clenched teeth. "I suppose you'd better take care of that immediately,"

"Oh, right. Lou had the unmitigated gall to give John a B in Honors and require that Jamie do her homework," Anneka said. "Yeah, I better get on that, right away, Maggie,"

"It's galling, I know, but we can't have Clayton telling his attorney we didn't comply with his request."

"I know, I know," Anneka sighed. " It's just so damned infuriating. I'll call them in and change their schedules. I don't know how John remains so focused when the rest of the family is just plain nuts. Hopefully, he can get away to college and out of that sick environment."

"Oh, Anneka, did I tell you when I was interviewing one of Susanne's friends, she told me Susanne dated John Clayton a couple of times?" Nogood asked.

"Really? No I didn't know that."

"Yeah, according to the friend, he was still carrying quite a torch for Susanne but she wouldn't give him the time of day when she started running around with Nate.

"Another bit of information I picked up was Jamie Clayton had a giant crush on Nate. Nobody said she'd actually dated him, though."

"Fat chance!" Anneka said. "She's never out of her father's sight, apparently, not even while she sleeps! You know, if we can't report this as a crime against persons or child abuse, I think I'll just let Mr. Clayton know Jamie told me he's sleeping with her. She kept begging me not to tell him. If he knows the secret's out, maybe he'll stop and just maybe he'll think twice about his lawsuit too."

"Don't say anything yet, Anneka. Let's get Spinner to give us his take on it," Maggie suggested.

"Of course, you're right," Anneka said reluctantly. " I promise not to do anything rash. I'm seeing Spinner tonight. I'll talk to him about it, then."

"That sounds interesting, Anneka," Nogood said. "Seeing quite a lot of Dr. Hartmann?"

"Grow up, Nogood. Spinner's leaving Ollie at my house overnight. Having that big dog around keeps me company and makes me feel safer,too."

"If it's company you want, I could loan you Dirty Harry for a couple of days, too."

"Yeah, that's all I need to drive me around the bend. You keep that damn bird at your house. I hate that damn bird!"

"Okay, Okay. Jeez. "

"Yeah," Maggie laughed. "The dog sounds like a better idea to me, too. But please be careful, Anneka."

Anneka left the office and detoured back to the counseling center, avoiding the yellow tape strung across the hall.

* * *

The killer parked a few spaces over from Anneka's Durango and waited patiently. School was out for the day but there were still plenty of cars left in the lot.

It's safe to wait here awhile. See if she leaves and heads straight home. No point in surveillance till she gets there. I'll grab a sandwich first.

Maybe tonight she'll decide to go for a stroll along the cliffs. She'll never see me in all those trees off the boardwalk. It's a jungle in there. Of course, if she has the dog, that might be a problem. I'll have to kill the dog and I don't really want to do that.

Come on, Anneka. Get out of there and go home. You're in there prying into somebody's life, aren't you? Oh, how you love to do that. I bet you're pulling secrets out of some unsuspecting student right now. Someone who trusts you. I bet you just love gossiping about everything you hear, too. Gossiping with your bitch friends. Nobody's secrets are safe from you, are they,? Oh, it's going to be such a pleasure to watch you die. . . .

The killer wondered if it was safe to masturbate. Right here in the school parking lot. Just thinking of murdering the bitch was so exciting.

CHAPTER 10

ANNEKA WATCHED IN disbelief as two little black-and-tan cocker spaniels chased Ollie around her living room.

"What the hell are all these dogs doing in my house?"

Spinner's answer went unheard as the cockers unearthed Kitty Shameless from his hiding place and took off in mad pursuit. The cat made a dash for the stairs and was gone in a blur of fur.

"Jeez! Damn it, Spinner! Kitty—Kitty!"

Anneka took off, up the stairs, around the landing, pursuing the two barking cocker spaniels. Their little black-and-tan butts raced up the stairs ahead of her. Spinner brought up the rear. People and animals charged into the loft to find Shameless had escaped up the wrought iron staircase to the crow's nest. Ollie the Labrador, had followed at a more sedate pace and now he sat down , threw back his head and began to howl. The cockers did, too.

This cacophony was punctuated with the hissing of the indignant cat peering down through the iron railing at the cockers and Ollie. All three joined in a doggy chorus of frenzied excitement .

"Jeez, Spinner! Where'd you get all these damn dogs?"

Sinking back on her chaise lounge, Anneka tried to still her pounding heart and catch her breath. The two cockers sat side by side looking baleful, heads cocked. They were identical. All black but for tan feet, chests, eyebrows and cheeks. Ollie sat beside them. Three in a row, they stared Anneka down.

"Once again, where did these dogs come from and what are they doing here?"

"Let me explain..." stammered Spinner.

"Please do, just before you remove them from the premises."

"Well... you see, I happened on these two little cocker sisters at the pound."

"The pound. Why were you at the pound?"

"Let me tell you, okay? You see, back in Wisconsin, I was a supporter of the Animal Refuge and Humane Center? So... I went to the pound here to get on their mailing list or whatever, to help out, you know?"

"Go on."

"Well, that's when I spotted them, just sitting together, looking so damn sad and so cute...."

"Yeah, so?"

"They were about to have their last supper, Anneka."

"You mean...?"

"Adoptions have been slow at the pound lately. They're in a budget crunch. Laverne and Shirley were about to have their last meal."

Laverne and Shirley?" Anneka laughed in spite of herself.

The two cockers were now on the chaise. One sitting on each side of her.

"That's what I named them. Their actual names were C'est si bon! Get it? C'est si and Bon."

FOUL WEATHER

"Oh, yuk!"

"That's what I thought. But Laverne and Shirley kind of fits them, don't you think?"

"That's pretty cute. But which is which?"

"If you look closely, Shirley has a little more brown and her face is smaller. See that?" Spinner asked.

"Oh, yeah. Are they litter mates?"

"Uh huh. And they're inseparable. That's why the people at the pound wanted them adopted together. They're really cute, don't you think?"

Anneka stroked the cockers' silky ears and the tops of their curly heads and they wriggled closer to her on the comfortable, satiny chaise.

"They're completely housebroken and good little watchdogs—"

"— And they bathe and feed themselves and watch their diets. Why are you telling me all this, Spinner?"

"I was hoping . . . I was sort of hoping . . . you might consent to watch them for me for a little while?"

"No way! Take care of two dogs? C'mon, I work all day, Spinner."

Laverne and Shirley, dismayed by her tone, leapt into Anneka's lap and began covering her face with kisses.

"Anneka, calm down. It would just be till I find another place. My landlady won't let me have three dogs. Listen to me for a minute."

"SPINNERRRRRRRR!"

The girls were attacking her ears, kissing her wetly.

"Anneka, listen, you already have a cat door. I'll put in a larger dog door. That way Ollie will be able to use it, too, cause we hope to visit a lot? Then, I'll build a little dog run for them in the back. You can keep them in the kitchen and utility room when you're gone. Please? They won't be any trouble. They'll be good company, they'll alert you at night if they hear anything suspicious—"

"God, Spinner! Stop whining. All right. But only until you find another place to live. Then, they're out of here. Understand?"

"Okay, okay, sure! It'll work fine. I've got the food and everything you'll need in the car."

"What about my cat? He's not going to like this!"

"He'll be all right. Animals get used to each other. They just need a little time."

Kitty Shameless sat on the second step, staring at the assembly in a hostile fashion. He didn't like Laverne and Shirley. He didn't like them one bit.

* * *

Spinner, true to his word, provided an endless stream of amenities for the cockers. He paraded back and forth from the car with dog dishes, Kibbles and Bits, canned dog food, dog toys and dog beds with puffy mattresses in a bone print.

Laverne and Shirley immediately seized a rubber toy in the shape of a cat and pulled back and forth, a tug of war that sent them first one direction, then the other.

Shameless sat on the kitchen counter, his head moving back and forth in rhythm with the dogs' antics.

To prove Spinner's faith in them well-founded, the sisters went through the dog door, did their chores and banged right back, to receive Spinner's praise and head pats.

"See, nothing to worry about! They're such smart little dogs. Don't you just love them?" Spinner marveled.

"Yeah, yeah, they'll probably take this year's Pulitzer Prize. Remember, this is a temporary arrangement."

"Okay. Hey, do you still want the big guy here, too?"

"No, I'll be fine."

"Okay, the girls will bark if they hear anything but Nate Dupray's on the run. He won't show up here."

"I'm sure you're right. The more I think about it, the

more I think Nate's the guy. If Susanne told him I was encouraging her to break it off with him, he could have wanted revenge. He has a violent temper... Spinner, if you have a chance to stop at the women's shelter tomorrow, could you check on Destry Murphy for me? I'm worried about her."

"I'll try and find some time. I'll be at the high school in the afternoon. See you then. Why don't you let me take you to dinner? Repay you for helping me out with the girls?"

"Oh, okay... See you tomorrow, then."

"Lock everything up, Anneka."

* * *

Laverne and Shirley made the rounds with Anneka. She checked the doors and the windows and turned off all but the night lights. The cockers padded up the stairs after her, checked out their new doggy beds and then jumped to the foot of Anneka's downy comforter, snuggled and snorkled into position and fell immediately asleep. This new life was working out beautifully.

"Oh, all right, girls! Just this time, though."

When she switched off the bedside lamp, the moon was shining brightly on the bed. The comforter was all warm and cozy where the little cockers slept. Hmmm, tomorrow. Dinner... with Spinner. Anneka giggled. That rhymed. She slept. For the first time in a long while, she didn't dream.

CHAPTER 11

ANNEKA REACHED FOR the shrilling phone across her cluttered desk.
"Counseling office. This is Anneka Ericcson speaking."

"Hey, Paleface. Whatta you doin'?"

"Hey, Skye. Oh, I'm just entertaining college reps, getting ready for the next batch of SAT's, screening students for scholarships, writing letters of recommendation, seeing students and answering the stupid telephone . . . other than that, nothing."

"Why, throw in some crisis counseling and one enraged parent and that's been my day." Skye said. "How are you doing, otherwise? Excluding our crazy jobs?"

"Pretty well, considering. I have two new roommates, Laverne and Shirley. You should come over and meet them."

"Don't even tell me you've gotten more cats."

"Nope, two new dogs. Compliments of Dr. Spinner Hartmann. He rescued them from the pound yesterday. Spun me some yarn on how the poor things were about to be exterminated."

"Just what you need. They guard dogs at least?"

"They think they are. Actually, they're two identical little cockers. But not to worry. Soon as he finds a place where he can keep all three dogs, Spinner's getting them right back."

"Well, I'm thrilled for you. I would have told him to pitch a tent. Besides the animal connection, what's shaking with you and the good doctor?"

"He's invited me for dinner tonight, and you know... I'm kind of nervous about it. It's been awhile since I've actually been on a date. Usually we're with the Lemonade Ladies or at school."

"Anneka, you're a big girl now. I'm sure Spinner enjoys our company but he wants to see you by yourself."

"Why? I was comfortable the way it was. Maybe you and Charles could join us for dinner? Or meet us for a drink?"

"Nope. C'mon, Spinner's fun and attractive. Don't think somebody won't grab him fast, if you're not interested."

"I am interested , Skye. I'm just nervous!"

"What's to be nervous? You've got plenty of things in common plus two of his dogs."

Out of the corner of her eye, Anneka spotted John Clayton lingering by the office door. "There's a student waiting for me, Skye. Can I call you back?"

"No, listen. I need to tell you something I picked up from a couple of kids this morning. They told me Nate Dupray was into drug dealing, big time. Said they saw him Thursday night before the murder flashing a lot of money. Bragging he had five thousand dollars on him and a lot more coming."

"Wow, that explains why the police haven't got him. He's got connections and money? Probably took off for Portland or Seattle. I'll tell the district attorney. He may want to talk to those kids. Now we know who bailed Nate out of jail. His family certainly doesn't have that kind of money."

"Yeah, well, I wanted to let you know. Call and tell me how your date with Spinner goes. And relax about it!"

"I'll try."

"Love ya, kid. Bye."

* * *

John Clayton stepped tentatively to the open door of the office and knocked twice.

"Um, Ms. Ericsson, do you have a few minutes? Or can I make an appointment for another time?"

Actually, I've been wanting to talk to you, John. It's just been too hectic. Come in."

John was a tall imposing young man with none of his father's irritating manner. Unerringly polite, and always dressed impeccably, he looked ivy league. His shiny brown loafers with the little tassels were almost too preppy for Cook High.

"Your last SAT scores came in, John. Let me get them."

"I'd appreciate that. I have to have a high SAT to get a good scholarship. This is the third time I've taken it cause I wanted to improve my math score"

"Well, you didn't need much improvement, but your score is higher. Combined score . . . 1560." Anneka placed John's folder back in the file cabinet. "You've almost aced the thing. I'm so proud of you."

"Thanks, but my dad . . . I was hoping I could get a perfect 1600 this time. I wonder what I missed."

"John, it's very rare anyone gets a perfect score. You're in the very top percentage."

"I know , but I want to get into one of the top schools. I don't have that many extracurricular things on my college resume."

John was right. The top universities wanted students with high grade points and SAT scores but students with leadership qualities who excelled in extracurricular areas, as well.

In the three years Anneka had known John, she'd occasionally see him with other students, but most of his free time, even at lunch, was spent in the library or working in the science or math labs.

"Umm, the reason I needed to see you, Ms. Ericsson? I've *got* to keep my four point. So, I need you to take me out of history with Ms. Wagoner. Can you find an opening for me in another honors? Ms. Wagoner gave me a *B*. My dad wants me out of there."

John's anxiety was apparent in his voice. Anneka felt sorry for him.

"All right, John. It's bad timing. We're so far into the semester, but, okay. Pick up the change tomorrow morning."

"Uh . . . my dad wanted me to tell you to change Jamie from her class, too. Jamie doesn't like Ms. Wagoner and Dad says it's stressing her out."

John clenched his hands together. His knuckles turned white from the pressure. *The poor kid*, Anneka thought. *Now Clayton's got John taking responsibility for Jamie.*

"John, you know your sister's in special ed. Her schedule changes have to be done in an I.E.P. Have your dad call me, or better yet, have Jamie come in and talk to me. She's an adult now."

"She won't do it. She always has to have somebody else do it for her. She's twelve going on twenty. Sometimes I could just— um, well . . . I'll tell Dad what you said, Ms. Ericcson. I'll stop in before school tomorrow and pick up my schedule change. Thanks for your help."

What was he about to say? Anneka wondered. It was so seldom John showed any emotion. He must know his dad's sleeping in Jamie's room. What a perverted family. John needs out of there and fast.

The phone rang twice, signaling an in-school call.

"Hi, this is Anneka."

"Have you seen Nogood this morning?" Lainey asked.

"No, haven't had time. Why?"

"Holy shit. She's got a shiner bigger than a prize fighter."

"What!"

"Yeah, she says she stepped on a hoe handle— My Aunt Martha's drawers."

"Oh God, it's that damn Manny guy. She really knows how to pick 'em."

I think you should talk to her, Anneka. She always listens to you."

"I'll try but you know she's never had any sense when it comes to men. But I'll try... Lainey, I gotta go."

Anneka hung up just as Lou Wagoner rapped at the office door and ambled in. She draped her lanky frame over the office chair and threw a long leg over the chair's arm. The foot was encased in a canvas hightop, magenta and lime in color, untied shoestring dangling over the side. It looked like a cast-off from Dennis Rodman's closet.

My aching butt! Anneka thought. Now she was going to have to listen to another harangue from Lou. She'd rather have a root canal... But wait... the woman was smiling!

"I just had something I wanted to feel you out on, Anneka. If you've got a minute."

"Sure, Lou."

Today Lou had perched the artificial flower on top of her uncombed mop. Her make up was overdone, a scarlet slash of lipstick was smeared across her teeth. She looked like Delta Dawn, thirty years later, still waiting for the lover who had taken a powder.

"I was wondering, Anneka, if you're seeing Dr. Hartmann... exclusively?"

Oh shit. She didn't need this. What was she going to say to this woman?

"Dr. Hartmann and I work together, Lou. We're friends. Why?"

"Well, I've been wanting to ask him over for dinner since

he's new in town, and all. But I didn't want to interfere, you know, if you had an exclusive relationship with him?"

"Lou, I've only known him a few weeks."

"Good! That's understood then. He's fair game. I think he's very handsome."

And Lou sashayed out of the office, a much older version of one of Anneka's lovesick coeds.

* * *

When the outside door of the counseling center squeaked, Anneka came to with a start. How long had she been working at her computer? A quick look at the wall clock showed it to be five-thirty. It was pitch dark outside the windows, the only light came from her computer. Damn! She was alone in the building again. This wasn't supposed to happen.

When she heard the stealthy steps crossing the waiting room, Anneka totally freaked. *Who* was that and why were they being so quiet? Without even thinking, she took a nose-dive under the big oak desk and pulled the office chair in after her.

My God! Who is this? Fred or Maggie would have called out to me. They wouldn't scare me like this. Oh-my-God!

The quiet footsteps passed from the waiting room into the office and stopped before the desk. Whoever it was, it was a heavy breather. Anneka was grateful. Maybe they wouldn't hear her heart lurching around her chest!

She scrunched together in a tight ball. Then she saw it. A magenta and lime hightop still trailing a yellow shoelace. What the hell? It was Lou Wagoner! Could she just pop up now? Oh, hi Lou. Don't mind me. I usually spend the afternoon tucked under my desk? No, this was just too damn embarrassing. She'd have to stay here till the woman left. Wait a minute. Why is she rifling through the papers on the desk? Then in disbelief, Anneka heard the unmistakable sounds of the buckles on her briefcase being unsnapped and then, the rustling of papers. This was unbelievable! Embarrassing or not, she wasn't taking this! All of a sudden, the briefcase snapped shut. The tennis shoe retreated. Anneka heard the outside door close quietly and collapsed in relief. It was several minutes before she could gather the strength to begin unwinding her cramped limbs.

Anneka was about to crawl out from the confined quarters when she heard more footsteps approach. This time, the intruder was humming softly, and again, paused by her desk. The carefully shined loafer with the tassel could belong to none other. It was John Clayton! What did he want? Should she pop up now? Anneka could just hear the story repeated over the Clayton dinner table or to the student body at large. Guidance Counselor Puts In Overtime Under Her Desk. Nope, she was staying right here until he went away. The loafer passed and she almost gasped at the sound of her student files being opened. A couple of heartbeats later, the shoes glided by and out the door, followed by the sound of the outside door being quietly closed.

Without further delay, Anneka emerged shakily from beneath the desk. What had Lou wanted and what was John Clayton doing in her files? Checking for the top ten list, no doubt. Luckily, she kept that in the main office file. Grabbing her purse, she beat a hasty retreat out the door. Anneka didn't know if she should be feeling embarrassed or furious. Alternating emotions coursed through her veins.

But she was late for her first real date with Spinner. She'd think about it all later. Back at Tara.

* * *

Anneka stayed with Spinner that night. It was nice. He smelled like spicy soap and he didn't snore.

CHAPTER 12

*H*AVE TO STOP *smoking. Mother's right. It's going to kill me. Where is that bitch? Three in the morning for chrissake. I want to go home and get some sleep. Somewhere fucking her brains out with that psychologist, no doubt. Acts so, so pure and she's such a fucking whore.*

Damn cold in these woods. Stupid little dogs. Sniffing over here and yapping their heads off. They must smell me, damn it! Where the HELL is she?

Some women should never be born. So inconsiderate. Always thinking of themselves. Worthless tramps!

The killer sheathed the heavy gutting knife and crept away, shivering in the damp and early dawn. Nothing remained in the dark curtain of trees but a faint scent of smoke and the impression of heels in the moldering leaves ...

* * *

The day was cold and clear. One of those days on the coast that make up for all the rain.

They had crept into the house early. Early enough for the neighbors to still be tucked in their beds. At four in the morning, Spirit Cove was chilled and asleep. Not a person abroad in the brittle new day.

Spinner had insisted on following her home and checking the house before he left. Laverne and Shirley were ecstatic to see them both They were too smart to play favorites.

Anneka slept until nine, reveling in the fact that it was the weekend. She had the whole Saturday to unwind and spend on herself. Classical music drifted through the house and sunlight made silhouettes on the walls. She took her coffee and climbed to the crow's nest, Laverne and Shirley close behind. Kitty Shameless slept without a care in the middle of her desk.

Sinking into the easy chair, Anneka gazed out on a glistening sea. The cockers shared bits of her jelly doughnut and cleaned up all the crumbs. Probably bad for their teeth. Ah, well, their teeth were Spinner's problem. Relaxing and dreaming in the easy chair on this beautiful morning, Anneka felt positively euphoric. She could almost pretend things were the way they'd been, before all the horror happened.

Spinner had stopped by the women's shelter the day before and reported to Anneka that Destry Murphy was asking for her. Anneka planned to do some errands in Newport and then go see her. The girl was so depressed, the counselors were concerned about her mental and physical well-being. Anneka didn't know why, but Destry was never quite out of her thoughts.

She had told Spinner about Lou Wagoner showing up in her office yesterday and then coming back and scaring her half to death. Spinner had a theory. He thought Lou might have been looking for information about him. She had left three requests for his phone number in his mailbox and he'd ignored all three. Maybe she thought Anneka had his number written somewhere in her office. It was far fetched, but Lou's behavior, of late, was a bit bizarre.

Anneka still got embarrassed remembering how she'd hidden under her desk. In the light of day, the fear she'd felt seemed exaggerated. Nate was a fugitive. Unlikely he'd show up in New Albion again.

Anneka resolved not to think about it. She was just going to enjoy the day. The cockers and Shameless were all sleeping in the sun. Anneka relaxed and let her mind dance with the music.

* * *

She had errands and grocery shopping to do before she visited Destry. Anneka slipped into her favorite jeans, a pullover, wool socks with Birkenstocks, and a white downy jacket. She pinned her hair up under a soft floppy hat and she was ready to go. While she locked up the house, Laverne and Shirley dogged her every step. Oh, what the hell. She'd let them come along.

"Do you want to go bye-bye in the car-car?"

Oh brother, she thought. Listen to me.

In jest, she said, "Go get your leashes. Don't expect me to do everything for you."

She had not anticipated their reaction. They turned in unison, dashed into the utility room, and galloped back to their new mistress, leashes trailing from their mouths.

"I'll be damned! Where did you learn to do that? You're good girls. Yes, you are."

Wait'll she told Spinner. Laverne and Shirley were smart. Real smart.

The girls needed a boost into the back of the Durango and off they went, through the woods to 101.

The drive to Newport takes scarcely twenty minutes and is ocean view most of the way, but it was the weekend and there was traffic. She drove south, engine humming, the CD playing the velvety tones of Kevin Mahogany. The cockers pressed their noses to the glass, fascinated with the landscape whizzing by their rear window.

She knew it was Spinner when the cell phone chirped.

"Hello?"

"Excuse me, but could you connect me with the lady I saw last night?"

"Oh, you must mean Bon Bon? She's with a customer and can't be disturbed."

"Well, then, could you inquire if she'd let me fix her dinner? At her place?"

"Hell, yes. If you're cooking. Anything I can get at the store? I'm going for groceries."

"I'll pick it up . All I need is your kitchen and your company."

"What a deal. You give great therapy, Dr. Hartmann."

"Spinner, did you know Laverne and Shirley can fetch their own leashes? I was amazed. Who owned them? They're really well trained."

"I know. I didn't tell you because it's so poignant They were the pets of an elderly woman found dead in her apartment. Laverne and Shirley were standing guard over her. They had to be dragged away from her body."

"Oh, God. Oh, Spinner. That's so sad."

"I'm just glad I found them in time. Wonderful little dogs. See you tonight about seven?"

"Seven's good. I'm going to see Destry and then stop for groceries. Be home in a couple of hours. Bye."

Anneka pulled up in front of the women's shelter and left the cockers with the windows open. It was a cool day. They'd be fine.

"You guard girls. You guard!"

The cockers went on full alert status, staring intently out

the back window, little tails wagging furiously. They were *so* cute!

* * *

Destry sat dejectedly in a corner on an old ramshackle couch. Probably donated by some philanthropist for a deduction on a tax return. Poor kid.

Women and children were scattered about the living room. They all had the same demeanor. Some watched soaps on television. Others just stared into space. The whole place smelled of hopelessness.

"Hi Destry, honey."

Anneka gave the girl a hug.

"Oh Ms. Ericsson, you came. Have you seen Nate?"

"He hasn't been seen anywhere. The police can't find him."

"Something bad's happened to him."

"Why do you think that, Destry?"

Anneka watched Destry's fingers knead at the homemade dress, saw the anxiety and indecision play across her eyes.

"I shouldn't tell you. I promised him I wouldn't tell."

"Destry, if you know anything that could help the police find Nate, please tell me. If Nate didn't kill Susanne, he needs to come forward and clear his name. Otherwise, he'll be running for the rest of his life. Do you understand that?"

"Miss Ericsson, Nate isn't afraid of the police."

"Who's he afraid of then?"

"He was doing ... some bad things. I found money hidden in the trailer. I've never seen so much money."

Destry's face was deadly white and she was biting at her already bloody nails, but she took a deep breath and continued.

"He was getting drugs from Portland and selling them here on the coast. He said if I ever told, he'd be killed. And they'd kill me too and the *baby* ! I'm so scared, Ms. Ericsson. These people are really dangerous."

Anneka took the girl's shaking hands in hers and held tight.

"Destry, listen to me. You're safe here. Completely safe."

By now the other women were staring at them curiously. Anneka led the weeping girl to a far corner of the room, out of earshot.

"Did you ever see any of these people or get their names? Did they come to the trailer?"

"No, he always met them late at night. He said they'd bring the drugs to the cove."

"What cove?"

"Spirit Cove. He'd go through the coast guard cottages and take that wooden walk to the cove. At night, it's real deserted. There's a rusted old still left from prohibition, the one in the ferns next to the boardwalk? He met them there all the time."

"Destry, did Nate ever mention to you that I lived in the cove?"

"No, I don't think so. It's a wonderful place, though. My mom's native-American. She told me there are Indian spirits there."

It *must* have been Nate in her house that night, Anneka realized. He was using the cove to meet his drug contacts. She needed to get this information to the sheriff.

"Thanks for telling me this, Destry. It explains why Nate has disappeared."

"You think he's dead, don't you? *Do* you think he's dead?"

Anneka thought it more likely Nate was hiding out in Portland with his drug profits and his big-time connections.

"Destry, you need to face the facts. Nate's a criminal and possibly a murderer. He's going to prison, in either case. You have to think of yourself and your baby."

"But, Nate's all I have! I can't take care of this baby by myself! What am I going to do?"

"Let's talk about that. What have you discussed with the counselors here?"

Destry sighed and buried her face in her hands. When she looked up, her eyes were calm. Her voice was resigned.

"They don't say anything outright, but I can tell they think I'm too young to keep this baby. I don't have anywhere to go. I won't live with my brothers. What would you do?"

"Hard question, Destry. Do you have any other family?"

" My mom and dad live in Albany."

"Why can't you go there? Have you fought with them?"

Destry sighed heavily once more.

"No, but I went to live with my brothers to get away from my mom and dad. We used to live on the reservation but dad didn't like it so we moved to Albany. We stayed in a church shelter at night. There were a lot of homeless people there. The church gave us a blanket and we'd sleep on the floor. We got two meals a day. The rest of the time, we had to get out of the church. Mom had free bus passes so we'd ride around on the bus or hang out at the library till we could go back to the church. I hardly went to school at all after the fourth grade."

"Oh, Destry . . . When did you leave Albany."

"On my thirteenth birthday. There were a lot of homeless people sleeping at the church that night because it was so cold. I'd gone to sleep when I felt somebody pulling on my blanket. It was this old dirty man who smelled really bad. He was trying to feel my . . . well, you know, Miss.

My mom called my brothers and they said if I'd cook and keep the trailer clean, I could stay with them for awhile. But they drink a lot and they're always bringing women home and partying in the trailer. It's no place for a baby."

The girl's voice revealed a lifetime of misery. Anneka held her close. Destry slumped and was still.

"Destry, you asked me what I'd do. I'm going to tell you."

Anneka took a deep breath. "I'd give the baby up for adoption. I feel this would be the most loving thing you could do. Give your child the chances you never had. Then, you could go ahead and plan for your future and know that someday, someday you'd be prepared to have a real family."

Destry said nothing. She lay in Anneka's arms like a rag doll.

Anneka felt Destry's tears on her cheek, but the girl's head rested on Anneka's shoulder; the tears were her own.

"Hey, you don't have to decide anything right now. There'll be more time to think about it when you talk with the counselors. Go wash your face and comb that pretty hair. We're going to lunch."

In the seaside restaurant Destry relaxed and ate her fish and chips with a fifteen-year old's healthy appetite.

When they returned to the shelter, Laverne and Shirley covered the laughing girl's face with kisses. Destry clung to the older woman for a long moment before she climbed clumsily out of the car.

The afternoon was almost gone but there was still grocery shopping to be done. Anneka planned to call the sheriff and the district attorney when she got home, to tell them what she had learned from Destry.

* * *

The Safeway was crowded at this time on Saturday afternoon. Anneka whirled through the aisles, throwing the basic foodstuffs in the cart as she went. Having a new boyfriend helped her avoid a lot of temptation and she wheeled virtuously past the candy and bakery sections.

Anneka was so intent on her shopping, she smashed her cart right into the cart driven by Mr. Clayton.

"Whoooa! Slow down there, Ms. Ericsson! Where you going in such a hurry?"

Anneka didn't answer. She was staring at Mr. Clayton's feet . . . in a pair of shiny, brown loafers with little tassels.

FOUL WEATHER

* * *

In bed, that night she tossed and turned. She couldn't get over the idea that it might have been the senior Clayton rooting around in her office, looking through her files during a time he knew the building was probably deserted. It was really weird.

Her last waking thought was of Destry before she drifted into dreams.

* * *

On the other side of town in her borrowed bed, Destry dreamed as well. Oddly, she dreamed of the little cove. That secluded and beautiful place where she had gone with Nate. Climbing and laughing they had scaled the side of Big Whale Cove and taken the path that wound down to Spirit Cove. There was a totem pole standing above the shore. Nate had explained the totem was in homage to the Indian tribe that had first inhabited the surrounding area. Destry had run her hand over the carved figures in wonder, remembering her mother's stories of the spirits that roamed the cove. Each time she and Nate returned, she would stop to caress the totem.

They had made love here for the first time. Nate had been so sweet, so sincere.

It was so clear, the night, the stars ... In her dream, she saw a fire in the distance and a girl, a slim girl who stood at the top of the path and looked longingly out to sea, her face wet with rain. No, not rain, tears. Her face was wet with tears ...

The spirit of Dancing Rain

The dogs have found the bones of my dead baby.

MARY ANNE LARSON

My dead baby. No larger than a bird.

There is an outcry in the camp. The men talk in loud voices and I hear the old women muttering as they warm themselves by the fire. They say the spirits will be angry.

But I have done my dance to the guardian spirit. She will lead the baby to the country of souls, will help her cross the river to the other side. There, the river will always be filled with fish and there will be beautiful birds and many days of sun. And someday, my guardian spirit will lead me there and I will be with my baby again.

I used my hooded cloak for a shroud. I needed to wrap something around her. She looked so cold. No time for mourning but I left a piece of my hair in the shroud. It will bind us for all time. I will not think of the bones . . . her spirit has already crossed the river.

They will recognize the cloak as mine. Such fine cloth woven with golden threads. It could only have come from the ship. My gift, from Drake, the man from across the sea.

It won't be long now. He will come for me in the cove. Tomorrow, I will rise early in the dawn and purify myself in the waters.

I will wait in the cove.

CHAPTER 13

ANNEKA WAS A few minutes late when she pulled into the *Whaler's Landing* restaurant. Outdoor steps led from the back parking lot to the upstairs bar that looked out on the little harbor. The tourist brochures called it the smallest harbor in the world.

Across the street from the restaurant were the famous "spouting horns." These were a phenomena of the sea, caused by rushing waves entering holes in the rocks. As water filled the rock's crevice, a spout would shoot into the air, effectively drenching the hapless tourists standing on the bridge.

Ocean going vessels used for whale watching excursions ferried tourists in and out of the harbor. Mostly gray whales traveled up the coast from Baja to their home in the Bering sea. Orcas were less frequently seen, but occasionally, they would sweep into the bay snapping up seals in their massive jaws.

Anneka was meeting the Lemonade Ladies. They had lured Nogood here under false pretenses. They were having an "intervention."

Anneka's quick glance at Nogood confirmed she had a shiner, all right. Sitting at the end of the table, she was throwing back a highball that Anneka suspected was not her first. The friends had agreed to talk to her, all of them together, hoping it might have some impact.

"Hey, Skye. On my way over, I think I spotted Elvis at the Texaco Station," said Nogood. "Maybe he's not dead, after all."

"C'mon, Nogood," said Lainey. "Skye and I don't want to hear any cracks about Elvis. He's our idol."

"Well, you should hit on some men that are alive. My idol's Johnny Depp."

"Since you brought it up, Nancy-George, we've been wanting to talk about who's hitting on *you*," Maggie said. "Let's hear about the eye?"

"My eye was an accident. Where's that girl? Hey, how about another drink over here?"

"Nogood, we mean it," Maggie said quietly. "We're worried about this guy."

"No need to be worried. It's none of your damn business, anyway. I can take care of myself."

"Then why this scene straight out of *Looking for Mr. Goodbar*? said Anneka. "This isn't the first time some man's used you for a punching bag,"

"Listen, I threw Manny out on his ass. He won't be back! Now, does that make you all feel better?"

"No, not really. We've heard it before," Lainey broke in from the other end of the table.

"All right!" Nogood sank back in her chair and sighed, "I know you're my friends. You mean well or I wouldn't listen to this for a damn minute. The fact is, most nice men bore me. Too predictable. I like a few thrills in my relationships."

"A black eye is thrilling? Get real," Lainey said.

"Goddamn it! That's enough!" Nogood slammed her glass on the table and glared. "It's really not any of your fucking business who I see, is it? I said I told Manny to take a hike and that's all you need to know. Now, can we have another drink here and change the subject—or I'm leaving. I mean it!"

* * *

The Lemonade Ladies had tried but they knew when to shut up. You could only push Nogood just so far. She said Manny was gone and they'd have to be content with that. Still, everyone was in a lighter mood when they left the restaurant.

Skye couldn't resist one parting shot as everyone went to their respective cars.

"Remember, Nogood, if they don't remember when Kennedy was shot, they're too young to date!"

"Up yours, Bellingham!"

But Maggie followed Anneka to her car and pulled her aside.

"Do you think Manny's really gone, Anneka? I mean, what does anybody know about this guy? He just shows up in town from who knows where. He's prone to violence on women..."

"What are you thinking, Maggie?"

"I don't know, how do we know he's not some kind of a predator, or something. It wouldn't hurt to mention his name to the police, would it?"

"I think he's just another of Nogood's bad choices but no, it wouldn't hurt. Don't tell her, though."

* * *

It was about eight p.m. when Anneka turned south on 101 and headed home. Still early, but the night was black and stormy. The sturdy Durango tunneled through the dark, its headlights the only light on the coast highway.

She had expected to go home directly after school. She'd left no lights on and the animals must be getting hungry. Kitty Shameless would fend for himself but the cockers required more care. Anneka had to admit she was going to miss the little sisters when Spinner found a new house. Maybe they could work some kind of arrangement where the pups stayed with her on weekends or something. Sort of a joint custody kind of thing...

She hit the remote control for the gate, maneuvered the winding narrow road through the trees, past the recreation center and turned left on Breaker's Scarp.

The headlights illuminated her front door and she brought the Durango to an abrupt halt in the drive. The front door was open!... Maybe she hadn't pulled it tight when she left this morning? The wind off the ocean could have blown it open. It had happened before. Her arms had been filled with records and a briefcase. Yes, she could have neglected to pull the door completely closed. Had it clicked? She couldn't remember.

Popping the back door of the Durango, Anneka rummaged under the floor carpet for the tire iron she kept there. She made as much noise as possible approaching the door. She felt foolish. How many times had she been in a hurry and forgotten to lock the door? She was certain this was nothing. Still, Anneka rang the doorbell twice and called out in a loud voice.

"Anneka? Anneka, we're here! Are you home? Fred and I are here. Hello? " The last hello she pitched in a low, gruff tone.

Clutching the tire iron, Anneka went inside, switched on the lights and stared.

The place was in shambles.

She stood motionless and strained for sound. Nothing... only the muffled crash of the sea against the rocks.

Slowly, she absorbed the scene before her.

FOUL WEATHER

Glass shards glistened on the hearth, her prized crystal sailing sloop had been torn from the mantel. A vase of fresh cut flowers had been smashed; water stains dripped from walls and strewn petals bled on the wood floor. Down feathers from the ripped couch and pillows had settled gently on broken picture frames. A large picture of Anneka's sister, Margit and her family was torn in half. Her brother Arne and pictures of Marilyn and the children ripped in pieces.

Books were flung helter-skelter. She trembled as she reached for a piece of paper on a pile of hardcovers.

The lined paper was stained dark brown in places. It was a poem of some kind, scrawled in curling, girlish script across the page.

The air was not so clean
The sea gone gray, not green

Gulls had shed their gleaming white
The stars shone not so bright

It was November . . .

When last I saw the sea
It sparkled

Sunlit waves

Gulls soared
And children laughed with glee

But that was June
And June is gone from me
Author
Susanne Slocum

Anneka's hand shook violently. The poem slipped through her fingers and fluttered to the floor, coming to rest among the books and flowers and fractured bits of glass.

Several seconds elapsed before the dread pushed forward in her frozen brain. The animals! Where were the animals?

"Laverne, Shirley! Here Kitty, Kitty! Oh my God! Please!"

She picked up the dropped tire iron and raced through the downstairs rooms into the utility room. Pictures of old psycho-movies flashed through her mind. A cat nailed to a door. Hideous scenarios flickered in her brain like silent cinema on fast forward.

Maybe they were outside. Maybe they'd all run out through the dog door. She threw open the utility room door to the garage. Behind her, a small chirp of a sound.

"Kitty? Kitty Shameless? Where are you?"

Another muted meow from the upended paper bag on the floor. Shameless stared at Anneka from inside. His unfathomable green eyes revealing nothing.

The tire iron clattered to the floor. Anneka pulled him out and hugged him tightly.

"Oh thank you, God. Thank you!"

She wiped her tears on the cat's velvety head.

The cockers!

She lowered the cat to the floor and raced to the outside calling frantically. Again and again she called, her voice thrown back by the wind. In minutes she was soaked with rain.

Maybe they were upstairs! She took the stairs two at a time to the loft.

She spotted the cockers first. They were hidden under the chaise lounge. Two black noses rested between four tan paws. They whined pitifully, and looked at Anneka with mournful eyes.

There was no time to feel relief. Anneka stared with horror and disbelief at her bed.

On the pale-green muslin coverlet was a reeking pile of human excrement.

She knew it was human because in the middle of the steaming mess, someone had placed a fresh yellow flower.

CHAPTER 14

SHE SANK TO the chaise and rocked back and forth while waves of nausea rocked her body.
Staggering, Anneka returned downstairs and poured a large dose of whiskey from the wet bar.

Incredibly, there was another glass on the bar, half filled with bourbon. The visitor had stopped for a drink as well. Anneka swept the heavy glass to the floor.

The bourbon hit like a hot avalanche. Bending double, she retched on the floor, sickness coming in waves.

When the nausea passed, Anneka remembered the drawer on her bedside table hanging open. She climbed again to the loft.

It was gone, of course. The gun was gone.

* * *

Hope you liked the present, Anneka. Just a little hostess gift. And I might add, thank YOU for the lovely gun. I did you a favor, really. Loaded guns can be dangerous.

Your home is lovely. Pretty pricey, too. Money from your former husband, no doubt.

Ah well, a home's a castle, isn't it? That's what my fucking mother always says.

Did you enjoy Susanne's touching little poem? Teenage girls are so sappy. It make's me want to puke.

A bit risky for me to be here. The cops are watching you really closely. But I'm so fond of my little hiding place in the trees. Like being right in the room with you. Did you know with my scope, I can see you naked? Yes, I can.

I've got to leave for a while. Got laundry to do or mother gets her underwear all in a bunch.

The killer slithered from the sheltering trees and disappeared.

Just the illusion remained, thick, black and secret.

* * *

Anneka called Spinner first. He came right away, called the police and supported her through questioning that went on for hours. The crime team took the gun's registration number. Nate Dupray was now both armed and dangerous.

The poem had to be left by Susanne's killer. The clue showed a cold calculation that chilled Anneka. She remembered the blood-soaked papers from the girl's backpack. Nate obviously felt no remorse for killing Susanne. And her bed . . . that was the act of a psychopath.

The detectives said she had probably missed him by minutes. They theorized he had been waiting for her to return and went into a rage when she did not. The search network had been widened and the cove was cordoned off to traffic. Dogs could be heard baying in the woods. The crime team put her house off limits while they searched and combed, probed and poked. It was like having her bones picked.

When the last man packed his kit and left, Anneka stood

and looked helplessly at the chaos in her living room. Spinner gathered all the animals together. He deposited the cockers in the back of his Jeep and helped her gently into the front seat. Shameless was quivering and mewing pitifully as Spinner placed him carefully on Anneka's lap.

"We'll all camp out at my apartment tonight, Anneka. My landlady be damned."

Too tired to protest, Anneka sank back in the Jeep. It felt so good to let someone take care of her. Shameless curled up in her lap and they comforted each other. From the back seat, Ollie placed his big gentle head on her shoulder. The cockers snuffled and curled up together.

They all went to Spinner's place.

CHAPTER 15

ANNEKA HAD TAKEN a day off after the break-in. She had used the time to replace her gun. Spinner advised she replace the magnum with something a bit more manageable. Anneka remembered the powerful kick from the magnum only too well and settled for a pearl handled thirty-eight snub-nosed revolver. It fit her hand better and was still an efficient weapon.

Her house was put back in order and the broken things replaced by the Lemonade Ladies. They showed up after school and worked way into the night. They were such great friends. Her bed now boasted a sparkling new white duvet and a towering heap of snowy pillows of all shapes and sizes to match. All the hideous reminders were gone. Only the vibrations of violence lingered.

* * *

The mailroom was filled with teachers hurriedly collecting their mail before the first bell of the school day. Several of them gave Anneka sympathetic hugs and reassurances. She fought to keep from bursting into tears. Her emotions were still too close to the surface.

Jason Peabody, a first year teacher in the science department, lingered.

"They'll get the son-of-a-bitch, Anneka. The whole state's looking for him. I had Nate in Physical Science. He's not that smart. He'll be back behind bars where he belongs."

"Did you have problems with him, Jason? In class?"

"Nah, he never did any work but he was pretty laid back. Spent most of his time coming on to the girls or letting them come on to him. I got concerned about Jamie Clayton, though. She had a thing for Nate. Completely moony around him. You know what an innocent she is!"

If you only *knew* what an innocent Jamie is, Anneka thought.

Anneka's mailbox was crammed with the accumulation of two days. She reached for a folded paper caught in the back of the narrow box. It was stapled together across the entire flap. Anneka Ericsson was written in decisive black ink on one side.

> Anneka, I thought you said you weren't seeing Dr. Hartmann exclusively? That's not what the word is around school. You could at least have been honest with me! Thanks for letting me make a complete fool of myself!
> Lou Wagoner

Oh Jeez! That poor woman. Anneka crumpled the paper in dismay. She'd better talk to her. Damn!

FOUL WEATHER

* * *

The counseling center was filled with students, many waiting to talk to Anneka. They were always top priority. Anything else would have to wait.

Nick Cobos was one of Anneka's favorites. A senior, he was a National Merit Scholar and one of Cook High's top athletes.

Nick's freckled, boyish face looked concerned as he shrugged off a backpack that must have weighed fifty pounds.

"Ms. Ericsson, are you okay? Everybody's talking about Nate Dupray breaking into your place. I wanted to let you know some of us guys on the team are planning on watching your house at night."

"Nick, that's so thoughtful but you don't need to do that."

"We feel like there's not enough we can do for you, Ms. Ericsson. You're always here for us. The college rep from Penn State said you wrote me the best letter of recommendation he's ever seen and last year when my folks split up? You kept me going. Ms. Ericsson, you've been the "wind beneath my wings.""

Nick's speech ended in a gush and he reached over and patted Anneka's hand awkwardly. She couldn't bring herself to speak. Sometimes, the sweetness of these kids just knocked her out.

Anneka made sure she could keep her voice steady before she replied.

"Nick, you and your friends are the best. But the police are watching my house tonight and for as long as they need to. Please, don't worry about me. You'd be surprised at how tough I am."

"Are you sure, Ms. Ericsson? We don't want anything to happen to you. Nate's a jerk. You know, I saw him hanging around the night Susanne was murdered."

"Where?"

"I'd gone back to school to try and find Coach and I saw Nate parked in back by the auto shop."

"Did you tell the police?"

"I will, if you think it's important."

"I do, Nick. It could be important to prove their case."

"Okay, but remember now, if you need us for anything, you'll let us know?"

"My word on it, kid."

And Anneka's knight in shining football jersey, slung his heavy backpack over his shoulder and ducked out the door.

* * *

The phone rang once. An outside call.

"Counseling office, this is Anneka Ericsson."

"Ms. Ericsson, this is Detective Enger. We've finished combing the area surrounding your house. We need to let you know what we've discovered."

"Tell me."

"The trees and undergrowth are real thick but we found a place on the east side of the house that we think someone's been using to spy on you. There's a lot of footprints and trampled leaves and the area's littered with cigarette butts and debris. Even apple cores and banana peels, like someone's been camping out in there. Ms. Ericsson, we think the perp's been watching you, pretty regularly.

"My God!"

"With binoculars, he'd have a perfect bead into your living room, kitchen and bedroom."

* * *

Anneka was thoroughly shaken after the call from Detective Enger. When she finished seeing the last student, she slipped next door to Lainey's office .

FOUL WEATHER

"You got a minute for a friend who needs to run a few things by you?"

"Hey, you're white as a ghost. Don't tell me something else has happened."

Lainey was a great sounding board. In spite of her flighty exterior, she had a cool and analytical mind. She'd put things in perspective and come up with solid viable options.

"To begin with, this was in my mailbox this morning. How do you think I should handle it?" She handed over Lou Wagoner's note.

"Holy Shit."

"Yeah, I feel sorry for Lou, you know? And a little guilty, too. She asked me about Spinner and told me she was interested in him. I didn't know what to say; I'd just met him. Now, after all that's happened, Spinner and I have gotten, well, pretty close. He's been there through all this nightmare and I'm pretty involved with him at this point."

"You two click, Anneka. That's been obvious to all of us. You can't stop seeing Spinner because of Lou. The poor woman doesn't have a clue. That hair! Like a blow-dry with a Mixmaster. She looks like a joke. The kids are complaining about her classes, too. She's very critical of them and they don't like it."

"Yeah, my kids say the same thing. The way she's acting? I just don't get it."

"It's called recapturing lost youth," said Lainey. "I think Lou's lonely. Her mother died about a year ago and that was her only family. Sure, a boyfriend would be great but hey, she needs to face reality."

"Well, yeah, but how to tell her that?"

"You'll have to be candid with her. Write her a note."

"That's not the coward's way out?"

"No, might be easier for her that way. Give her time to absorb the facts without embarrassing either one of you."

"You're right. That's what I'll do. Now, listen to this. A

125

detective just called to say I'm being stalked. Apparently, Nate's been watching me from the trees by my house."

"Holy Shit! That scares my pants off. Anneka, you must be terrified!"

"I'm numb, actually. More angry, than afraid and I've got plenty of protection. I got another gun and the police are watching the house. So's Ed, our security guy at the cove. Plus, the neighborhood watch and Spinner's leaving Ollie at night. Spinner wanted to stay, too, but I don't think that's a good idea."

"Why?"

"There's two members of the school board who live at the cove. I don't want any talk. It's not good for the students to hear that kind of stuff. I know I'm not pure as the driven snow, don't even have to be, but I want to be a good role model for the kids. You know what I mean..."

"Anneka, I think your students adore you and realize you're an adult, but yeah, professionally, I see where you're coming from."

"Well, back to work. Thanks for the counseling session. And thanks for helping with the mess at the house. I don't know what I'd do without you guys."

"You're welcome. Hey, I love your hair today. It's got that casual, just-got-out-of-bed look. Verrrrry sexy!"

Lainey was such a bull-shitter, but Anneka patted her new "do." She felt better.

* * *

The phone rang. Anneka glanced at her watch and realized it was almost quitting time.

"Hey girl, what's it like at the office?"

"Busy as hell, Spinner. But I'm about finished for the day."

"Good! Because I want to take you to dinner. Why don't you meet me in Old Town at *The Captain's Table*? They've got a good seafood pasta there. Then we'll pick up Ollie and I'll take you home early. You need your sleep."

"Oh, that sounds wonderful. Five o'clock, okay?"

"Your vodka martini with two olives will be waiting."

She had purse and briefcase in hand when the phone rang again.

"Hi, Ms. Ericsson, this is Destry. Is it okay for you to talk!"

"Destry! Sure, good to hear from you. Are you doing all right?"

Destry's voice brought back Anneka's anxiety. She needed to see the girl.

"Yes, I'm doing fine. I wanted to let you know I thought about what we talked about. You know, about the baby? Then I talked with the counselors here and I've decided to give the baby up for adoption. I wanted to thank you for being so nice to me and helping me think things through."

"Oh, Destry, I know that was a tough decision. So what happens next?"

"I'm being sent to this girl's home in Portland. The counselors say it's real nice and I can live there and go to school. They have real good doctors, too, and they'll send me to a hospital to have the baby."

"Destry, that's great!"

"I know. I feel so much better about everything. The counselors say the people who adopt my baby will be really good parents and provide a wonderful home and everything. When I've had the baby, I can live at another home and keep going to school. And they'll give me more counseling, so I can decide what I want to do after I get out of school and—"

"Whoa! Hold on. I want to hear all about this in person. When do you have to leave?"

"Two days from now. Do you think I could see you before I go? I feel like you're my friend and I'm kind of lonely right now."

"Destry, I'll come tomorrow right after school. We'll go out to dinner. I want to see you too."

"That would be great. I'll be all ready . . . Ms. Ericsson? I saw what happened to you. It was on television. I'm so sorry. I can't believe I didn't see what kind of a person Nate was. I mean, I knew about the drugs and everything, but I never knew he was . . . crazy. How could I be so stupid?"

"Destry, we grow and we learn. That's what life's all about. I'll see you tomorrow and you can tell me all about your plans for the future. Remember, women need to be able to take care of themselves. It's a wonderful feeling when you know you can. My favorite expression? 'I am woman, hear me roar.'"

"'I am woman, hear me roar,'" Destry repeated slowly. Then she giggled.

Anneka smiled as she replaced the receiver. God, it felt good to hear that girl laugh.

CHAPTER 16

JAMIE CLAYTON CAREFULLY placed her left foot on the slippery ladder rung. The makeshift structure was precarious and creaked ominously as she climbed from the sandy beach floor of Big Whale Cove up the steep rock wall of the cliff. At the top of the ladder, she grasped the thick rope hanging over the side to hoist herself up over the edge. Brushing sand from her jeans, she peered into the blackness and made out the path which led down into Spirit Cove.

Where is he?

Shouldn't have come. It's creepy here at night. Hard climbing up that cliff, too. Good thing there's a ladder and a rope for that last part. I'm all dirty now. I probably look just awful.

This cove's blacker than any place I've ever seen. Like a jungle. You can't even see the sky. Trees dripping all over me. Cold. Should go home . . .

But Nate needs me. He'd never murder Susanne. He'd never hurt anybody. The police are so dumb.

I don't want to deliver that package for him, though. It's clear over to South Beach. Wouldn't do it, but might be the last time I see him, ever. I've got to see him one more time.

God, what if Daddy wakes up? He'll call the police, I know he will. I've got to get back. Where is he? Can't see my watch, it's so dark. I'll really be in trouble if they've found out I'm gone.

Please, God. Just let Nate take me with him. I won't ask you for anything else, just this. Please.

Hate it at home. Mama and John don't love me, anyway. It's always been just me and Daddy. He's changed, though. I don't really like being so close to him and everything. I could tell Ms. Ericsson didn't think it was right either. I hope she doesn't say anything.

If it got around school, John would be so mad at me. Say I was ruining his future. So smart, but mean. He's always been mean. I'm afraid he's going to hurt my little bird just like he said the last time he was mad at me. I hate him. I'll be so glad when he's gone to college.

If I could just go away with Nate! That would be so awesome. I'm going to ask him again. Have to figure out a way to bring Sunshine with me though. Nobody'd take care of him if I was gone.

Mother says birds are a dirty mess. She's mean too.

What's that?

Must be Nate. Thank God.

"Na-aaate! I'm down here. On the board walk, by this old tank thing. I was getting really scared... Nate?

"Hey! What are *you* doing here? Well, I'm just meeting somebody but what are you—

"Why are you pushing me? It's all wet down there. Stop it! I'm going to tell Daddy —"

* * *

When Jamie Clayton turned up dead, she'd been missing for two days.

Her body was in the rain forest, just off the wooden walkway, directly north of the old still. Anneka only had to walk a short distance to help the police with the identification.

The area was clear of evidence now. The rain had washed the blood stains from the needled floor. The entrails that had spilled on to the ferns and moss had been carefully scooped back into the body cavity by the forensics team.

But nobody could put Jamie back together again.

Anneka had trembled as she watched. They'd zipped up the body bag and carried it down the length of boardwalk, to the waiting ambulance at the end of Breakers Scarp.

Jamie had been wearing lavender-and-white striped overalls with a pink bandanna around her neck. The overalls had bloody holes in their bib.

Anneka remembered the outfit well. It must have been Jamie's favorite because she wore it so frequently... The color brought out the lavender in her dark-lashed eyes.

In fact, the last time Anneka had seen her, she'd worn those overalls.

She could see Jamie so clearly still, standing in front of the desk in her office, asking to use the phone to call her 'Daddy'. Saying he'd forgotten to give her lunch money again. Anneka remembered her lecture; about her lunch money being Jamie's responsibility.

How pompous she'd been. Come counsel with me, children. I'll give you good advice to carry to your grave. First, Susanne and now, Jamie. They'd needed her. She'd failed them. The guilt sucked her down like heavy stones. She couldn't bear it.

Forensics showed Jamie had not been raped. There was no physical evidence of sex before she died, but the tests revealed she had not been a virgin.

Anneka could have told them that.

*   *   *

She was sitting on the cliffs overlooking the cove. Today, the little sandy beach was strewn with great patches of sinewy kelp washed in on the waves. The surface of the water reflected no sun. Like the surface of my soul, she thought.

The sky was steel-gray. There was an eerie isolation in the fog and mist. Silent gulls hovered in the sheltering rocks.

Anneka shivered and hunkered down in her fleece-lined sweatshirt. Its hood protected her from the wind, but more importantly, it gave her more privacy from the watching policeman. The man seemed to respect her aloneness and stayed a good distance away, down in the cove. He had not climbed to her high perch on the rocks.

She felt a certain amount of sympathy for the policeman who waited so patiently in the mist. He reminded her of Ollie, who was patient with her, also. She had not brought the dogs, though they had longed to come. She couldn't stand their enthusiasm, found their joy unbearable. She wanted no one around her. Like gulls disturbed, her thoughts shrieked and screeched. She needed no one to hear them. They were private thoughts, private ghosts that swirled and eddied around her in the mist and the fog.

Anneka had stopped shedding tears. The night before she had cried herself to sleep. She shook and sobbed and wept and pounded her pillow till all feeling was gone. At first light, the pillow was sodden but the tears had stopped.

The second funeral had been too much. Voiced platitudes had fallen on her deaf ears. She was in a black rage.

She felt, she too, could kill without a moment's hesitation. She didn't care about the golden rule. She didn't give a fuck about turning the other cheek. She could have wrapped her hands around Jamie's father's neck and watched him die. She felt no sympathy for the weeping mother, a mother oblivious to evil in her own house. She felt no empathy for John, who stared so emotionlessly ahead.

And the young man, Nate Dupray, the killer in their midst, she wanted him found. She would have the bastard's liver.

But revenge escaped her. So she sat by the sea. Removed from human sins and sorrows.

Like the words of the psalm, "I would dwell in the uttermost parts of the sea...."

Far down the seawalk, at coves's point, she glimpsed a shrouded silhouette standing precariously on the very edge of the rocks. In the swirling mist, it looked like the person in her dream. She thought she heard a chant or the snatches of a melody. Not a ghost, then. Dead spirits do not sing.

Anneka started to call out to the police escort but the figure was gone. Vanished, as it vanished in her sleep.

She continued her seawatch. She continued her seachange.

CHAPTER 17

WELL, THAT WAS some stone face you put on at the funeral, Anneka, dear. One would think you were totally devoid of emotion.

But then, you probably won't miss Jamie all that much, will you? She was such a whiner. A stupid little girl, really, and so dependent on Daddy. I was surprised she'd venture out to the cove. Looking for a tryst with Nate, no doubt. Snooping around until she saw me. It just wouldn't do.

I thought I conducted myself very well at the services. All those police milling around. Such bad taste. The mourners were quite distracted.

I've missed spending my evenings with you but it's just too risky. My nights are quite dull. I am so sick of playing gin with mother. Perhaps, things will quiet down so I can resume my visits.

I understand your friends cleaned up the mess I made of your house. I'm sure the dear ladies were quite appalled. Oh, well , dear girl . . . Shit happens.

And the killer laughed heartily, convulsed with mirth. The noise reverberated inside the dark, warm car.

* * *

Anneka forced herself to return to work. This time of year, there was so much to do. Graduation to plan, pre-registration for next year, a thousand things to get done, to get underway. She had to go back. After the first day, it got better.

But Anneka was also anxious about Destry. Destry, who carried Nate Dupray's child.... He had murdered Susanne and Jamie. Both of whom had loved him. Was Destry safe? So far, Nate had eluded the growing network of law enforcement with astonishing ease. Anneka began to worry obsessively for Destry's safety. The sooner she was out of the vicinity, the better. The administrators at the shelter said they were moving her within the week. It wasn't soon enough for Anneka. She made arrangements with Spinner to drive the two of them to Portland.

The night before the move, Spinner and Anneka took Destry to dinner at the Salishan Lodge, an exclusive resort on the outskirts of Lincoln City. Anneka wanted the evening to be especially nice, A break from the austere and desperate setting of the women's shelter.

Destry looked so pretty. Her face at first so pale now had a healthy glow.

She carefully placed the fine linen napkin over her burgeoning stomach, and inquired earnestly about the extra silverware.

"Ms. Ericsson, do they give you two forks and two spoons, in case you drop one on the floor?"

What innocence! Anneka ached for her. Thank God, Spinner had come. He kept the evening light and fun.

Destry talked briefly of Nate. "It's hard to believe the father of my baby is actually a murderer but I can't understand why he'd desert us like this, otherwise."

"You have no idea where he's gone?" Spinner asked.

FOUL WEATHER

"No, I remember him hinting he always had a place to stay but he never told me where. Just that it was a big place and these guys were very rich."

"Well, let's enjoy ourselves tonight, Destry," Anneka said and lifted her wine glass. "Here's to your new future."

* * *

The next day Spinner and Anneka took her to Portland. They made a day of it, sightseeing and shopping. Afterwards, they settled her in her new quarters, a marvelous facility, with a caring staff and a wonderful educational program. She even had a room of her own, the first one she'd ever had.

She hugged them both tearfully as they said their goodbyes. Anneka had promised to be with her when the baby was born. Susanne and Jamie were lost. She was determined there'd be a happy ending for Destry.

* * *

Spinner was quiet on the way back to the coast, a two-and-a-half hour drive. When he finally broke the silence, his voice was grave.

"Anneka, I've been debating whether I should tell you something. After his sister's murder, I was asked to sit on the interview with John Clayton. You've been through so much, but you work with the boy, and I think this is something you should know."

"Nothing's going to surprise me about that family. John's a great student but how can the poor kid help having emotional problems? He must be grief stricken over Jamie."

"Well, he hid it well, if he is. But you never know with kids. They all express grief in different ways. I couldn't help noticing a peculiar lack of affect in his tone. If he's emotional, you can't tell."

"You know, I've never noticed much emotion in John, either. But then, he only comes into the office to talk about academic concerns. Once, before Jamie was murdered, he came in to see me and he acted angry. I thought he was going to say something about Jamie and her father but he just stopped mid-sentence."

'The police have an old juvenile record on John. Happened when he was fourteen. It's buried in juvenile law, but the police filled me in because I was the sitting psychologist. They wanted to see if I could get some kind of reading on the kid."

Anneka had been lounging back in the seat. She sat up and looked at Spinner with surprise. "Now that's difficult to imagine. John in trouble with the law? What did he do?"

"He pleaded guilty to one count of Animal Abuse I, in connection with the death of a sea gull. According to the court records, he put a firecracker in a hot dog, then fed the hot dog to a gull. It exploded in the gull's throat."

"My God!"

"Several people witnessed it and reported the incident to the police. He was sentenced to a year's probation and some counseling sessions. According to the therapist's report, he never showed any remorse and kept saying the counseling sessions were a big waste of his time. No problems reported after that, but the counselor thought he was one cold personality. Said he was happy when he didn't have to work with him anymore.

Anneka was silent. Digesting this new information, the memory of a pair of shiny brown loafers with tassels did a rerun in her brain. A pair of loafers glimpsed, as she crouched hidden under her desk. She'd thought John was trying to find the top ten list, he was so fiercely competitive. Then she'd even imagined Mr. Clayton might have been the intruder. He had the exact same shoes when Anneka had seen him at the grocery store. Was it John and was he there for another reason?

She shivered, and moved closer to Spinner. There were so many pieces to this puzzle. She hated puzzles. With effort, she cleared her brain of them and concentrated on the solid comfort of the man beside her, and the stability he lent her life.

* * *

That night, back in Spirit Cove, Spinner prepared dinner, "Scallops Oliver" named for Ollie, the adoring Labrador. They washed it down with a chilled chardonnay.

Anneka was beginning to appreciate this fine cuisine. Much tastier than the TV dinners she routinely consumed.

The two ate in the living-room, in front of the fire while shadows danced on the walls from the candle light and the dogs snoozed in front of the hearth. The blinds were drawn against the night. Anneka always kept them closed, now.

When Spinner went to the kitchen for more wine, Kitty Shameless jumped to his chair. Delicately, he scooped a scallop out of Spinner's dish with a careful paw.

It was so cute Anneka didn't rat on Shameless.

Dessert was an elaborate concoction of chocolate from Spinner's latest Julia Child Cookbook. The man was a find.

After dinner, they took the dogs for a run. It was a dark night and the fog curled around the cliffs.

In the cove, Anneka glimpsed the nightwalker again, standing on the edge of the scarp.

The figure was clothed in some kind of long hooded garment and seemed to drift above the cliff in the swiftly moving mist. It appeared to have no feet, to walk on air.

"Spinner, look up there! I see that person all the time."
"Where? I don't see anything."
"On the cliff."

The fog swirled, seemed to suck the figure up and it was gone.

"How weird! It was right there." Anneka strained to see through the thick clouds surrounding the rocks.

Spinner took her arm. "Gone now. Someone out walking, just like us."

Ollie growled low in his throat and nuzzled Anneka's leg.

Suddenly, she wanted away from the chill night and fog. Wanted to be home in her warm house, sitting by the fire.

CHAPTER 18

ANNEKA RECOGNIZED MR. Clayton's voice immediately.
She couldn't believe he was calling her. But of course, he had no knowledge of the afternoon when Jamie had dropped her bombshell.

Now she listened in utter disbelief to his opening statement.

"Ms. Ericsson, I was unable to reach Ms. Ramirez so I decided to call you and you can pass the message on. I'm calling to inform the school administration that I have consulted with my attorney and am filing a suit against the high school and its staff for gross noncompliance with special education laws that pertain to my late daughter's educational needs. I think the school's failure to monitor my daughter's emotional state and her academic needs, in a large part, contributed to her death.

Anneka sat down slowly in her desk chair, took a notepad and wrote the date, time and Mr. Clayton's name. Next, she retrieved a small tape recorder from her desk and turned it on. Then she took a deep quivering breath. When she finally spoke, her voice was low and controlled.

"Ms. Ericsson? Are you there?"

"Explain this further, if you would, Mr. Clayton. You believe the school to be responsible for Jamie's murder?"

"Yes, I do. If Jamie's self esteem and confidence level had not been so seriously undermined, she never would have sneaked out of the house to meet that boy! And furthermore, Ms. Ericsson, my attorney agrees with me!"

"Oh, I just bet he does."

"Pardon me?"

"You must have missed Jamie almost immediately, when you retired for the night, didn't you, Mr. Clayton?"

"I most certainly did. I reported her absence immediately to the police. I knew right away, something horrible had happened to her."

"Something horrible happened to her, all right. Even worse than her father sleeping with her, in her bedroom, in the same bed!"

"*What* !"

"Mr. Clayton, I know you were sleeping with Jamie. She told me. Oh, quite by accident. She was horrified that she let it slip. She said you'd made her promise not to tell.

"Jamie's educational needs are over. Her self-esteem? Her self-confidence? You took care of that.

"You are a perverted man, Mr. Clayton. You make a travesty of fatherhood. You took advantage of a vulnerable and emotionally confused young girl. That, in itself, would be an outrage. But the fact that you were her father and she trusted you, makes that crime even more heinous."

Anneka paid not a bit of attention to the blustering sounds on the other end of the line. She just turned the recorder's volume up further.

"I called Social Services and reported it, the very day Jamie told me. I told the other administrators in the building, as well. Unfortunately, Social Services were quite explicit that there was nothing we could do because Jamie was already nineteen years of age. But, I promise you, Mr. Clayton. I will have no qualms about taking the witness stand and telling the court and this community every word that Jamie told me. Oh, I would welcome the opportunity.

"Don't speak to me of the school being responsible for your daughter's lack of self-esteem. Don't threaten me or the school with defamation of character or any other trumped-up charges, you and your damned attorney dream up. I promise you, I will go right for your jugular. I don't give a damn about your threats, from you or your attorney.

"I despise you Mr. Clayton. You are a loathsome excuse for a human being. I would give anything to see you in a jail cell. If there's a way to bring that about, I will make every effort.

"In the meantime, stay out of my sight and stay out of this school.

"And finally, you can go straight to hell, Mr. Clayton."

There was a click. The phone went dead.

CHAPTER 19

WHEN TIME PERMITTED, Anneka liked to get out of her office and mingle with the students on their lunch hour. Frequently, she happened on a kid who really needed to talk and who wouldn't normally come to her office.

Since Susanne and Jamie's murders, Anneka and Lainey had been doing a lot of grief counseling, mostly, with friends of the girls, but sometimes with students who were badly frightened by the presence of violent death in their young lives.

The entire community was traumatized. The news media were everywhere. Maggie had done a good job of keeping them away from the school, but they accosted students in other areas of town. New Albion had achieved a notoriety that was completely unwelcomed by its citizenry. Although, order had been restored in the town, the reminders of violent death remained, like the headmarkers on graves after the battle was over.

Most people wanted a return to the commonplace. They wanted their old lives back.

The mayor had gone on television, requesting the press respect the grief the townspeople were feeling. This was a particularly powerful appeal, since one of the murdered girls was his own.

A wealthy man, the mayor had offered a huge reward for information that would lead to the arrest of the killer. New Albionites who watched the television programming were struck by the change in Mayor Slocum. He had shrunk in stature, as if he'd been pricked with a pin till the air leaked out. Mrs. Slocum never emerged from the estate that was the family home. She reportedly was tended by a nurse around the clock. The house was always lighted, lighted in every room as if festivities were planned, as if company were coming; illumination to dispel the gloom, the sorrow for an only child lost forever.

The Clayton family had made no appearances to the press. Anneka knew the reason for Mr. Clayton's silence. She knew Jamie's family must grieve for her but she felt no empathy for Mr. Clayton. Jamie's mother had always been a quiet diminished little woman. Anneka wondered who would share her sorrow and if she felt guilt for Jamie's death. It was difficult to believe she had known nothing of the relationship between Jamie and her husband.

John Clayton had returned to school and carried on much as before, his academic performance not diminished by grief for his sister. Anneka had been shocked by Spinner's revelation about John's arrest for animal abuse. She made several attempts to talk with John about his father and Jamie's deaths, but she got nowhere.

He would talk only of school matters and the college offers he had received. The last time he had been in Anneka's office, she had touched his hand as he was about to leave. He had visibly withdrawn from the contact, seemingly, another victim of his family's pathology.

But all the citizens of New Albion had undergone a change.

FOUL WEATHER

Suspicion and uneasiness permeated the little town. Anneka carefully check her windows and doors each time she left the house. Each lock and latch must be secured. At night, she booby-trapped the doors and windows. The last thing she touched before sleep, was the new revolver on the bedside table, its weight comforting, the cold steel almost caressable. An ugly object that had taken on a beauty in Anneka's eyes for the measure of security it offered.

Anneka turned a corner of B wing and ran smack into Lou Wagoner. Anneka had been walking at a fast pace, head down. The collision was inevitable.

"Watch where you're going, you damn fool— Oh, Anneka. Thought you were a student. They don't care who they ram into. Sorry."

"Whew! Sorry, too. I guess we were both lost in thought."

Anneka hadn't seen Lou since she had written the note of explanation about Spinner. Lou hadn't replied but Anneka had hoped she accepted the explanation in the spirit it was intended. She made the decision now to not bring the matter up if Lou didn't.

Students were still complaining about Lou and wanted to be changed from her classes. Anneka had denied the requests, citing the time into the semester as explanation. So far, that had worked. She hadn't had to say anything to Lou about her current lack of popularity. She hadn't mentioned the complaints to Maggie, either, hoping Lou would resolve the problem on her own.

Lou's appearance was unorthodox, as usual. Maroon lipstick was smeared on her large teeth. The outfit of the day was camouflage fatigues worn low on her lean hips. She looked like a recruit from a paramilitary group.

"You've got a new hairstyle, Anneka."

"Um, yeah, I do."

"Does Dr. Hartmann like it like that?"

"Well, yeah, I guess."

149

"Hmmm, well, see ya."

Lou proceeded on down the hall, her tall figure moving with athletic ease.

Anneka breathed a sigh of relief. God, that woman was weird! She'd been afraid she'd light into her about Spinner again. She must be getting over it. Where had she found those pants? Did the woman *have* a mirror? Jeez.

"Hey, Anneka, babe. Did you decide to do guard duty with the rest of us peasants?"

"Oh, hi, Nogood. Felt like talking to the kids and stretching my legs. Besides, it gets me away from the phone."

Nogood's black eye was beginning to turn an ugly shade of yellow. She'd promised to shed the violent boyfriend but the Lemonade Ladies weren't sure he wasn't still around.

"Nogood, have you gotten rid of that damned jerk? I haven't had a chance to talk with you."

"Yeah, don't worry about it."

"But I do. Is he gone, or not?"

"Well, he keeps calling but I don't talk to him."

"Damn it, Nogood! Tell him you'll call the police!"

"I *said* don't worry about it. Speaking of the police, are they still watching your house? You're the one who needs to be careful."

"Yeah, they show up every night when I get home from work. They come in and check the house and check periodically through the night. At first, I was happy to have them but I don't think it's necessary any more. Nate's not hanging around here. It's silly.

"Don't be so sure. I think he may still be somewhere nearby, maybe some stupid girl's hiding him. I wish they'd find him. Everybody's spooked. He's a vicious killer. Remember that."

"I will. I'm taking every precaution."

Nogood took off after some unruly students and Anneka headed back to her office. As she passed through the large

FOUL WEATHER

atrium filled with teenagers sprawled in comfortable chairs, she thought back to the night when all the horror had begun and she shuddered.

The atrium was filled with sunlight and the laughing students lent a far different atmosphere than the black hell she'd stumbled through the night Susanne was murdered. How easily she, too, could have died that night. Something as simple as deciding to find her mail in the dark. That clap of thunder had saved her life. Poor Susanne. How had they all failed to see the boy was completely mad?

In its place of honor on the atrium wall hung the picture of the current senior class, a picture taken in a happier time. Susanne and Jamie were seated together in the front row, their smiles bright. Seniors forever.

Anneka avoided the picture and turned into the counseling center, greeting the kids waiting to see her.

Mike Kowalski shouldered a freshman aside good naturedly. "Whoa, hold it there, dude. Seniors first."

"Wait a second, Mike. Let me get my phone."

"Counseling office, this is Anneka."

"This is Spinner, "We are Borg," Hartmann. How about me fixing dinner tonight? I've missed you."

"Hey! I've missed you too, dude."

"Guidance counselors sure talk funny. How are things there?"

"They're coming to take me away, ha, ha. Actually, things are pretty calm. I walked around during lunch. Ran into Lou Wagoner. She seemed to be all right after the note I sent her."

"Well, that's good. You don't need that kind of action from her. I wish she'd stop calling me, though. If I'm not home, she calls the landlady. It's getting pretty annoying."

"Hey, I didn't know that! I thought she'd gotten the picture."

"Ah well, you know, I'm such a charming fellow."

151

"So, charming fellow, what we having for dinner?"
"I'll surprise you. About sixish?"
"Cool, totally, dude."

* * *

I am bored with this surveillance. Following Anneka around in the car just doesn't do it for me. I miss my little place in the trees. So much more intimate. Titillating, even.

Well, things should calm down soon and I can go back to my night watch. Anneka will be feeling completely safe and then, SURPRISE!

I could sneak back in easily enough. Cops are such boobs. They aren't capable of guarding their own assholes. I wish they knew how clever I am. How superior. The sheriff and crime team are a joke. Gotta write a book about this, honestly. It's comedy. I'm having the time of my life.

The cops, the dogs, the fucking psychologist, none of them can protect you from me, Anneka. The only thing I worried about was the gun. And I have that now. A nice weapon but not my choice. I've been so successful with my knife. A bullet is so quick. Not fun.

The bitch always stays late. Who's she trying to impress? Other counselor left a long time ago. But then, Mrs. Dillon needs to get home to keep an eye on her husband. That fellow's quite a Casanova. I couldn't believe who he's screwing around with. Guess he thought he was pretty safe way down the coast in Florence. Maybe I'll write his insipid little wife a letter. Let her know what hubby's up to these days. Yup, I'm gonna do that.

What an institution that school is. All run by women. God, I wish I could be on the school board. I'd get rid of all of them. I hate those fucking women. Maybe I should just off them all.

Parking lot's emptying fast. I've got to be careful nobody notices me just sitting here. There goes that damn assistant principal. Ass principal for short. Ass principal Wardy. Hah, that's a good one! Wonder where she got that black eye? I hope somebody decked her. I'd like to black the other one. And the principal's worse. Margaret Ramirez! What a bitch she is. Doesn't even use her married name. Like she should be proud she's a greaser. Ramirez. A damn Mexican woman, principal of a high school. She thinks she's such fucking hot shit!

Calm down, calm down. Maybe I should be taking that medicine, listen to my mother's nagging. Can't afford to lose it now. Anneka's my top priority.

Here she comes! Here she comes! Damn, I wish I could follow her home . . . Patience, patience. Not much longer. . . .

CHAPTER 20

ANNEKA WAS UP before the sun and on the road to Portland.

Destry had called late the night before from the hospital. Her labor pains had started. She sounded like a fearful child.

She *was* a fearful child.

Anneka offered to stop in Albany to see if she could find Destry's parents, but Destry said she hadn't heard from them in months and didn't need them now.

Anneka called Maggie to tell her she was taking emergency leave. Bad time to be gone from school, but there was no alternative. Destry hadn't asked her to come but she'd promised to be there.

Never having had a baby, Anneka wasn't sure how much help she'd be. But she could be Destry's friend. She felt such a strong attachment to the young girl. She reminded her of someone. Anneka was haunted by Destry's eyes.

In her profession, she had learned not to dwell on the

problems of the people she counseled. She didn't take them home with her.

But it was not like that with Destry. They had bonded. They'd be a part of each other's lives from now on. That was just the way it was.

The night before, in her restless sleep, she'd had a dream so vivid she remembered every detail. A shadowy young girl cradled a baby wrapped in a shining cloth. She clutched it to her and wept. Her eyes . . . that was it. The dark limpid eyes could have belonged to Destry.

She'd dreamed of that same girl before. So strange. She must remember to ask Spinner about recurring dreams. There had been more and more of them lately.

It was eight o'clock sharp when Anneka arrived at St. Vincent's Hospital in downtown Portland. Visiting hours were not until afternoon but a nurse told her she was expected and could go directly to the room.

A young doctor was just leaving the room and asked if she was Ms. Ericsson.

"I'm glad you're here. A counselor from the Marie Constanza Home's been with her, but Destry's asking for you."

"How is she, Doctor? Are you expecting any problems?"

"So far, so good. However, it's always a concern when such a young girl gives birth. She's very mature and composed for being just fifteen, but there's no family with her and she needs you."

"I'll stay as long as I'm needed, Doctor."

A crisp voice signaled the need for Dr. Elliot to report to the nurses' station. And yet again.

"Dr. Elliot, please come to the nurses' station."

He consulted his watch. "I'll check back after I do my rounds. We're monitoring her contractions. We can induce labor if nothing happens in a few hours. She's fairly comfortable right now."

* * *

Anneka tiptoed in to find Destry with her eyes closed. Quietly placing the package she had brought next to a large plant on the bureau, Anneka sat in the chair by the bed.

The young girl looked even more vulnerable as she slept, the huge mound of belly so incongruous with the child's face. Anneka wanted to give her a hug but didn't want to awaken her. Then, Destry stirred and cried out and Anneka grasped her hand.

"Are you all right, Destry?"

"Oh, Ms. Ericsson, you're here."

"You bet! I don' know nothin' bout birthin' no babies, Ms. Scarlett, but I'm stayin' right here till we have this one!"

"That's from Gone With the Wind," Destry giggled. "I saw that movie at the shelter."

The girl looked pale and exhausted but her smile was genuine. Anneka was relieved the girl wasn't hysterical. If she'd been about to have a baby, Anneka thought she'd be hysterical.

"I'm so glad you came. Everybody's real nice to me but I don't have any close friends yet. I guess being alone's the scariest part.

"How's Dr. Hartmann? And the puppies? And Kitty Shameless?"

"The menagerie's fine, Des. So's Spinner. He wanted to come but he couldn't get away. He'll stay with the animals and call us tonight. But, hey, how do you feel? Are you having pain now? What's that machine for with all the lines?"

"That's to measure my labor. The pains aren't really too close together yet, but the doctor wants me here. I told him you'd come. I feel a lot better now."

She shifted slightly and the machine blipped, the colored lines peaked and a grimace of pain crossed Destry's face.

"Should I call for the doctor, Destry? Are you okay?"

"I'm okay," Destry relaxed and grinned at Anneka. "You really don't know much about having babies, do you, Ms. Ericsson? It's all right, though. I know exactly what's happening. We had classes at the home. I'm not too scared. Everything's happening just like they said it would."

With an effort she reached over and gave Anneka's hand a reassuring little pat.

"Destry, enough with the Ms. Ericsson, already. Just call me Anneka. We're having a baby together, here. We need to be on first name terms."

"Really? I'd be so proud to be your friend, Ms. Ericsson, whoops, I mean Anneka! It'll take me awhile to get used to that.

"But I wanted to tell you . . . Anneka, about last night. I had this scary dream. No, it wasn't scary, exactly, but it was so real and so sad. This girl. She was young and she looked like an Indian. You know, like a Native-American? She looked . . . she looked sort of like me. I have some Indian blood, you know, on my mother's side? Well, anyway, this Indian girl had a baby in her arms and it died. She buried it in this beautiful long cloth that had gold threads in it. I felt like it was happening right then. I woke up and I was just so glad I was in the hospital and the doctors could make sure my baby's okay, but the dream, it was so—"

At that moment the door flew open and all hell broke loose.

"Destry! Baby! Mummy and Daddy are here!"

Anneka was shoved roughly aside by a man and a woman who looked and smelled like the streets.

It was the Murphys.

They fell on Destry with protestations of love and loud all-will-be-wells.

The Murphy family was re-u-ni-ted.

"We'll take care of you and the little one, Destry, honey," Mr. Murphy said. "Don't you worry none, now. No grandson

FOUL WEATHER

of your daddy will go without. We'll be one happy family!" Mr. Murphy beamed with a mouth full of nothing but gums and a big wad of tobacco. This last, he disposed of in the potted plant.

Mrs. Murphy was patting her daughter's belly like it contained a jackpot of prizes.

"As soon as you have this baby, Destry, we're all going back to Albany together. I've already told the welfare people we'll need more money. There's another mouth to feed. They were telling your dad he had to go back to work, you know. They found him a job. Can you imagine? Your poor dad working with that bad back of his? Well, this is gonna change things. Everything's gonna be okay. We'll take care of everything."

Destry opened her mouth to scream and the waves on the machine went haywire.

Anneka rang for the nurse.

* * *

The physician and several orderlies got rid of the Murphys. They stopped protesting their parental rights when threatened with court charges for neglect of a minor. Dreams of a fat welfare check gave way to their fear of jail or the loss of any existing benefits.

Destry was adamant she was not changing her mind.

She looked her mother in the face and said she would never let her baby grow up like she had. If they ever wanted to see her again, they'd better leave the hospital right away and not try to interfere in the adoption process that had already begun.

The chastened pair left the room quietly and Destry proceeded to handle everything from there on with a quiet courage Anneka found amazing. She didn't know where Destry found such strength.

* * *

It was late when Anneka finally left for home. The baby had been born. A baby girl who was going to make some lucky couple very happy.

Anneka had held her breath when Destry held her. She thought it would be too hard, it was such a beautiful little baby.

Destry had taken the child in her arms and said the most extraordinary thing.

"Baby girl. I didn't know it would be you!"

Then, she had laughed softly and cradled the baby to her breast.

That morning, before Anneka had left for Portland, she'd taken a wrapped parcel from her old family trunk. It contained a baby blanket brought from Sweden by Anneka's mother, Alfreda. The blanket was old and had been in the Ericsson family a long time. It was made of a soft fine wool. Anneka had washed it carefully in a mild baby soap. but when she held it to her cheek she imagined it still smelled faintly of the sachet and ancient scents from her mother's cedar chest, the chest that had come from across another sea. She thought it would be perfect for Destry to give to the baby when it went to its new parents.

Destry wrapped the baby carefully in the soft blanket and smiled at the child.

"Baby girl, your life is gonna be so fine," she said.

CHAPTER 21

"Anneka, get over here right away." She hardly recognized Lainey's voice on the phone. It didn't sound like her at all.

"What's happened? Are you all right?"

"No. Please come. I need you now."

She broke the sound barrier getting to Lainey's house. Screeching up to the curb, Anneka spotted Lainey's husband Trevor pulling away. The sleek black Lexus did a U turn and streaked off with a squeal of tires. Trevor didn't even acknowledge he'd seen her. He must have recognized the Durango. What the hell was going on?

Lainey stood in the doorway of their upscale glass and cedar home, clutching a bathrobe to her throat, tears streaming down her face.

What was wrong here? It was unusual for Lainey to let anything rock her like this. Something really bad must have happened, but then, why had Trevor left? Anneka's mind churned as she hurried to her friend's side.

"Lainey! Come on, honey. Let's get out of the doorway. It's cold. C'mon in. Please."

Lainey allowed herself to be pulled into the house, out of sight of the neighbor's children playing on manicured lawns.

"Lainey, what is it? Where are the kids? Are they okay?"

"Yes, they're all right. They're at Mother's."

Anneka pulled two wrinkled tissues from her purse and began mopping the tear-ravaged face before her.

"I saw Trevor leaving as I drove in, Lainey. What—"

"He wasn't just leaving, Anneka. He was *fleeing* the scene!"

Lainey pulled a wrinkled sheet of paper from the pocket of her gown.

"Read this. It was in the mailbox when I got home from school on Friday. I've been carrying it with me ever since, trying to think of the best way to handle it. I was going to confront Trevor right then and there but I needed more time to think."

It was an ordinary piece of typing paper. Anneka smoothed the paper and began to read.

> What well-known professional about town is engaging in a little hanky-panky with a teacher in our local high school?
>
> And what well-known counselor in said high school is totally ignorant of her husband's affair with her much younger colleague?
>
> Said couple was certainly enjoying themselves holding hands over a candlelight dinner in a quiet little cafe down the coast—naughty, naughty!
>
> Is this any way for a married man to act? With a teacher? A teacher of impressionable adolescents! A role model for our children!
>
> Something must be done! People must be told! The school board! The school board must be informed! It's my civic responsibility!

What a scandal!
What an embarrassment for the poor wife!
What a f-u-c-k-i-n-g shame!

"Lainey, this is a damned anonymous note! From some cowardly sicko. Let's just throw it away, for God's sake."

Lainey's face turned hard and she snatched the paper from Anneka's hand.

"Come on, Anneka! Let's stop pretending. We all know Trevor has had his little indiscretions in the past, but I ignored them, just prayed they'd soon go away. But I can't ignore this. A teacher at school? Anneka! I can't ignore this. I can't!"

"Hold on. We don't know it's a teacher. We don't know that. Let's not just assume everything this scum-bag's written is the gospel truth! "

"Come here. I want you to hear something."

Lainey's voice had suddenly gone dead calm.

"I was still in bed when I heard Trevor on the phone downstairs. I guess he thought I was asleep. I thought it was odd, a phone call so early on Sunday morning. My first thought was something's wrong with one of the kids so I went downstairs. Trevor was talking very softly to someone on the phone. When he saw me, he just hung up.

"Come here, Anneka, I want you to hear this."

Lainey led her to the phone on the hall table. Anneka watched as she pushed the redial button. With a resolute look, she handed her the phone.

It was answered on the first ring. The voice was young and very irritated. Anneka recognized it immediately.

"This is Stephanie. Who is this? Damn it, stop calling here!"

The phone slammed in Anneka's ear. She looked at Lainey and the disbelief was written on her face.

"It's Stephanie Myers, isn't it, Anneka? I knew it the instant I heard her voice. She's in our offices often enough. She asked if it was Trevor. She said, 'Trevor, is that you? Why did you hang up?'

"You're right, Anneka. Whoever wrote this note *is* a scumbag. But a scumbag who knows what they're talking about. It's Stephanie Myers, all right. The little bitch! I just can't believe it! *What* am I going to do?"

Anneka just looked at her... She was speechless.

CHAPTER 22

IT HAD BEEN several days since Anneka had last seen Miranda. At their last meeting Miranda had just sat, mute and sullen, totally different from the sunny happy girl she had once been. Her teachers said she did her work in class but didn't communicate with her classmates.

Miranda had been Susanne's best friend since childhood. Although Anneka was unusually adept at getting students to open up and talk about their feelings, the girl sheltered her anguish like a precious gift, sharing it with no one.

Before Susanne's death, the girls had made plans to go to the same college. They had pored over countless college catalogs in the counseling center, Susanne's blonde head touching Miranda's red curls as they talked, their words spilling over each other excitedly as they discussed the pros and cons of each college, the various sororities, the cute college guys they would meet on campus weekends.

When they had finally made their choice, they giggled and flirted with the college reps and made plans to visit the campus for orientation and sorority rush. They talked endlessly about the prospects of coed housing and planned every detail of the dorm room they would have together. Neither girl had to worry about scholarships or college tuition. Both had wealthy parents anxious to give them everything they needed and wanted.

When Susanne became involved with Nate Dupray, everything changed. Susanne no longer looked forward to college or a future away from Nate. She had fallen hard.

Now, one girl was dead and the other mourned, mourned Susanne as much or more than an immediate family member.

Miranda's parents had asked Anneka to see her and she did, frequently. But the girl remained silent, locked in misery, deeply affected by her friend's death, the fabric of her daily life and future plans a tattered shroud.

So, when Miranda asked to close the door because she needed to speak with her, Anneka was surprised and grateful.

The girl's eyes were red and swollen.

"Sit down Miranda . . . You've been crying."

The girl swiped at fresh tears impatiently and dropped her cumbersome bookbag to the floor. She wore black. Black jeans and a black sweatshirt. Her face was devoid of makeup. She didn't look like a teenager anymore.

"Ms. Ericsson, I have to trust you. I have to talk. Susanne trusted you. She said she could tell you anything and you'd listen and you never judged her or acted shocked."

Miranda pulled the chair closer to the oak desk and sat.

Anneka said nothing. She just held her breath.

"I miss her so much. She was my best friend since the first grade. We did everything together. We had a ball. If one of us had a date, we'd usually find another guy and we'd all go out together. Afterwards, we'd sleep over at each other's houses and pick the guys apart and laugh for hours. We were always like that. You know how close we were."

Miranda took a shuddery breath and clasped her hands

together in a prayer-like gesture. She cast her brown eyes to the ceiling and sighed. Then she looked again at Anneka and her eyes were cold and the tears were gone.

"That's why it was so hard when Suzie went ape-shit over that bastard Nate Dupray. He split us apart. I didn't like him. I didn't trust him. But Sus' wouldn't listen. She thought he was such a fox."

Miranda's praying hands now became clenched fists and her voice turned as cold as her eyes.

"He was sexy. I'll give him that. All the girls thought he was hot. I think that's what attracted Susanne so much. His looks and his bad reputation, you know? She didn't see the danger in it. She thought she could reform him!"

Anneka just nodded.

"Ms. Ericsson, Susanne told me some things that were so scary about what Nate was involved in and who he was involved with. I told her she had to break it off, but she wouldn't listen!"

The girl's voice dropped to a whisper and Anneka had to lean forward to hear her.

"Nate was the major drug pusher around school, you know. The kids could get anything they wanted from him, if they had the money, that is. He even had a network of the fringe element around here . . . you know, the losers? They'd help him spread the drugs and let people know what he had for sale."

Miranda gulped in breath and continued, her words rapid and eager.

"He wanted Susanne to help him. She wouldn't do it but she wouldn't break up with him either. I begged her but she said he'd never had the breaks in life that she had. That if she was just understanding enough, if she just loved him enough, he'd give it all up. For her! Hah!"

Miranda's voice quivered with rage and she tore at the

tissue in her hand. Her fingernails were bitten and the polish was chipped.

"Jamie Clayton was involved too, you know. She had a gigantic crush on Nate. She was always hanging around us, hoping she'd see Nate. It was pathetic. But you know, Jamie. She wasn't awfully bright, you know? And Susanne felt sorry for her, so we let her hang around."

Miranda's nose was running and her hands shook as she swiped at her nose. The words were tumbling out of Miranda now and Anneka prayed she wouldn't stop.

"Is that why Jamie was at the cove, Miranda?"

"Uhhuh, Jamie was helping Nate with the drugs. They'd pass them off in Spirit Cove. Jamie'd do anything Nate asked her. Susanne found out about it and she told me. She swore me to secrecy. I wanted to tell the police or come and tell you, but Susanne got real pissed and she said she would never forgive me if I did that. That Nate would get in trouble and she wouldn't be able to see him and she loved him and all that crap!"

Anneka remained motionless when Miranda's fist hit the desk.

"I was so happy when they arrested the bastard. Course I didn't tell Sus' that. But I was. I was so afraid she'd get in trouble or get pregnant or something horrible like that. But then the police let him go! Susanne said it was those creepy men we saw that paid off his bail!"

"What men?"

There was a knock at the door and Miranda froze like a frightened deer.

"They can't know I'm here! They can't know I'm . . ."

"It's all right, Miranda. The door's locked. No one knows you're here!"

The footsteps passed and Anneka hurried to hang her "Out To Lunch" sign on the other side of the door. The girl's face had turned white at the interruption, but still, she continued to talk, the words coming even more rapidly.

"Ms. Ericsson, the day before Susanne was murdered? I was with her. I didn't tell the police or anybody this. I haven't told anyone. It's been driving me crazy but I was afraid!"

"It's okay, Miranda. It's okay. You want me to get you some water or something?"

Miranda got up and began to pace back and forth in front of the desk. Anneka went around, took the other chair and drew Miranda back to her side. The girl's breath was ragged and she was shaking violently.

"Take some deep breaths, Miranda. None of this is your fault, you know. Anyone would have been frightened. Nothing's going to happen to you, I promise, Miranda. I promise."

Miranda clung to Anneka. Her thin body trembling, but after a minute or so, she went on.

"Well, Susanne wanted to go for a walk on the beach after school. It was cold and really rainy. I thought she was nuts, nobody goes on the beach this time of year, but she kept begging me to go with her, you know? She said she needed me to be with her because I was her best friend. And . . . *they* were there!"

"Who? Who was there?"

"First, Nate. He'd just been released from jail. And then these guys from Portland showed up—They weren't even kids! They were old! Like in their forties or fifties? And they were driving this humongous black Mercedes. Really well-dressed but they talked like gangsters, you know? Susanne and I were so scared. You could tell Nate was scared too. He tried to act real big but his voice kept cracking . They said there was money missing from the last supply of coke they'd given him? And they wanted to know who we were, Sus' and me, and where was the rest of the money? I was like petrified! These men . . . they were like movie gangsters. Like the drug guys you see in the movies? You could tell they didn't fool around. I think Nate was trying to get us involved in it, you know?"

Miranda shuddered and swallowed hard. She was perspiring and breathing in huge gulps of air. Anneka thought she might be hyperventilating.

"It's okay, Miranda. Stop for a minute and try to calm down. We have plenty of time."

Anneka tried to keep her own voice from shaking. Miranda waved her hands in front of her face, like she was trying to wave away the fear.

"Well, they told Nate they'd be back in a couple of days and he'd better have the rest of the cash. And then, they just drove off! Back to Portland, or somewhere. I was so scared! And I was so mad at Susanne for dragging me down there. Nate just tried to laugh it off. Like *he* wasn't scared. But I could tell he was. He couldn't even light a cigarette, his hands shook so bad. Oh, God! If I'd only said something after that, maybe Susanne would still be alive and poor Jamie too! I can't forgive myself for that! It's all I think about!"

"You were afraid. It's easy to understand. I'd have been scared, too."

"I'm still afraid, Ms. Ericsson. They saw me. What if Nate tells them they'd better get rid of me too? That I could identify them or something? Jamie and Susanne are both dead. I'm afraid I'm going to be next!"

"Miranda. I can't let you keep this to yourself. You might need protection. We have to tell the police."

Miranda looked Anneka straight in the eye. She seemed to be trying to make a decision.

"There's something else . . . I have to tell you something else."

"What?"

"I've been too terrified to say anything. I know I should've but I was so scared. I keep seeing those horrible men in my dreams. I keep seeing that long black car. It looked just like the hearse they took Susanne in! Oh, you've got to help me. I can't keep this secret any longer. I can't!"

"Miranda, what is it? Here, hold on to my hands. What is it you need to tell me?"

"... Ms. Ericsson... I know where Nate is." Miranda's voice was low and her teeth clenched. "I know where he is and I want the police to go get the fucking son-of-a-bitch!"

CHAPTER 23

OCEAN OVERLOOK DRIVE wasn't really a drive at all, just a weed-choked path barely wide enough for a vehicle to maneuver. It plunged down a steep grade and wound around a large two-story house on the edge of the sea. The house, obscured by thick foliage and trees, stood in solitude on at least five acres of prime waterfront.

In the sunlight, the house would be a splendid sight, but it had rained incessantly for three days and this late afternoon the place appeared untended, uninhabited, almost haunted in the drenching downpour.

The rain fell. It fell on the walkways and trails. It flattened the foliage and ripped leaves from the trees. It battered the weathered cedar siding of the house and gushed in miniature falls from the eaves. Rain pounded on the huge dark windows and ran like tears down the panes. As the path neared the house, it all but disappeared in a profusion of bent and dripping rhododendrons.

At the side of the house sat an old truck, its doors wide

open to the rain. Close by, a beat-up four-wheeler was covered with streaks of mud. The rain beat a steady drum on the hoods of the cars and their tires sank further into the saturated earth.

Amid thick purple hydrangeas, a black Mercedes gleamed darkly. Like some malignant growth.

* * *

The officers approached the house on foot. Mud sucked at their heavy boots. Guns drawn, a string of men serpentined in and out of the bushes and trees. They paid no heed to the rain. They moved like guerrillas through a foreign forest.

Somewhere inside, low music drifted, the silky sounds of some long-ago crooner.

From out at sea, came the moaning lament of a fog horn.

A man in plain clothes reached one side of the door . He flattened against the rain-wet wall. His partner nodded his readiness from the opposite side. They held their weapons high.

"J. C., you stay cool now," Wiley whispered. "We're waiting till we get the signal. We're not going in alone, you got that?"

J. C., the younger of the two men sighed. "Yeah, wait till that fat-assed sheriff blows his megaphone and our cover along with it. Sure as shit, it'll be the two of us left with our asses hangin' out."

* * *

In the house, a lean figure paced behind the closed blinds.

Nate Dupray was sick of hiding. Sick of the jerks from the city. All they did was play cards, drink beer and listen to that fucking Frank Sinatra. They'd probably off him if he tried to leave, though. They liked all the heat centered on him. Besides, they always kept their gun belts on under their fancy suits. Just like the gangster movies he'd watched when he was a kid.

* * *

Dim light filtered through the shaded windows and sounds of broken conversation floated out to the porch, muffled by the driving rain.

Nate's shadow passed swiftly by a window.

"Did you see that?" Wiley asked.

"Yeah, let's kick the door down and go in. Dupray's a breed. He can probably smell us out here, for Christ's sakes!"

"We don't know how many are in there, J. C. The sheriff wants to try a no-harm situation, if he can. If they see how many men we've got out here, they might just give up without a fight. No need tryin to live up to your initials, big shot." Wiley was sweating profusely even in the cold driving rain. He was getting too old for this shit.

More men circled around the house. They were armed to the teeth. At a signal from the sheriff, they took cover behind the trees and lowered themselves to the muddy ground, carefully keeping their weapons above their bodies. The rain stung their faces as they sank slowly into the mire. The men were nervous, their adrenaline high. They were ready to break loose.

* * *

"What's with you, kid? You'd make a corpse nervous. All that pacing back and forth. Wanta play a game of cards?"

Nate didn't answer. He drew closer to a window. His hair gleamed blue-black in the lamplight. His attention was drawn to a movement behind the blind. Slowly and delicately, he peeled back a corner and there they were. Camouflaged by trees and mud, but cops, definitely cops, lined up like a shooting gallery at the arcade.

And here we are, Nate thought. Sitting ducks.

* * *

Through a megaphone came a reverberating voice.

"This is the sheriff. You're surrounded. Come out with your hands over your heads."

The magnified voice seemed to linger, hang suspended on the driving rain.

"You've been warned. Come out with your hands over your heads."

Little puffs of heated air came from the nostrils and mouths of the crouching men. Rain ran down the backs of their necks. Fingers tensed on triggers.

Then Nate Dupray exploded through the door behind the protective fusillade of a ratcheting AK-47.

J. C. was knocked flat by the door. His gun sailed off the porch.

"*SHIT* !" yelled Wiley. "Hold your fire!" He dove over the porch rail.

The officers were firing wildly, struggling to gain their feet in the sucking mud.

J. C. took two shots in the shoulder before he rolled off the porch and disappeared from sight.

Nate ran, his weapon spitting deadly ammo, making it off the porch and halfway up the road before the officers nailed him.

He stopped short. His head jerked. Shouting an obscenity at the sky and the trees, the last words he would ever speak, Nate dropped to his knees, caved to one side and lay still.

Rivulets of blood ran from the bullet holes.

The rain fell on the warm red blood steaming down the

FOUL WEATHER

heavy ruts in the road, a widening stream taking on life of its own as it fled the body, diluting thinner and lighter in the rain.

The boy lay like a stone-felled animal.

The birds and creatures of the forest had flown and fled from the gunfire.

The woods were strangely still.

* * *

"Christ! Is he dead?" one officer asked.

"Nah, I think I got a pulse."

"Let's get him in an ambulance. Call 'em in. C'mon, let's have some help over here."

"Where's J. C.? He was hit!"

"I got him. He's alive. Get the ambulance quick!" yelled Wiley.

"Is the house secured? Anybody else in there?"

"We've got two in here. They're cuffed!" another officer shouted.

Two men were led from the house. Older men in expensive shoes and gold watches. Quiet men. They gave no resistance. They made a request to call their attorney. After that, they didn't speak.

A squad car, wheels spinning in the slick earth, came to an abrupt stop. The men, with hands cuffed behind their backs were shoved in. They glanced just once, at the fallen boy on the ground.

"Who's the kid, guys? A friend of yours?"

The question came from a jeering cop, his face and uniform caked with mud.

The men remained silent.

"Looks one hell of a lot like Nate Dupray, don't it? Ya know we've been lookin' for him a long time. Appears you boys been harboring a fugitive. 'Fraid we'll have to book ya for that."

The men said nothing.

Paramedics slid Nate's bloodied body through the open doors followed by the stretcher bearing an unconscious J. C.. They paused long enough for Wiley to jump in and the ambulance screamed from the scene.

* * *

New Albion learned of the capture later that day.

Nate Dupray was alive, but in a coma, and under heavy guard at the New Albion Hospital.

The other occupants of the house were jailed, but would probably make bail. A squadron of Portland attorneys following the scent of trouble and money arrived by private plane a few hours after the arrest.

The little town was playing host to big time drug traffickers, all right. But a search revealed no drugs of any kind. There was a large cache of weapons and money. It was not revealed how much.

The phone lines hummed. The reporters swarmed. The lawyers bargained.

The mothers of New Albion hugged their daughters and felt immense relief. The big bad wolf, if not completely dead, was at least mortally wounded.

Nate Dupray breathed on, hooked up to numerous smoothly purring machines.

CHAPTER 24

THE CAT HAD one hazel eye and one green one. Right now, they were both trained on the man. He had just moved the cat's favorite chair away from the bird, dumping the cat out most unceremoniously. Earlier, the man had forgotten the cat's noon-day meal of seafood morsels with just a bit of people tuna sprinkled on top. There had been nothing in his bowl. All in all, it had been a most unsatisfactory day. But the cat began his bathing ritual anyway, a pink tongue lapping carefully at a dainty white-mittened paw. He was a most fastidious cat.

Jamie's father was rearranging the furniture in Jamie's bedroom.

It was such a pretty, feminine-appearing bedroom. He positioned the chair again carefully. It looked good just there, directly across from the door. It gave the room a focal point. That was the decorator's term for it, wasn't it?

He didn't know why the arrangement of the room had become so important. It had never mattered to him before. Of course, he was a completely different person now.

Before, Jamie would have been eager to help. She would have made suggestions on how to change the room. They had always had such a close and loving relationship.

Many people would probably say their relationship was too close but they just didn't understand. His wife certainly would never understand. But she was like that. Such a cold woman and John was just like her. Mr. Clayton didn't care for his son at all.

John hadn't given a damn when Jamie died. He hadn't shed a single tear. He had never showed his sister any affection or tried to help her in any way. All he ever worried about was getting into a prestigious college. John could go to hell. Mr. Clayton wasn't going to miss him. Not one bit.

There! The chair looked perfect there. Exactly across from the door and in a central part of the room. The silken pulls from the drapes were a colorful touch. Did the chair sit just a tad too low? How about adding these throw pillows?

Ah, that was perfect. Just perfect.

One more thing. His gaze fell on Jamie's bright little yellow canary in its gilded cage. He could swear that bird was looking back at him with complete understanding. Jamie had named the bird Sunshine. She had really loved the tiny bird. She would want this for him.

Mr. Clayton carried the cage to the open window. With a careful finger, he lifted the little wire door and shook the cage gently. He watched, his eyes awash with tears, as Sunshine flew free. He imagined the bird could fly as far as heaven and be with Jamie.

Next, Mr. Clayton hitched up his pants, straightened his tie and smoothed back his hair. He had just had it styled and his beard trimmed.

He looked damn good. He smiled at his image in Jamie's dresser mirror. The beard gave him a distinguished look. No doubt about that.

Carefully, now, James Clayton climbed the chair, knotted

the silken cords to the hook in the ceiling and twisted them tightly around his neck.

He took his last breath of air on this earth and stepped off the chair.

* * *

The cat had watched the bird's flight with great interest. Now, he stretched and jumped from his warm nest on the downy comforter. He tread daintily over the mauve carpet to where the man's body turned slowly from its twisted bonds. The cat stood on his back legs and with a playful paw swatted at the swinging feet. But he soon lost interest and resumed his nap on the soft frilly bed.

The body was still swaying gently when Mrs. Clayton opened the door.

After she stopped shrieking, Mrs. Clayton continued to stare at her husband's body.

She took a long careful look at the blue distended face, at the bulging, blood-red eyes.

"I never liked you very much, anyway," she said.

CHAPTER 25

"Really, Anneka, I don't believe the way I'm being treated in this school. Like I'm public enemy number one or something. It's so unprofessional! They should grow up, these people. Like Trevor's the first man who ever wanted to leave his wife. Is it my fault he's unhappy? Can I help it if his wife works in the same place I do? God, it's just so unfair!"

Anneka was seething. Stephanie Myers had the gall to sit in her office, complaining to Anneka about people disapproving of her affair with Anneka's best friend's husband? And Lainey in the next office? My God, this bitch had sunk to the lowest level of bitchdom. Anneka wanted to pull her hair. She wanted to kick her ass.

"Stephanie, Ms. Geoffreys told me you needed to discuss the behavior of a student. I'm not comfortable, for obvious reasons, discussing your personal affairs. And that is not a pun."

"Oh, right. Like you and Lainey Dillon only talk about school related things during school hours. Get real! I know you and your friends are bad-mouthing me every chance you get."

Anneka said nothing. Stephanie was not going to have the satisfaction of getting a rise out of her.

"Well, fine. Trevor's moving out and nothing anyone says is changing his mind He's been totally miserable for years."

Stephanie's emancipated breasts were heaving with indignation. She was losing her cool but Anneka wasn't losing hers.

"Ms. Myers, is there a student you need to discuss? Something of an academic nature I can help you with?"

"Um, excuse the interruption, please. This will just take a minute."

Spinner leaned through the office door and waved some documents.

"I've got to get this paperwork to Lou Wagoner. One of her special ed. students. I need it right away or we'll lose funding on this kid."

Stephanie unwound from the chair like an oiled snake. She pushed the offending boobs right in Spinner's face. The man had no room to maneuver. No where else to look.

"Dr. Hartmann," she breathed. "I've been hoping to talk to you about a student. I need someone with more professional expertise than just a school counselor. Could you give me a few minutes of your time?"

"Uh, I'm sorry. I'm late for an appointment. Perhaps Ms. Ericsson could fill me in later?"

"Oh, could I make an appointment for another time, then? Maybe tomorrow? It's very important."

Stephanie took Spinner's arm, gave him a radiant smile and walked him right out of the office. The man was defenseless. Where was a cop when you needed one?

Anneka watched as Stephanie propelled the good doctor right past Lou Wagoner who was walking into the counseling center. Spinner was able to get out a few words about the paperwork waiting in her office. Then, he was gone.

The scent of perfume lingered in the air, so heavy, it was enough to make a person wretch. Probably covering the scent of musk from an early morning roll in the hay, Anneka muttered uncharitably.

She threw open her windows. She didn't need any reminders. Anneka was already imagining Spinner succumbing to the old siren call. In her mind, he was gulping for air and going under for the last time.

"Well, you can kiss that man good-bye!" Lou Wagoner crowed.

"I guess she's working the counseling center this week."

"Here's the paper work from Dr. Hartmann." Anneka shoved the papers at her. "The meeting's in just a few days. Leave it in my mailbox before you leave today. Now, if you'll excuse me, I'm going to lunch."

Anneka stormed out of the office. Lainey was still at her desk, pale and tight-lipped. Anneka wondered if Trevor had already told her he was leaving.

"Going to lunch. You okay, Lainey?"

"I'd like to take a pair of pliers to the nipples showing through that slut's slinky blouse. Then, I'd feel a *whole* lot better," Lainey replied.

"This whole thing sucks," muttered Anneka. "Men suck."

She was in a very bad mood.

* * *

There's some kind of physical law in the universe that says bringing order to one thing will just result in disorder somewhere else. That must be what's happening here, Anneka thought. Even with Nate Dupray captured and in a coma, there's still crisis everywhere.

185

Anneka had come back from lunch to find Mrs. Clayton waiting in her office. Anneka didn't think she'd been out of the house since Jamie's funeral except to attend services for her husband. At least, that was the impression she'd gotten from John the last time they talked. Anneka hadn't attended Mr. Clayton's funeral. Dead or alive, she hated the man's guts.

Mrs. Clayton looked agitated and apprehensive, like she was expecting another catastrophe. In normal circumstances, she wasn't a woman anyone much noticed. At school conferences, she'd sat at her husband's side, never expressing an opinion.

"Ms. Ericsson, I don't have an appointment...."

"No problem. Come in."

Mrs. Clayton settled herself in the office chair and pulled at her skirt nervously. She was much thinner than Anneka remembered. She cleared her throat several times before she spoke.

"I scarcely know where to begin. I'm so worried about John. I try to talk to him but he ignores me. It's like nothing has happened, like Jamie's death and his father's suicide have had no effect on him. He comes home, shuts himself in his room and studies. In the morning, he's gone before I even get up. It's like I've lost everyone. I'm totally alone now."

Mrs. Clayton cried like she did everything, quietly, unassumably.

Anneka spoke gently. "It may just be John's reaction to traumatic events. Everyone reacts differently. He may lose himself in school work to shut out the grief."

"Oh, I know. But some of his reactions are so strange. He's never cried. Not once. And he's never acted depressed or unhappy."

Mrs. Clayton shifted her chair closer and lowered her voice. "For instance, I tried to involve him in the arrangements for his father's services. I thought maybe it would help him, give him something concrete to do. So I asked John what he thought about cremation. And he said, 'I think it's fine, for dead people.' And then he gave me this odd smile."

Her voice broke and she fought for control. "I just dropped it. I took care of everything myself. I never brought his father up again."

It was very quiet in the office. There was rain falling in gentle patter against the panes.

"As soon as John goes off to college, I'm selling the house and getting out of New Albion. Somewhere far, somewhere sunny, away from the rain. Both John and I need a fresh start. If only I'd left when the children were small. My marriage wasn't good but I stayed for them. My God, if I'd only had the courage to leave. I had some suspicions . . . I shut my eyes to everything— It's my fault, my fault!"

The rain had intensified. It beat against the windows accentuating the tension inside.

"Mrs. Clayton. You didn't kill Jamie and you didn't put the rope around your husband's neck. Those events were totally out of your control."

The woman had covered her face. All her fingernails were chewed to the quick. Anneka was reminded of Destry's fingernails, Miranda's . . . So many victims . . .

"When you do get settled elsewhere, please get counseling . Maybe a support group for women. Don't drown in guilt. You can still have a life."

Anneka went to the file cabinet and pulled out John's file.

"Let's call John right now. I need to show him these letters that came in the mail this morning. These colleges are definitely interested in him. I want to know which ones I should write letters of recommendation, so let's discuss it together."

* * *

John greeted Anneka politely and nodded at his mother. He wore his brightly polished loafers, the ones with the tassels, and Anneka wondered again if it had been John or his father in her office that afternoon.

"John, I wanted to share these letters with you and your Mom. I think you'll be excited about some of the colleges we've heard from."

"Great, Ms. Ericsson. Thanks for taking your time."

Unfailingly polite as usual, Anneka thought. She noted John took the chair farthest from his mother. She studied his face, his eyes. His eyes . . . they were like polished glass.

Some of the schools were interesting to John and others he discounted as not important, or places he wouldn't pursue. With the letters dealt with, Anneka took a stab at the other concern.

"We've never talked about your dad's death, John. Your mom's worried about you."

"I don't want to talk about that, if you don't mind."

Anneka tried again.

"If you don't want to talk to me, that's okay. Maybe another counselor, such as a grief counselor?."

"Look, I don't need a grief counselor. I don't feel any grief." John's voice was nonchalant, as if he was discussing the weather. "If you really want to talk about my father, let's start with the fact that he was screwing my sister. What makes you think he didn't kill her, too?"

Mrs. Clayton gasped and began to weep.

Gathering his books, John unwound his tall frame from the chair in one fluid motion. He didn't even glance at his mother, but at the door, he turned and gave Anneka a sunny smile.

"Sorry about the bad scene, Ms. Ericsson. It won't affect my letters of recommendation, will it?"

* * *

Anneka tossed and turned and tried to sleep.

Spinner had called. He said he was sharing brats and a beer with Ollie and turning in early.

But her imagination had taken control. She saw Spinner twisting and turning in sweaty sheets with Stephanie Myers, legs akimbo and screaming in passion. To the side, lay an exhausted Trevor Dillon softly crooning love songs for lovers. The refrain "That old black magic has me in its spell . . ." wafted through the night. She even dreamed of Stephanie's perfume, imbedded in her nostrils for all time, a particularly aromatic hell.

The rain pounded and the wind howled. The knarled fingers of the tall hemlock scratched and fumbled at the window. The waves shook the bed like a boat in a stormy sea.

CHAPTER 26

NEW ALBION SLEPT under a frosty starry sky.
In the small hospital behind the marina, Nate Dupray lay white and still, enveloped in a heavy fog.

Dreams terrible and twisted whirlpooled through thick chunks of gray. Dazzling bolts of light would strike without warning, jumping Nate back to consciousness, making him struggle against the restraining belts and tubes and the constant pain screaming in his gut; pain that rose and fell with the ebb and flow of morphine through his veins.

Dying is hard, Nate thought.

He knew he was dying. Would have known even if the sons of bitches by his bed didn't keep reminding him. Day and night they were there. Every time he came to.

"You'd better make your peace with God before you go, Nate."

"You're checking out of here, buddy. Better to meet your maker with a clear conscience."

"C'mon, give us what we need, Nate. Do at least one thing right in your miserable life."

The sons of bitches never stopped.

Sometimes he tried to form words but they wouldn't come. They took too much energy. He was too tired. Otherwise, he'd tell them to go to hell. Go fuck themselves. When he dropped back into the black void, he was glad. It got him away.

Nate's stirrings brought warning bleeps from the machines. Needles peaked and plunged in alarm.

"Is he dying? Call a nurse, damn it! The little bastard's going to croak before he tells us anything."

"No, I don't think so. Look, the line's even now. He's just unconscious."

Even in his pain, Nate felt a certain satisfaction, but it vanished with a swell of sadness.

He wanted Destry to know. Know that he didn't kill them. Not Susanne or that dumb little shit, Jamie, either. He wanted his baby to know his father hadn't murdered anybody. Oh, sure, he'd run a few drugs but he didn't kill girls.

He'd hidden the car in the parking lot, behind the school shop. Susanne never showed up. He waited a long time, smoked a lot of cigarettes.

Oh, he knew who killed Susie, all right. Knew who he'd seen. Even through the pouring rain, through the steamy windshield. Wouldn't everybody just be too surprised?

But the fuckers would never believe him.

He felt the blackness coming and struggled against it. He wanted to talk to Destry. He'd tell her who. . . .

* * *

The machines registered a warning blip, blip. The signal brought the police woman. She stared down at Nate Dupray with a certain amount of sympathy. She guessed he wasn't coming around, after all. He'd never pull out of this. Too many bullets in too many vital organs.

Nate's eyes fluttered open, just for a moment. Blue, blue eyes.

If you didn't know better, you'd feel sorry for him, the woman thought. Such a good-looking kid... He didn't look like a monster.

He looked like an altar boy.

CHAPTER 27

DRASTIC CIRCUMSTANCES CALL for drastic measures. The Lemonade Ladies were meeting. The line had been drawn. They were going to brainstorm a strategy to get Trevor back.

A twenty-three year old girl was no match for the Lemonade Ladies. The thing was as good as done.

Anneka maneuvered the Durango between two cars parked right in front of the River Road House. What luck. The parking lot was full.

The tide was up and the Siletz river was running high, close to cresting at sixteen feet was what the radio was reporting. Waves pulled restlessly at the pilings holding the scenic restaurant right above the water. There were no boats on the river. This morning the flag in the village harbor had ripped its warning of high winds and heavy seas. Experienced fishermen were safely at home. The river so placid on a quiet day could turn lethal in a heartbeat. The huge salmon that swam in the river were clearly off the hook.

Anneka spied her friends in a quiet corner just off the lounge. Meetings as sensitive as this required a little privacy.

Skye stood and motioned to a chair.

"Hi kid."

"Hope you haven't started without me," Anneka said.

Lainey was at the other end of the table. Maggie had a protective arm around her shoulder.

Nogood raised her wine glass in greeting. Her black eye had almost disappeared. They all hoped Manny had faded along with it.

"C'mon, Anneka, you're always the last damn one to get here. Let's not waste time. We gotta work out a plan and fast," Nogood said.

"You think the girl's really that formidable?" Skye asked. "She's scarcely out of Pampers. What could Trevor possibly have in common with her?"

"Trust me, Skye, " said Anneka. "I've seen her in action. This girl can process men like a food blender."

A harried waitress arrived at the table. Anneka ordered her usual, a vodka martini, straight up, two olives. Everybody ordered another round. Lainey's hand shook as she handed her glass to the girl.

Maggie got right to the point. "What's happened so far, Lainey? Give us the latest."

"Well, Trevor's gone. He just packed a suitcase and left. He didn't say anything other than he'd be in touch and not to worry about the bills. I don't know if he's at a motel or already moved in with her. He hasn't even called."

"Just like that, huh? What a bastard." Nogood shook her head in disgust, reached in her purse and drew out a cigarette.

Everybody glared at her.

"Oh hell, that's right. I'm with the nicotine police." She reluctantly shoved the cigarette back in her purse.

"I can't believe he'd leave without some discussion. What about the children?" Skye asked.

"I haven't said anything to them," Lainey said. "Just Daddy had to leave for awhile. They're so young. They don't understand."

"That damn Stephanie! I wish I'd never hired her!" Maggie said.

"Where did she come from anyway?" Skye leaned forward and offered a tissue to Lainey whose eyes had filled with tears.

"She came from Portland. Started teaching in a high school there right out of college. The principal gave her a good recommendation."

"Well, it's certainly not your fault, Maggie," Anneka said. You couldn't know what a carnivore she is, it's not like it'd be on her transcript or anything. So, let's concentrate on what we can do now. We've got a Lemonade Lady in jeopardy here."

The group strained their brains for ideas, some serious, some in jest. Lainey's problems were their problems. If it happened to one of them, it happened to all of them.

Anneka told them about seeing Stephanie in the parking lot of the local super market. She and Nogood had been loading up the back of the truck with refreshments for a student council meeting the next day.

"So, then Nogood yells, 'Hey, Stephanie, you been seeing any *single* men lately?' And then we both ducked down behind the Durango before she saw us! Gawd! She looked all over with a real mad look on her face but finally went into the store. I could have died. And Nogood, I could have strangled you."

"Well, I'm sorry, but I just can't stand the little bitch."

The story made Lainey laugh and the group's mood turned silly.

"I know. What about this suggestion?" Skye asked. "Some students were telling me about this lesbian biker gang in Portland? I guess they're really tough. The leader's called Big

Mama Mavis and she's supposed to be one scary lady. We get in touch with them and suggest Stephanie has the hots for Big Mama. See if she'll just roar down to the coast and carry the little slut off. How's that?"

"Let's drink to that," laughed Maggie.

"Let's drink to anything," everybody chimed.

"Ha! You girls are amateurs! I got an even better suggestion," said Nogood. "Lainey, when Trevor shows up at the house, you tell him this. You tell him he can have a blowjob just any old time he wants one. I guarantee the man will be back before sunup!"

There was total silence at the table. The Lemonade Ladies stared at Nogood.

"Well . . . I bet it would work."

Skye regained her speech first. "You know, she's probably right. Men are animals."

"Yeah, but they've got their bad points too," Nogood said.

CHAPTER 28

STEPHANIE MYERS WAS getting ready for her early morning jog. Running was a natural high and necessary to maintain her svelte shape, as well. She never missed her early morning run.

It's certainly paid off, she thought to herself. She wriggled and writhed into a skin-tight purple spandex body suit and tucked her long blond hair beneath a baseball cap with New Albion High in gold letters.

The high school colors were purple and gold. She was glad. She looked great in those colors.

Studying herself in the full length mirror, Stephanie turned to each side and sucked in her already flat stomach. She turned away from the mirror and gazed over her shoulder at her shapely rear and long lean legs. She was satisfied with the view. It wasn't every woman who could look this hot in spandex.

Stephanie laced up her running shoes humming a tune from an old muscial. In high school, she'd played the leading role of Maria in *West Side Story*. "I'm so pretty, I'm so pretty. I can't tell you how pretty I am. Ta da da dum, ta da da dum." She tripped lightly down the stairs to her living room below. She lovingly caressed the back of her elegant new sofa and swept by to the kitchen.

The condo was new and in a lovely neighborhood. A trifle small and she couldn't afford an ocean view, but she hoped to remedy that situation very soon. *If* everything worked out like she'd planned.

Stephanie frowned. She'd been so annoyed with Trevor last night, she hadn't even let him sleep over. All he'd wanted to do was stay home and spend a quiet evening by the fire. God, like she couldn't do that when she was old and wrinkled, like fifty or something.

What she had always liked about Trevor, what she had *loved* about Trevor, was he took her out to the nicest places and he had plenty of money to spend. Not like the young guys she'd dated. Lately, though . . . lately Trevor hadn't been nearly as much fun. Said they shouldn't be seen out together until the divorce. There'd be time enough to live it up after the financial settlement was done, he'd said.

Stephanie poured herself a fresh glass of juice and popped her vitamin. This was her usual breakfast. She'd have a light lunch at school later and save her calories for dinner. Last night Trevor hadn't taken her to dinner, either, and now, she was famished. There was nothing in the fridge but juice and some salad stuff. Damn Trevor anyway! He could be so thoughtless sometimes.

On the way out, she stopped to clip a tiny cell phone to her belt, just in case Trevor called. She didn't want him to stay hurt and angry. Sugary sweet is how she'd be. Call him her sexy big bad teddy bear and crap like that.

Stephanie banged out of the apartment and headed for the carport. The five-year-old Honda wasn't her choice for a car. She wanted a new sports car. But second year school-teachers didn't make enough money to support new car payments and a fancy condominium. Well, this was the last year she'd have to teach school. She hated it. Trevor had mentioned she'd probably want to continue her career. Hah! Fat chance of that.

The morning was cold but at least it wasn't raining. Very foggy, though. Still, she ought to be able to get in a good run. She'd run in much worse weather than this.

There were no other cars in sight when she turned on to Highway 101. This early, there shouldn't be any other runners in the park, either.

Cape Foulweather had a trail that wound along the ocean and through heavy forest for almost two miles. Back and forth would get her a four mile jog. A good work-out, but a breeze for Stephanie.

She had her free conference period first thing in the morning. If she didn't have a parent conference, she usually didn't get to school until the second period of the day. Maggie Ramirez didn't like that. She had made a pointed remark in staff meeting that conference periods were duty periods like any other. Stephanie didn't give a rat's ass. The principal and all of the rest of Lainey Dillon's damn friends could just go to hell. Stephanie knew she was as welcome at New Albion High as piranha in the family pool. She didn't care. The women were all jealous, just because they were loaded with cellulite and ugly. She couldn't stand any of them.

She parked in the rear of the parking lot. She never paid any attention to the sign requesting payment in the box provided. Ha, like she was going to pay three dollars every day she ran in the park. Dream on.

There were no other vehicles in the lot. She loved this about the coast in winter. Portland had been so crowded, everywhere you went, wall to wall people. Everybody wanted to move to Portland or Seattle these days. Working out in the gym there had been a nightmare. Wait for this machine, wait for the sauna, wait for the exercise equipment. The Y in New

Albion was very well-equipped and you never had to wait for anything.

The results of her efforts were obvious. She was buff.

Before she ran, Stephanie went into an elaborate series of stretches. She never ran without stretching. She took plenty of time with her warm-up.

The ocean winds were bringing in huge drifting banks of fog. Visibility wasn't more than a few feet. But it didn't matter. Her feet knew the route intimately. She could run it blindfolded.

The trail was slightly hilly and wound through towering spruce, hemlock and cedar that were hundreds of years old. It was just a few short feet from the cliffs that dropped precipitously to the ocean below. A drop of fifty to sixty feet, sometimes more.

The winter surf was high. The tide was in. Waves thundered against the rocks, unseen in thick fog.

Stephanie's sleek running shoes scarcely skimmed the asphalt trail as she flew recklessly along the path, exulting in the speed, in the effortless stride. She felt all bone and muscle, aglow with vitality. She felt she could run forever.

Stephanie never saw the black-garbed figure. Patient and still, it waited behind the gnarled hemlock that crouched over the trail.

When it jumped directly in front of her racing form, the collision was violent.

"TA DA! Hello, Stephanie!"

Stephanie went sprawling in a tangle of purple legs and arms. Her cell phone came unclipped and fell to the side of the trail.

"You IDIOT! Oh God, my elbowwwww! Look, you've torn my tights too, damn it! What are *you* doing here anyway? God!"

"Waiting for you, you brainless little whore."

Stephanie felt a jolt in her stomach like a hard punch. It took her breath away and lacerated her liver. Another blow and another, this time lower, in her belly. Feces began to leak through the ripped colon. She gazed in disbelief at the abhorrent gore streaming out of her body, at the torrent of blackish-red that mushroomed through the slashed gold jersey jacket. She put both hands to her chest and met hot sticky wetness.

"Whaaaat? What are you doing?" Stephanie screamed and screamed. Her hand fell on the cell phone lying in the path. Her blind searching fingers tapped out 9-1-1. The heavy punch came again. She lost her breath and could scream no more.

The killer calmly picked up the phone to answer the insistent queries of the operator.

"Never mind. I was just testing my new cell phone. Thank you operator."

* * *

A solitary seagull sat atop the weathered signpost above the churning sea.

The seagull had watched, head cocked, beady eyes blinking, as the squawking purple thing flopped over the cliff and plunged headlong to the rocks below.

The gull sat motionless.

The sign read,

> DANGER.
> DO NOT GO BEYOND THIS POINT.

CHAPTER 29

NOGOOD SLAMMED HER coffee mug on Anneka's desk and plunked down in the chair in front of it.

"This has been one hell of a day."

"Yeah? What's goin' on?"

"Well, first off, Little Miss Oregon, a.k.a. dipsy Stephanie Myers, never showed up for work. I found her second period class just standing in the hall. Lou Wagoner called my office because they were making so damn much noise. We've had to cover all her classes so far and she had no lesson plans anywhere. What a mess. Maggie is so pissed."

"Wow, she didn't call in sick or anything?"

"Nope, we've been trying to reach her all day. Just get the message machine with all this stupid music and then Stephanie comes on sounding like she's giving phone sex. I need this today like I need a root canal."

Nogood took a slurp from the coffee mug, emblazoned on the side, the words, "I'M BAD WITH NAMES. MAY I CALL YOU SHITHEAD?"

"Nogood, you *gotta* get rid of that mug. Jeez."

"Ah, nobody sees it. I keep it in my desk. Cardboard and foam cups can give you cancer."

"You're the damn assistant principal of the school. You can't walk around with that mug—"

"Yeah, yeah. Don't worry about it. Hey, do you think Stephanie's run off with Trevor?"

"I hope not. Lainey called to tell me she had an appointment with her attorney first thing this morning. But she said Trevor's been calling since last night and wants to talk to her."

"Hey, maybe he's coolin' it with Stephanie huh? Maybe that's why she didn't show today. The poor girl's depressed."

"Pray it were so. I don't know, though, Lainey doesn't seem too hot to talk to Trevor. She told me if he wants to come back, she'd have to think about it, hard. She's pretty much had it with him."

"Good for her. I hope she hangs tough. He's been such a bastard.

"Well, gotta get back. I've got an office full of problems." Nogood hauled herself from the chair but turned in the doorway. "Anneka, if I can't find anybody, would you take Stephanie's last period? We don't have any teachers free today."

"Sure. Let me know. I'm pretty much here all day."

* * *

Lainey walked into her office at the same time as Anneka's phone rang.

"Counseling center, Anneka Ericsson."

"Hi Babe."

"Hi, Spinner."

"Has Lou Wagoner given you that special ed paperwork I needed?"

"Not yet, no. Want me to ask her for it?"

"I've got a kid I need to see there this afternoon. I'll just leave her a note in her mail box.

"Hey, Anneka, I was thinking this weekend, we might go to the antique fair in Toledo. I've never driven up the old Siletz river road. Might be kind of fun. And we can stop for lunch at this place on the river. It's supposed to be pretty good."

"That sounds fun. I love to explore those old shops. Can we take the dogs along? We could walk them along the river."

"Sure. Ollie's been missing Laverne and Shirley.

* * *

"Lainey, I thought I heard you come in. Come sit a minute and talk to me."

Lainey looked tired. She'd looked tired a lot lately. The last few weeks had taken a toll.

"Are you all right, kid? You look like you need a vacation."

"Yeah, some sun and a couple a months on a deserted island would be nice."

Lainey sat down in a despondent heap, as if her legs had suddenly given way.

"I look like a hag, I know. I don't sleep much and the kids are really a handful since Trevor left. He's coming by to take them out for dinner tonight, though, so I can just collapse when I get home."

"Hmm, isn't this the first time Trevor's been back since . . ."

"Yeah, he's been calling a lot though. I know he misses the kids and he says we need to talk. But I don't think I want to talk to him right now. I'm too tired and too damn mad. I don't want to deal with any of it."

"That's understandable."

"I started a separate checking account and froze all our mutual funds, so he couldn't pull any nasty surprises on me. Trevor found out and he was quite insulted. Said he couldn't believe I had such little trust in him. Can you imagine? He had the nerve to talk about trust!"

Lainey laughed, a laugh that had nothing to do with amusement. She put up a hand to smooth back her hair and the hand shook.

"Stephanie didn't show up today and she didn't call in to the substitute service," Anneka said. "Nogood's been scrambling to cover her classes. They just get her machine when they call. Maggie's really annoyed."

"Well, gee. Maybe the poor girl broke a nail or something."

CHAPTER 30

RAIN OR SHINE, summer, winter, spring or fall, the *Whale Watch Inn* is usually overrun with people. Tourists and locals alike flock to the scenic inn to consume cinnamon rolls the size of footballs with melted butter oozing down the sides and overflowing the plate.

The inn hangs suspended above Big Whale Cove, a stunningly beautiful place. Across the cove, up from a sandy beach strewn with driftwood and over a rocky ridge there is a steep path, treacherous and overgrown with salal, but if the climber perseveres, the path winds down to the shelter of Spirit Cove.

The big cove is decorated with attractions that delight visitors to the restaurant. Sea lions and seals frequently rest on the rocks of the inlet, seeking surcease from the pounding open sea. From time to time migrating and resident gray whales swim lazily within its borders.

Sometimes, on their twice yearly journeys between sunny Baja and the freezing arctic seas, killer whales may decide to explore the cove. This can result in a few tasty sea lions or seals being snapped up in the gaping jaws of the hungry orcas.

Locals watch stone-faced as tourist mothers cover the eyes of their shrieking children and snatch up napkins to catch the pieces of buttery bun dropping from their astonished mouths.

Of late, a wave of publicity has made *Whale Watch Inn* even more of an attraction.

There is speculation Sir Francis Drake may have anchored in the cove in 1579 and spent the winter there sheltered from the winds and high seas. He named the small harbor "Albion" after the Celtic name for England and socialized with the Indians who lived in round earth huts on the peripheries of Big Whale and Spirit Coves.

An English historian theorizes that Drake put up at New Albion for five weeks and built a stockade to hide his looted treasure.

In 1996, a group of archeologists uncovered the foundations of what may have been Drake's wooden stockade. Ground-probing radar located a 2-foot thick wall in the land above Whale Cove and scientific study confirmed the timbers were the right age to have been placed in the 1570's.

During the summer, crowds of people gathered at water's edge to watch divers search the floor of Whale Cove for further evidence that Drake may have left behind some 400 years ago. The sea was turbulent that day and nothing was found.

* * *

On this early morning , a young mother was trying to interest her young son in these fascinating bits of history but he was far more interested in his dripping cinnamon roll and the old rustic boat that rocked below him in the gentle surf.

The inn had placed the small rusted-out fishing boat on the shore as a maritime attraction for the tourists. Its hull lay half submerged in the surf, an ancient anchor hanging from the side, partly visible even at high tide.

FOUL WEATHER

Mikey had tuned out his mother completely. He had a new pair of binoculars and was leaning close to the window to scrutinize the side of the old boat.

"Mom, what's that purple thing by the boat there? Mom? MOM! That's hair. Euuuuuuuh, that's hair, Mom! "

His mother pushed him aside, grabbed the binoculars and leaned to the window. She screamed.

"My God! That's a body! Mikey, don't look, DON'T LOOK!"

* * *

Stephanie bobbed gently in the surf, her long yellow hair entangled in the rusty anchor. Her entrails were still somewhat intact and undulated in the sunlit-dappled waves. A banquet for the little crabs and fishes.

CHAPTER 31

MAGGIE AND NOGOOD were waiting in her office when Anneka arrived shortly before eight.

"What's going on? What are you guys doing here so early?"

"Anneka, come on in and close the door," Maggie said. "Have you seen Lainey yet?"

"No, what's wrong with Lainey? Has something happened?"

"Lainey's fine. It's Stephanie Myers."

"Oh God, *did* she run off with Trevor?"

"No, listen, Anneka! Lainey will be here any minute and we need to decide how to tell her this. Stephanie's body washed up in front of the *Whale Watch Inn* early this morning. People in the restaurant spotted her. She was tangled up in the anchor of that old boat they keep on the beach."

"My God!"

Maggie paced back and forth in front of the window.

"A man from the Coast Guard recognized her. The sheriff was waiting for me in the parking lot when I got to school. They want to keep the details quiet and they want us to prepare the students, of course."

"Keep what details private?"

Nogood spoke for the first time. Her voice tense. Her lips tight.

"It wasn't an accident, Anneka. Stephanie was murdered and probably pitched from the rocks above Cape Foulweather State Park."

"Murdered! Who'd want to murder Stephanie?"

"Who, indeed?" asked Maggie.

Anneka sat down slowly. This was just too damn much, she thought. Too many deaths. Too many murders. Just too damn much. How could this be? Nate Dupray was dead. He was buried last week.

"Another murder? It doesn't make sense. Just statistically, how can there be another violent death in such a small town?"

"Oh, c'mon, Anneka. Remember those two college girls murdered at Foulweather State Park five years ago?" Maggie answered. "That's still unsolved. They've never found the killer or killers. Living right off Highway 101 these days can be dangerous."

"Yeah, I read this article some time back about the Northwest wilderness having the highest number of unsolved killings per capita of any place in the country," Nogood said. "Thick lonely forest areas are said to be perfect places to kill somebody; the bodies can remain undiscovered for years. And the sea, the sea's really a friend to murderers because the bodies are often not found at all. And if they are, the salt water's obliterated all traces of the crime." Nogood nodded her head emphatically and took a gulp of her coffee. "Stephanie was a very good-looking girl. Shouldn't have been running alone. The parks are totally deserted that early in the morning."

"So, along with two of our students murdered by a vicious killer, we now have a teacher killed by a psycho in the state park. That seems rather too much of a coincidence, doesn't it?" Anneka asked.

"Okay, if not a random killer, then who?" said Maggie. "You know the sheriff was asking me some pretty pointed questions about Trevor,"

"Trevor! That's ridiculous! Are you telling me the police seriously think Trevor could have murdered Stephanie?"

Maggie had continued to pace back and forth in front of the window. Now, she stopped and faced Anneka.

"You've heard of a crime of passion? Trevor's going to be the first person considered as a suspect and that's why we've got to get Lainey as soon as she comes in."

"Oh God, as if Lainey hasn't been through enough already." Anneka stood and joined Maggie and Nogood at the window. All three women stared out at the parking lot. Lainey's reserved space remained empty.

"Maggie," Anneka asked. "What did the police say other than they found the body? Was Stephanie raped? How do they know she didn't just fall off the rocks? Hell, that can happen. Why couldn't it have been an accident?"

"Because she'd been stabbed repeatedly in the chest and stomach."

"My God! Will this... horror never end?" Anneka returned to the comfort of her old desk chair, clinging to its familiarity.

"They don't know if she was sexually molested," Maggie continued in a low steady voice. "They're doing an autopsy, of course. They can tell she was in the water over twenty-four hours. They think she was thrown off the rocks and died from the impact. Her head was... They'll know when they determine if there was water in her lungs."

Nogood drew a long breath, "OK, Maggie, how do you want to handle this? We've got about ten minutes to come up with a strategy. What do you want us to do?"

215

Maggie reached across Anneka's desk and grabbed a pen and notepad.

"Right. Anneka, you take care of telling Lainey. Tell her its all right to go home. I don't want the police questioning her at school. I'll take care of that with the detectives. God knows, I've gotten to know them well enough. They'll want to talk with some of the teachers, too. Maybe, even some students, But they'll have to get permission from me and the parents for that."

Maggie was thinking out loud, pulling together a plan to contain this last crisis.

"When you've finished with Lainey, call Ruth in Toledo. Ask her and that other counselor to come down and help us with the students. Call Spinner, we can use him, too. If any students want to go home, that's okay, but have someone in the attendance office call their parents first."

Maggie turned to Nogood.

"I'll write something for morning announcements. We don't want a whole lot of rumors circulating out there. We'll announce Stephanie's death and say they'll be more details when we know more about it.

"Okay Maggie," Nogood said. "I'll get a substitute for Stephanie's classes. Lou Wagoner can keep an eye on them till the sub gets here. She's right across the hall and she's got first period conference."

"Okay, but remember, I don't want the police talking to anyone without my knowledge. I'll call the newspaper and radio station and tell them not to come on campus. Any information they get, they'll have to get from me."

Anneka watched Lainey's car swing into the lot.

"Here she is."

Maggie and Nogood started for the door.

"All right, let's get to work," Maggie said.

* * *

"Lainey, I need to talk to you."

"Sure. I'm running a little late this morning. It's hard not having Trevor around to help get the kids ready. They're running me ragged, you know?"

Lainey was standing at her desk sorting through the papers there and simultaneously booting up her computer, preparing for the day. She looked bone weary.

"Uhh, Lainey, we had some bad news this morning about Stephanie Myers."

"She's not here again today? What's the matter with her? Wait a minute . . . is this about Trevor?"

Lainey sat down and looked at Anneka warily.

"Well, no. Something really bad has happened. Stephanie was found dead this morning. Washed up on the beach in front of *Whale Watch Inn*.."

"Oh, wait a minute!" Lainey held her hand up as if to stop a fast moving truck. "Stephanie's dead? DEAD? Are you sure?"

"The police were here when Maggie got to school. We'll announce it to the students and faculty first thing. We're just saying we don't have all the details. They'll think it was an accident."

"What do you mean Anneka?" Lainey said slowly. " Is there reason to believe it *wasn't* an accident?"

"Stephanie was murdered. Lainey? Are you okay? Stay right here. I'll get you some water."

She looked dangerously close to fainting. Anneka took hold of her shoulders.

"Take a deep breath. Are you okay? Do you feel faint? "

"Give me a minute. Just give me a minute."

She put her head in her hands while Anneka watched helplessly. Lainey, the eternal optimist had vanished.

A long moment passed.

"Anneka?"

"Yes?"

"Do you think people are going to think Trevor did it?"

"I don't know. Maybe. But we know that's impossible. Trevor's been a jerk, but he could never murder anybody."

"Of course he couldn't. That's ridiculous. It's so ironic, though."

"What's ironic?"

"Trevor's been calling and calling to talk to me. I think he wants to come home. He was having second thoughts about this thing with Stephanie."

"That's ironic, all right."

"No, that's not what I mean. What I mean is, I don't really want him to come back. At least, not right away. And now, Stephanie's dead. So, Anneka, if he comes back, I'll never really know if he chose me and the kids... instead of... you know what I mean?"

The phone made both of them jump. Anneka reached for it first. It was Rita, Maggie's secretary.

"Is Lainey there with you?"

"Yes, but she can't talk to anyone right now. And, Rita, she'll be out of the office for awhile today."

"She'd better take this one. It's her husband calling from the police department. He says he has to talk to her. He says its an emergency and he only has one call."

* * *

9:35 Morning Announcements

"Students and faculty, we regret we have some tragic news to announce. We've just been informed of the death of one of our faculty members. The body of Ms. Stephanie Myers was found on the beach near Cape

FOUL WEATHER

Foulweather early this morning. We'll give you more details when they become available.

"We will be following our regular schedule but students may be excused from classes to see the counselors or to call their parents.

"Times for funeral services will be announced. If they are to be held in Portland where Ms. Myers' family resides, we will have a memorial service for her in the school auditorium.

"All other announcements will be given this afternoon before last period.

"Please stand for the National Anthem."

CHAPTER 32

BENEATH ANNEKA'S HOUSE, a brooding horror lay in wait. It listened as she went from room to room absorbed in everyday tasks. It was patient and grinned beneath Anneka as she slept.

I couldn't have planned it better than this.

A trap door under Anneka's pantry, a concealed trapdoor to the crawlspace. How perfect.

I could have been down here all along, dry and warm and safe. Froze my ass off outside in those trees. A little creepy and dark, but I've got my flashlight. A cinch to get in, too. Just zip right through the dog door. What a trip. I can get in any time I want and hide down here.

Until I decide to surprise her.
I'll come right out of the floor.
Like out of a cake at a party.
TA DA!

* * *

Home, Anneka just wanted to get home. The day had been a nightmare; students, parents, teachers, reporters, police, an unending stream.

The team of Anneka, Maggie, Nogood, Spinner, and Ruth had worked non-stop handling the office traffic and manning the phones.

Lainey had returned in mid-afternoon and pitched right in. There had been no time to talk. She had assured Anneka she was all right and then led a weeping student into her office and closed the door.

It was not only the students who were shaken by the sudden violent death of someone who had so recently lived and breathed among them. The faculty and staff suffered the same shock. Dwight Ridout, the young handsome coach so beloved of all the adolescent girls, broke down in Anneka's office.

He'd dated Stephanie for several months. He thought they had a commitment to each other and then, suddenly she dropped him for Trevor Dillon. She told him she was just being practical. The older man was established, had more to offer her, a life of upper-middle-class amenities, comfort and leisure. She wouldn't have to work as a teacher anymore. She wouldn't have to work at all. She talked about maybe even opening her own gym.

"She was really excited about that. I never had a chance."

Anneka could hear the bitterness in Dwight's voice. He didn't sound much different from her teen-age boys who felt jilted and betrayed when they lost a girlfriend.

"I guess that must have been difficult to accept, Dwight, after all that time together?"

"I was really down but lately, she'd started getting friendly again. Giving me that smile of hers, you know? No, I guess you wouldn't. But anyway, I was beginning to think she had changed her mind, maybe wanted to get back together. I should have known better."

"What do you mean, Dwight?"

"Ah, Stephanie was such an indiscriminate flirt. She gave the come on to guys just for the hell of it. She was shallow and self-centered, but damn it, in spite of that, I loved her."

He buried his head in his hands. When he spoke, his voice was muffled and thick with emotion.

"I ran with her in the mornings a lot, sometimes along the beach and sometimes in the park along that same trail she must have taken yesterday, when someone, when someone—If I'd been with her, this never would have happened!"

Dwight sat for several minutes, then gathered his lanky body wearily from the chair and left.

You didn't really know a person, Anneka thought. She'd always thought of Dwight as rather vapid, good-looking but immature. He seemed to thrive on the adoration of the teenage girls. She'd never have suspected his feelings had run that deeply for Stephanie.

The young people she talked with were less emotional about the person herself and more concerned about the death, the demise of someone not much older than they. If it could happen to her, to Susanne, to Jamie, could it not also happen to them? How could this be? People died when they were old, not when life was exciting and new.

The students shed tears and gave comfort to one another. Then, they returned once more to the routine of their classes, to their activities, to their own interests. Because, after all, there was a dance after the game Friday night. Life went on.

Parents had besieged the administrators with questions about Stephanie's death. They were told what the police had said to tell them. Details would follow. The death was being investigated.

It would be morning before authorities would release the real facts about the murder but rumors were already creeping over neighboring fences, coiling through phone wires, waiting on street corners. Fear and suspicion enveloped the little town once again, thick as sea fog.

At five-thirty in the afternoon with rain pounding the windows of the Durango, Anneka was finally on 101 heading home. As she took the curves over Cape Foulweather the wind shook the big truck with unusual force. El Nino had wreaked its chaos last summer and now weathercasters were blaming La Nina for a winter so furious and extreme as to be a rarity even for the Northwest coast. The flags in New Albion were flying in the harbor, two square red flags with a black circle in their centers signifying a serious storm with gale-force winds.

Everyone was on edge. Murders and rain and wind and not a ray of sunshine for weeks.

She hit the remote for the gate at Spirit Cove, swept through to Breaker's Scarp and into her garage. She was home. In for the evening.

Anneka flipped switches for lights, music and the gas fireplace, dropped the shades on the dark, tumultuous night, and slipped into her oldest, snuggly robe with a pair of fluffy warm socks. All the while, Laverne and Shirley capered around her and Kitty Shameless wound in and out of her feet.

Home. Peaceful haven. She poured a glass of mellow merlot and sank into the deep recesses of the soft sofa. Shameless immediately jumped on Anneka's chest and proceeded to purr with rapture while he kneaded the rough textured chenille.

She felt the wire in her spine relax. She vowed to think only of pleasant things as her mind began to drift.

Spinner... he'd been so great today. He had such a way of putting people at ease. She was so lucky to have found him. She hadn't been looking but there he'd been. What a break.

They'd had such a good time the previous weekend. It

seemed like such a long time ago, a day so removed from all the tragedies and stress.

They'd piled the dogs in the Durango and driven up the old Siletz River Road that wound along the river's banks. They pulled over when they felt like it and let the dogs run. For once, it wasn't raining. The day was clear, if not sunny, the air crisp and clean as the first taste of cold dry wine.

A curious thing had happened as they explored the river's edge. Hidden in a shelter of trees was an old wooden historical marker, the letters so worn as to be almost indecipherable.

The marker commemorated a Native-American woman named Mourning Ann, the bride of an early settler of the region. Wed at age thirteen, she'd borne thirteen children in as many years.

"Strange," she'd said to Spinner. "She is a real woman then. I must have read about her somewhere. I dream about her. And the name ... I thought it was Morning. It's Mourning ... How odd."

"What's that? You've had dreams about this woman? This woman on the marker?"

"Oh, it's nothing. Just something I read ..."

Spinner had rushed off then, through the trees to rescue Laverne and Shirley perilously close to falling into the river.

Anneka stared into the flames of the fire. She could still see the woman's face so vividly. Strange, the memory in a dream to remain so sharp. The woman was always somber, a quiet presence. In Anneka's dreams she roamed the ocean cliffs to the cove's edge and stood alone in the fog.

Last night she'd come again. This time, waving her arms at Anneka. Waving frantically, as if in warning. She seemed alarmed. Very, very odd ...

Anneka could feel herself falling asleep. She was so warm, so comfortable ... She hoped Destry was all right. So young.

So alone. Destry, whose dark eyes revealed an old, old soul . . . as if she'd lived myriad lives in her scant fifteen years. . . .

Anneka hadn't talked to Destry for a couple of days. She'd stayed with her every minute through the birth of the baby. Destry, connected to all those tubes, the monitor sensing the baby's heart rate. Destry, breathing the way she'd been taught and clinging to Anneka's hand. Just one time she'd looked at Anneka and said, "This is hard. I'm too young to be doing this."

When the doctor finally placed the baby girl in Destry's arms, she had looked down and laughed, a surprised delighted laugh. Then she said the most mysterious thing.

"I didn't know it would be you!"

What had she meant? What a strange thing to say. She'd ask her, next time they talked. . . .

* * *

Anneka slept, curled in her warm cocoon of couch, with dogs slumbering beside her and the cat curled in a snug little roll at her feet.

She woke once to hear the groaning of the trees as they rocked in the wind. Still raining. The sound a beating drum on the skylights above her head. She had a fleeting thought about the huge tree next to the house. Its roots were becoming more exposed. She needed to have that tree looked at. But worries seemed far away and that's where she wanted them to stay. At least for the night . . .

> Mourning Ann was running, running. She should not have left the children for so long.
>
> They were asleep by the fire. By the fire in the cove. If they awakened, they would be frightened.
>
> At one time, she could run like the wind. Now worry weighed her down . So many children, so much to do.

FOUL WEATHER

Her feet felt like heavy stones.

The worry clutched and grabbed. As she ran, the twisted branches whipped at her face.

Mourning Ann stopped running at the very edge of the scarp, paused on the precipice that plunged to the sea below and breathed hungrily of the cold salty air. She heard the whales sounding, singing their ageless song. They were right below her feet. So near. The mist from their blow frosted her face like tears.

The moon.

The moon was about to set into the sea. The wind billowed Mourning Ann's long cape behind her as she strained forward. She felt she could soar to the sinking moon.

It was so close.

She could reach it.

She knew she could.

As she fell from the cliff's edge, a piece of her cloak caught on the ragged rock and tore.

Just that last remnant remained on the scarp. Just that one remnant remained of Mourning Ann.

She sank into the blackness of the swirling pod and brushed against the barnacle encrusted side of a gray whale. Her long cloak swam around them and they locked in watery embrace.

Face to face, she stared into the enormous cloudy eye.

She drank sea water in thick swallows as she tried to breathe the teeming life all around her.

All the time she clung to the gaze of one big beckoning eye.

Mourning Ann had her one moment of sweet pure communion. And then, too soon, she drifted to the depths.

Dawn broke.

CHAPTER 33

MARCH 1, 1999

NEW ALBION COAST NEWS

HIGH SCHOOL TEACHER FOUND MURDERED BRUTAL SLAYING AT FOULWEATHER STATE PARK

A tense meeting with the press today as investigators for the sheriff's department vowed. . . .

* * *

NEW ALBION SHUDDERED and hunkered in, drew its blinds and cast wary backward looks down rainy night-time streets.
Captain Cook High School simmered, a stew pot flavored with equal portions of fear, anxiety and that curious voyeuristic need that is part of the human personality.

High drama has particular appeal to teenagers. Although horrified by the death they were at the same time intrigued. Students flooded the counseling center with faces that were earnest and sad appearing but revealed curiosity and excitement, as well. Although the event was certainly horrific, it removed them temporarily from the ordinariness of the school day; freed them from civics, from physical science, from government. That Geometry test? Oh, too upset to study for that.

"How could this be? Ms. Myers was teaching me history three days ago!"

"Do you think the killer's still around?"

"My parents won't let me out of the house!"

"Yesterday, after school? I stopped at the Dairy Delight and there was this dude that kept looking at me *really* funny. Do you think I should report it to the police?"

"My parents say we're going to move. They want us brought up away from crime and stuff. I don't want to move!"

"We rented this scary video last night? And we like had to turn it off! Right in the middle, you know? We got so freaked!"

"I don't think I'll go to church any more. How can God let stuff like this keep happening? . . . I don't understand how God can."

In the middle of all this, John Clayton, who stood and faced Anneka across her desk and said in a voice as cold as ice, "Harvard turned me down. Said although my qualifications were *exemplary* , I didn't quite make the cut. Are you responsible for this, Ms. Ericsson?"

* * *

The crisis team, worked non-stop. Some students coped on their own, strong and flexible as young saplings in a storm. Others sought comfort from their peers, their parents or their clergy. The center provided a place to come. The counselors attempted to assess when to offer sympathy or advice, when to encourage an outpouring of emotion and when to draw back, listen and do nothing.

As the counselors labored, the administrators fought to restore the normalcy of routine. Teachers continued to teach but their words went mainly unheard. Hard as anyone tried, there was nothing normal about that day.

During a short lunch break, a decision was made to meet at Anneka's house after school. The friends needed to talk, to get support from one another. They needed to sort out the events of the last few days.

* * *

Anneka busied herself in the kitchen preparing a tray of enchiladas for the evening while Spinner worked on the guacamole dip. They were carefully concentrating on mundane, necessary things, like food.

The main attraction would be Spinner's famous Margaritas, made with rum, not tequila, plus beer, lime juice and triple sec.

"Spinner, don't give Laverne and Shirley any more of that cheese. They're starting to look like little meatloafs."

"Ah, hell. You only live once."

"Maybe, but better to live with a less elevated cocker-cholesterol level.

"Why's Ollie snuffling around the pantry like that?" Anneka asked.

The big Lab had been pacing back and forth in front the pantry door.

"Because, he knows that's where you keep the dog treats."

"Well, he sure seems anxious about it. Give him some. Better dog treats than cheese."

But Ollie continued to nose around the pantry door and

only went to lie down by the fire when Spinner gave the order twice.

"Ollie's usually so laid back, Spinner. What's wrong with him anyway?"

"He's picking up on the vibes around him. We've been under a lot of tension."

Anneka caught the phone on its third ring. It was Destry, calling from Portland where the news had hit the morning papers.

"I'm worried about you, Anneka."

"Destry, hi! Hey, don't worry about me, kid. The police think the killer was a drifter, someone who happened along. Stephanie was all alone in a deserted park and she—"

"Yes, I know. I read that in the paper. But Anneka, I had this dream last night. This Indian girl keeps appearing in my dreams and . . . well, I felt she was trying to warn me and I'm worried about you, that's all. There's something— "

"Destry, what do you mean? What Indian girl?"

"My dreams, they're just so . . . oh, it's too long to go into on the phone— but Anneka, you know I never really thought Nate killed those girls. He was bad. I know that. But, I never thought he could do something like that."

"I know, honey, it's a really hard to understand when you think you know someone, and are as close to them as you were to Nate, but the evidence was pretty substantial. There's just no doubt that—

"I hear car doors," called Spinner. The Lemonade Ladies are here."

"Hey, I'll call you back, OK? In fact, you should come to the coast this weekend. We'll catch up on things. Miss you. Don't worry about me. Just take care of yourself, Des. "

* * *

Skye and Nogood arrived together.

Nogood pulled up in her neglected, disreputable looking vehicle, the right rear tire wobbling precariously.

But Skye was first at the door, emerging from the misty rain, moisture gleaming in her blue-black hair. She shrugged out of an elegant trench coat, "Gawd, Anneka. Do I need a drink."

Anneka and Skye both jumped aside as Nogood shook her raincoat vigorously in their faces.

"Damn it, give me that. I'll hang it to dry." Anneka said.

Maggie and Lainey arrived together, faces tired and drawn as soldiers after a battle.

The group settled around the living room with the stereo playing low and easy and the fire casting shadows on the walls, its glow a dream-weaver. Tension released its grip. Anneka felt the camaraderie of the women friends encircle the room like a physical presence.

"Oh man, this is wonderful! " said Maggie as she wriggled out of her shoes and fell back in the couch. "And Spinner, this is the best damn Margarita I ever had. I swear!"

"Thanks. The secret is a little bit of beer."

"The guacamole ain't half bad, either," said Anneka.

Maggie raised her glass. "Here's to all of you. I want to say, you've all been great the last two days. And Skye, Spinner, I'm so grateful for your help. We managed to keep the lid on, I think."

"The teachers did a wonderful job as well," added Nogood. "They were troopers. Even Lou Wagoner. She handled both Stephanie's and her own history classes for two days. I get so annoyed with her but, hey, she was great under the circumstances. They all were."

"I feel sorry for Lou," Maggie said. "She must be very lonely since her mother died . . . and now, her poor dog. Nogood, did you tell them about Lou's dog?"

"Oh yeah, I'd forgotten about that, with everything else that's been going on.

"I came in one morning, must be a couple weeks now and I had students waiting to tell me there was a dead dog in Ms. Wagoner's car. I thought it was probably just sleeping or something but I go out to the parking lot to check. And sure enough, there was a dog and yeah, that dog was as dead as my last blind date."

"Good God! What was it doing in her car?" Skye asked.

"She said the dog was old and had died during the night. She didn't want to miss school so she decided to bring him along and take him to the shelter as soon as school was out. She has first period conference, so I told her to take him right then. Can you believe it? What a trip that woman is.

"Oh, you guys..."Nogood's voice took on the beseeching quality she did so well. "Ah, speaking of trips, I'm driving up the coast this weekend and I wondered if—"

"Don't even ask me," said Skye. "No way, I'm not having that damn bird in my house again!"

"That infernal bawck, bawck and his filthy language," Maggie groaned. "He can roll over and croak for all I care. I'm not taking him, either."

"C'mon, you guys? Please? I've got a weekend invitation. You know Dirty Harry goes ape shit if I leave him alone. Anneka, would you take him?"

"Hell, no. Shameless hates that damned bird. And as for me, the last time he was here? If he had said, 'Fuck you. Make my day,' one more time, I was going to slide him on a skewer and make shishkebob out of him. Nope. Throw a rug over his cage and take him with you."

"I can't. He's very insulting to my dates and this guy's an evangelist, you know what I'm saying? Lainey? The kids would have fun with a talking parrot and he can recite the alphabet, even."

"Nogood, I'm not having a bird that says f-you every five minutes around my children. Forget it."

"Oh, jeez! Now I'm going to have to find a house sitter for Dirty Harry."

Nogood looked dejectedly at her empty glass. Spinner poured her another frothy Margarita from the pitcher and patted her shoulder.

"I'll take the bird for the weekend, Nogood. How much trouble can a little bird be?"

Spinner didn't catch the looks of amusement that passed between the women. He was new to the group.

* * *

"Lainey, how you doing?" Anneka asked.

Lainey had been very quiet, just sitting on the hearth, her back to the fire. Anneka thought she was throwing back Margaritas a bit too enthusiastically. Time to get some food in her.

"I'm okay, Anneka."

"We haven't even had a chance to ask you what's happened with Trevor."

"Well, the police didn't keep him. They just questioned him and let him go."

"Was he able to tell them anything?'

Lainey sighed and took another healthy swallow.

"They think Stephanie was murdered early, about six a.m. They asked Trevor where he was but he said he hadn't stayed over at Stephanie's. Said he just went back to his room, went to bed and slept till 7:30 the next morning."

"Did anyone see him?" Anneka asked.

"No, he's been staying at the marina on the bayfront. There's a lot of activity there. People going in and out because its partially time-share, tourists and that sort of thing. No proof."

"Well, do they believe him?" Maggie asked.

Lainey shook her head wearily.

"I don't know. They didn't hold him. Just told him not to leave town. You know, the usual thing. I believe him, though. I know the children's father couldn't be a murderer, even in the heat of passion, as they say. Besides, the thing with Stephanie was cooling. He'd been talking about coming home."

"Is he planning on coming back, then?" Maggie asked.

"No, we agreed it would be best if he stay where he is for the time being. This is no time to make decisions about our marriage.

"Spinner, how about a fill-up? These are so good."

"Is he pretty shaken up?" Spinner asked and dutifully refilled Lainey's glass.

"Being questioned by the police in a homicide can't be very pleasant, but I didn't get the impression he was overcome by grief."

"You know, I wonder if anyone but Stephanie's family will be particularly sorry," Skye said. "She was a singularly selfish girl from what I've heard."

" Coach Ridout was pretty distraught," Anneka said. "He'd been dating her before she and Trevor got together, I guess. But even he said she was her own number one priority."

"They had Dwight Ridout in for questioning too. Along with some other men from town. Trevor wasn't the only one she'd been dating, not by a long shot. Stephanie's been a busy girl," Lainey muttered and took a gulp from the salt-rimmed glass. "Still, Trevor got the impression the investigators weren't all that interested in him. They were putting out a net for all the transients in the area."

"What a grisly death. Stabbed repeatedly and pitched off the cliffs. I can't believe it still. Just out running in the park. God!" Maggie shuddered.

Everyone fell silent. It was such a surreal scenario and to have happened in New Albion...

"Don't you guys think it's unusual?" Anneka asked suddenly, breaking the peaceful silence. "I mean, so many deaths in such a short time. Such a small town?"

"You keep saying that, Anneka. New Albion should be immune to deviants wandering Highway 101? The police aren't that surprised. They told me lonely stretches of the coast are pretty dangerous," Maggie said.

"I know. But it seems strange we should have both Nate Dupray *and* a roaming psycho too."

"Have they released any more details?" Spinner asked. "Was she sexually molested?"

"They're not totally sure because she was in the ocean for so many hours. Salt water pretty much erases any evidence like that, I guess." Maggie said.

Again, the group fell silent, everybody immersed in their own thoughts.

Lainey's glass spilled from her fingers and in liquid motion she slid slowly from the hearth and lay supine on the floor in front of the fire.

"Oh shit," she giggled and passed out cold.

* * *

This is soooo much fun. I don't want this to end. I can even hear most of the conversation down here. What a charge. Right under their feet!

A little risky, maybe. I barely beat Anneka home and that damn big dog sniffing around. I may be pushing my luck here.

I'm stalling, I know, cause this is so exciting. Like tonight. Almost like being at the party—Fat chance of that, though. Nobody's ever liked me. So, the fuckers, sit around and call me names. Psycho, that's what they said. I hate, hate, hate them all.

Do it soon. Time to leave this town. Too bad, but it got pretty hairy the last time. That other place. I've liked it here much better.

Better to move on while things are still going well. It couldn't have worked out any better. But now, with that little shit Nate Dupray gone, we can't just keep having murders, can we? Too suspicious. Ah well, the coup de grace. Tomorrow night, I think.

The killer grinned.

CHAPTER 34

5:00 p.m.

> *This is Radio KST coast emergency broadcasting.*
> *We interrupt our regular programming to bring you this warning from the weather service.*
> *An unusually bad storm with winds of hurricane force is expected to hit the coast later this evening. Currently gusting at 60 to 70 miles an hour, the winds may reach 90 to 100 miles an hour as early as nine p.m. tonight.*
> *You are advised to stay in your homes and remain tuned to this station.*
> *Coastal residents should expect power failures and be aware of the danger of falling trees and landslides.*
> *We will keep a constant update on the storm.*
> *We repeat. winds reaching hurricane FORCE . . .*

LOU WAGONER WAS pissed off.
 If this wasn't the last straw. Pouring rain for days and now a fucking hurricane. Oh, they'd call it a

storm. Hurricanes didn't happen in the Northwest. Didn't matter if the whole town blew off the map, it'd just be a "bad storm."

This past week had been one nightmare after another. She'd been forced to teach her own classes and Stephanie Myer's classes as well. Like she didn't have enough work of her own. Everybody in the damn school was expected to be so fucking helpful.

As if she gave a flying rat's ass that dumb Stephanie got herself pitched off the cliffs. Nobody had liked her. She was a real pain in the butt, that one. But you'd think she was Princess Di the way everybody was acting. There was all this crying and moaning and kids having to go to the counselors "to talk about it." It made her want to puke.

"Oh, Ms. Wagoner, could I go to the counselor, please? I just have to talk this out. This is so sad!"

Gag me! Half the time, the kids hadn't even had any contact with the stupid slut. What a bunch of hypocrites!

There'd been the same bawling and wailing for Jamie and Susanne. Those two over-sexed girls. Nate Dupray's little whores. That's all they were.

And then, there was Mr. Clayton. The school had even sent sympathy cards for *him* . He'd put the noose around his own stupid neck and stepped off a chair, for God's sake. *Everybody* knew what a royal prick he was.

"You must understand Jamie's special needs, Ms. Wagoner. You have her all stressed out over this exam. She can't possibly be expected to do this long paper you've assigned. Remember, she has a *modified* plan, Ms. Wagoner."

Special needs, my aching ass! And that cold fish son of his, the fucking genius, if you believed his father.

"My son is a brilliant scholar, Ms. Wagoner. I won't accept that you think his classroom performance is worth an inferior grade. My son has never earned anything less than an A in his life, Ms. Wagoner."

And did talking to the counselor do any good? No way. Damn Anneka took both the Clayton kids out of my class. All the students had to say was "they felt uncomfortable" with the teacher and she'd custom-make their schedules so they didn't have a moment's worth of *discomfort*. Oh no, heaven forbid.

Did she give a fuck for my discomfort? Did she change Nate Dupray out of my class when he insulted me and my mother? Oh, that was different, wasn't it?

"That's an administrative decision, Ms. Wagoner. I can't do that. I can't take one teacher's problem and just give the problem to another teacher. Let's think of other ways to deal with it, Ms. Wagoner."

Was there even an ounce of sympathy coming her way when her dog died? He'd been the only friend she had in the world except her old crabby mother. Did anybody care about her darling dog? Did anybody comment on the fact that she was such a responsible person, she didn't take a single day off, no, not even a single hour off for her tragedy?

Did they think she didn't hear the comments about her leaving little Fluffy in the car like that? She had only wanted to take some time with disposing of his remains, to show some respect for his passing.

No, they carried on like she was some kind of weirdo or something. And that Geoffreys. That *damn* bitch.

"You've got to take care of this right now, Lou. You can't leave a dead animal in the car like this. It's upsetting the students."

So, she'd had to go just dump Fluffy off like some wad of garbage, like some smelly little turd. Bitch Geoffreys. It was okay for her to want my extra time and more, covering a double load of classes. Yeah, that was being "so very helpful."

Nobody gave a damn about her. Didn't she bleed like everybody else?

Couldn't she grieve for her little dog?

Lou slammed the hairbrush down on the bathroom vanity and stared in the mirror.

Why did those snickering kids always make fun of her? She had heard them today in the hall. Their voices were still there. In her head.

"Ms. Wagoner's hair? Did you see it today? What's she trying to prove? I mean, really. It's pathetic, you know?"

"And the way she dresses, like she thinks she's a teenager or something. Puhlease!"

"Yeah, all that camouflage stuff. Does she think she's like going on safari, or something?"

The little prigs. She'd gotten those clothes in Portland, at The Gap. She thought they looked good. She was tall and slim. She could pull it off. And her hair? What was wrong with it? She thought it looked like Sigorny Weaver's hair, kind of casual and sexy.

Lou leaned over the sink and studied herself in the mirror. She'd always tried to have her "own look." But she'd always been criticized for it. Her own mother made comments all the time. Nothing pleased that woman either. She was as bad as the bunch at school, those damn brats, her lousy colleagues, her mother. It was *JUST TOO FUCKING MUCH!*

* * *

Lou scrambled in the bottom drawer of the vanity. The smell of spilled perfume mingled with the dust.

Her fingers shifted through the debris. The drawer was a shamble of miscellaneous items that hadn't been used for a long time: old bottles of make-up, spilled talcum, uncapped, squeezed-out tubes of ointment, vials of unused medicine and unfilled doctor's prescriptions for her mother. She pushed aside a comb with distaste, caught in its teeth, strands of her mother's brittle, yellowing hair. A pair of glasses with one lens. She put them on.

There it was, the old electric razor. It should still work.

She looked in the mirror at the old Lou for a final time. She clutched her hands to her chest, holding the imaginary basket of hurts woven through with strands of malicious words and treacherous deeds. The basket had become too heavy to bear.

The one last shred holding her together, tethering her to the rest of humanity, snapped.

She connected the razor and methodically began to shave her head, making long even rows. Like a cornfield, she thought, and grinned at her image.

She worked the razor till every follicle of the wiry dyed hair fell into the dirty basin.

She sighed with enormous satisfaction.

Her skull was as white as a blanched almond.

She had the razor out; she might as well shave her legs, too. She couldn't remember the last time she'd done that. She carefully lifted first one then the other leg into the basin.

When her legs were as smooth and hairless as her head, she threw the razor on top of the heap of hair but hesitated and picked it up again. She lowered her underpants and carefully began to shave.

The vibrating hum of the razor made her smile orgasmically in the darkening room. When she was done, she felt cleansed, transformed. She had shed her skin like snakes do. She was BORN AGAIN.

* * *

Lou turned off the razor and cocked her gleaming skull.

The wind rattled the windows like a freight train but piercing the storm's roar was the sound of the doorbell.

There it was again.

Who the hell was it? Nobody ever came to see her and mother.

She decided not to answer. She turned off the bathroom light and sat down on the toilet.

She sat in the moth-soft shadows and thought of all she had left to do.

CHAPTER 35

"ANNEKA, ARE YOU all right? Looks like we're in for it this time."
"Hi, Lainey. Yeah, the wind's really ripping here. I just checked my trees. So far, no roots coming out of the ground but Laverne and Shirley about got blown into the next county."

"I'm kind of glad Trevor built our house away from the ocean front, but building on the side of a hill has its problems too. With all this rain, we worry about the land sliding out from under us and ending up in the middle of 101. But the reason I called is you're welcome to pack up the animals and come here. The kids and I'd love to have you. When the power goes out and it *will* go out, we can sit and tell ghost stories in the dark."

"I'm okay. I stopped after school and stocked up on candles. I've got batteries in the radio and the gas fireplaces work even if the power goes out. And Spinner's coming. He should have been here by now."

"I saw Spinner at school right after you left. He came in

to check if Lou Wagoner left those special ed papers on the Bailey kid. He was pretty annoyed. Said he's got to get that report written up."

"Damn! She still hasn't gotten that stuff to him? I gave her that packet a good two weeks ago."

"Well, you know old Lou. She gets to things when she's good and ready. Since her Mom died, she's been pretty spaced out, even weirder than usual."

Along with the annoyance she felt, Anneka had something else pricking at her memory. The last time she'd seen Lou, hadn't she said . . .

"You know, Lainey? Lou was in my office the other day . . . she said something that struck me as odd. I'd tucked it away in the back of my mind, but it's been niggling at me. She made some allusion to her mother, something like she had to get home, her mother always liked to eat early, or something like that. . . ."

"You must have misunderstood her. Her mother died last year. Remember, we all sent a sympathy card and flowers?"

"Yeah, I remember that. She took a couple days emergency leave. Still, I thought that was what she said. . . .

"Maybe she said her mother had liked to eat early so it still was a part of her own routine or something." Anneka changed the subject.

"What's going on with Trevor? He's not going to be there during this storm?"

"Oh, he offered, but I don't need him here. The kids and I are doing just fine without him. If the storm gets too bad, we'll go over to Mother's. By the way, have you talked to Nogood? Do you know if Merrill Grady called her? Did she say anything about it to you?"

"No, why?"

"Well, he came into my office yesterday, supposedly to talk about this senior in his history class but he ended up asking if I thought Ms. Geoffreys would be interested in going to the symphony with him Tuesday evening, and did I know if she liked classical music?"

"Get outta here!"

"For real. I thought that would be pretty cool, you know? I like Merrill. I told him Nogood was crazy about classical music and he should call her."

"Good for you, Lainey."

The Lemonade Ladies had made it their goal in life to hook Nogood up with some decent guy, but she'd succeeded in driving every one of them away, usually licking open wounds.

"I'm curious, now." Anneka said. "I need to call and make sure she's okay anyway."

"Yeah, call her. Tell her she can spend the night here if she wants. But tell her if she brings that damn bird, he'd better keep his filthy mouth shut."

"Okay, I'll tell her."

"You take care, now, you hear? If Spinner doesn't get there soon, let me know. Spirit Cove's a beautiful place with all those gorgeous huge trees but there's a reason they call it the widow-maker."

"Yeah, which is pretty stupid, if you ask me. Tree branches could fall on either sex. Why don't they call it the widower-maker?"

"You've got me there. Bye."

Anneka had planned a stir-fry for dinner. She had the vegetables all chopped and ready to go but was reluctant to start until Spinner got there. Stir-Fry was only good straight out of the wok.

She kept an ear tuned to the radio which had switched to constant storm warning format. They were reporting wind gusts at 70 to 80 miles an hour and 40 foot ocean swells battering the harbor. Several roadways were blocked by fallen trees and the Dairy Delight's enormous sign had fallen through the roof. Shelters were being set up in the area. People living in mobile homes were encouraged to go to a safe place.

Anneka listened nervously. The house shook and the rain was a solid sheet on the windows. She picked up the phone and dialed Spinner's apartment only to get the message machine, just like the last time. He must have been delayed. Maybe there'd been an emergency at the shelter or the jail. They were always calling him at the last minute. Unusual for him not to call, however. She was growing more and more concerned. The radio hadn't reported any accidents so far. No cars hit by trees, no big slides. Apparently some roads were blocked but none that would prevent him from getting to the cove. His cell phone should be working....

She picked up the phone again and dialed Nogood.

"Hey, kid. How are you doing? Is the sky about to fall?"

"Don't worry about me, Anneka. You're the one living on the edge of a cliff surrounded by falling trees. I, on the other hand, had the presence of mind to purchase property in the middle of town with the fire station right next door. I may even go over and play cards with the boys for awhile. You'd better come here and stay the night. Bring the animal farm. Bring Spinner. The more the merrier."

Anneka cast a nervous look out the window at her giant hemlock. Such a beautiful old tree, so sheltering, yet so menacing in a storm. She loved that tree. but she should have taken it down when she had a chance.

"It's just too much of a hassle with all the animals," Anneka said. "Thanks, but I'll be fine. This house is solid as a rock. I'm not worried."

"You should be, you're sitting right over the ocean. Do you know which way to run uphill if we have a tsunami?"

"Jeez, Nogood, we're having a heavy storm, not an earthquake. I don't think running uphill is the answer."

"Well, you'd better be prepared, just in case. You got flashlights, batteries, you got something to eat, extra water?"

"Yes, Yes, Yes, Yes. On all counts. I'll be fine. . . . Um, Nogood?

"Lainey told me Merrill Grady wanted to invite you to the symphony Tuesday night."

"Gee, news travels fast in these parts."

"C'mon, did he?"

"Did he what?"

"Did he ask you to the symphony?"

"Yeah."

"Well?"

"Well what?"

"Well, what did you tell him? "

"I told him Tuesday night is the night I clean out my vegetable crisper."

"You're impossible! I could wring your neck. Merrill Grady is an interesting and good-looking man and you—"

"Hey, I gotta go. Dirty Harry's really getting nervous with this wind. It's shaking the windows like—"

"Damn it, Nogood. You are—"

Anneka was still sputtering, but Nogood had hung up.

* * *

She poured a glass of Merlot and sat on the hearth, her back to the fire, trying to ignore the storm's din. It was getting pretty scary, but Anneka assured herself the house was sturdy and strong, and Spinner should be there any minute.

Kitty Shameless slept soundly, nose tucked under a soft paw, curled on the cushion of his favorite rocker by the fire. He was totally oblivious to the rain's barrage on the windows, the roar that was the wind. Not a worry in the world.

Anneka made a conscious effort to relax, to luxuriate in the solid warmth of the fire on her back. She held out her glass and watched the firelight burning in her ruby wine.

CHAPTER 36

Spinner sat in the warm car. The windshield wipers snick-snicked at a solid sheet of water pounding the windows. Through their frame, he could see the blurred vision of the house on the hill, a dismal silhouette in the pouring rain.

The radio issued yet another warning of the full power of the storm about to hit shore in a few hours. The Jeep rocked with the wind's force. The streets were empty. On the way he'd negotiated around fallen limbs, past flying tree branches and a couple of strong gusts had almost blown him off the road.

He'd wait a bit to see if the rain would let up. There'd been plenty of tornadoes in Wisconsin, but he'd never been in a storm like this.

Tornado warnings, if they came at all, usually came right before you had to run for shelter. He remembered the panic as he'd scrambled for the rusty hinge on the trap door to the storm cellar, tore skin from his fingers as he tugged at that stubborn door, the portable radio hanging from his neck urging him to hurry, to run.

He remembered the greenish cast to the sky, the electricity in the air.

Countless hours in that cellar, the dirt smell, the musty dampness were vivid in his memory. That hollowed-out place had been a refuge for many before Spinner came to live on the river. Their ghosts waited with him for that breathless time beneath the earth. The old ramshackle farmhouse in the woods, on a bend of the Tomorrow River. How long ago it seemed. Old rivers, lost woods . . . still treasured in his dreams.

Spinner sighed and patted the big Lab by his side.

"You wait here, Ollie. You guard, boy. I'll be right back."

He slammed the Jeep door in annoyance. Raindrops slapped his face as he looked once more at the house.

The afternoon had darkened quickly in the storm but there were no lights to lend a cozy glow. The house looked desolate, as if it mourned its very existence. It had no near neighbors for solace. It reminded him of some unpleasant memory. It reminded him of the house in *Psycho*.

Had this been Lou's mother's house? It must have been here for a hundred years.

Lou's car was parked at the end of the cracked and sunken driveway, in front of a three-sided shed. It'd be a miracle if that was left standing after the storm. Lou had better move her car.

He'd just missed her at the high school, damn it. Couldn't remember how many times he'd reminded her of the blasted paper work. Now the meeting was tomorrow and that meant doing the report tonight. If the packet wasn't done, she was just damn well going to sit down and do it now.

Spinner was fast drenched through by the rain. Water streamed from the bill on his cap. Still, he climbed the sagging slippery steps to the porch slowly. He was reluctant to be alone with Lou Wagoner.

She annoyed his landlady with phone messages, she left

messages on his home service and at his office. And in his mailbox at the high school he constantly found coy little notes with some invitation or another. Sometimes she just wrote "have a wonderful day " with smiling faces and hearts doodled on the paper. He'd tried to be polite to the woman, but she just wasn't getting it. Lately, there'd been a lot of hang-ups on his answering machine, too. Of course, that could be anyone.

Best to get this over with and get on to Anneka's. He didn't like her being alone in this storm. She was probably already wondering where he was. He should have called on the cell.

The front door was slightly ajar. He knocked firmly and the door partially opened.

Spinner peered into the shadowy interior
"Lou?"

He stood in the entrance to the hall. What he could see of the room beyond was littered with debris. It covered the floor and the furniture and trailed off beyond his line of vision.

The place smelled of neglect and worse. It smelled like a breeding-place for flies. Overcoming his distaste, he called out.

"Lou? Are you here? It's Rutger Hartmann... Lou?"

If he just didn't have to have those damn forms, he'd get the hell out of there.

"Lou?"

He ventured further into the silent murky interior and stepped into what must be the living room. Contrasted with the noise of the storm, the house seemed still, deserted.

He saw a source of the vile smell and skirted a small pile of what looked like animal feces. The thread-bare carpet was covered with suspicious stains. A saucer of hardened blackish dog food sat in the middle of the room. Boxes were everywhere, some covered with mildew. Others looked to be

255

packed with clothes. Others were filled to the brim with household items as if the occupant of the house were preparing to move.

He jumped when his reflection appeared in a gilded mirror. It was covered with streaks of grime as though someone raked their fingers down the glass in an attempt to see the image.

Next to the mirror, a calendar hung, permanently fixed on May, 1966.

He stepped on a large book open on the floor, pictures and clippings spilled about. He bent to one knee to sweep the items back in the book and a loose picture caught his attention.

THE WAGONER FAMILY ALBUM

What was this? Some kind of scrap book?

Pasted to the inside of the cover was a slip of gold bordered paper, lettered in old fashioned script, its ink faded into the past, its dates unreadable.

Spinner's senses shrieked for him to leave this place but his natural curiosity was getting the best of him. A part of any clinical psychologist is voyeuristic in nature. Lou would have made an interesting case study. She was such a unique personality. Spinner couldn't help but be intrigued by a family album. They offered such insight on family history, the genesis of the personalities.

He brushed off the newspaper articles and loose photos and looked at the picture on the first page. It was large and glossy. It wasn't a photograph. It had obviously been cut from a magazine. A svelte young woman posed on a beach, clad only in a scant bikini, hair blowing in the breeze off the water, teeth gleaming in the sun. Underneath, a caption printed in block letters.

LOU AT THE BEACH, SWEET SIXTEEN.

What the hell! This was obviously not Lou. What *was* this?

Below the girl was pasted an actual photo of a little white poodle-type dog. It appeared freshly groomed and stood in a patch of tall grass filled with wild flowers. The caption identified it as **FLUFFY**.

Fascinated, Spinner turned the next page. A fading black and white photo of a woman with a small girl. The picture was secured by four little black corners. Both the woman and the girl stood with their arms straight at their sides. Both wore shapeless dresses that hung to their shoes. Neither was smiling. Underneath, the same block letters.

MORE FUN TIMES WITH MOTHER

There had been other photos pasted on the page but now, all that remained were each of their four black corners.

Spinner slowly turned the page. Another shiny photo, again cut crookedly from some old magazine. A Norman-Rockwell-type picture of a plump woman with white hair, sitting in a rocker, her fingers poised over a piece of needlework, smiling benignly. The handwritten caption below read:

MOTHER ON HER 80TH BIRTHDAY

In growing disbelief, Spinner turned over the stiff pages of the album. He should leave this and go. This house was not occupied by someone of sound mind but, my God, this was intriguing stuff!

On the next page were pictures of two girls in their teens. Their heads had been cut off, separated from the rest of their picture. The school annual, maybe? Some school function? They were attractive young girls with beaming smiles.

Spinner leaned closer. He recognized the girls from the

257

town newspapers. These were pictures of the murdered students, Susanne Slocum and Jamie Clayton. The captions read:

LOU AS PROM QUEEN 1965 AND MOST POPULAR GIRL 1966

The small hairs at the back of Spinner's neck prickled.

Wait a minute! Wait a minute! What was this snapshot? That was Anneka's car. That was Anneka and him getting into the Durango. It looked like the day they drove up the old river road. The picture was blurred but he was certain that was what it was. My God! They'd left early, like 8:00 a.m.

There had been absolutely no one around that Saturday morning. Where had someone been standing to get this shot? Obviously hiding ... in the trees?

LOU, SATURDAY- SPENDING WITH SPINNER

Spinner's skin crawled. Go now. Get out. Still, with a shaking hand, he turned another page.

It was a shot of a young woman on a boat. It looked like the marina in Newport. Something familiar about the woman. He held the picture up to the fading light. Long blonde curling hair under a jaunty sailor hat, impossibly long legs wound out of abbreviated shorts. Legs with a runner's muscle. It looked like Stephanie Myers. It *was* Stephanie Myers. The caption read:

FUN IN THE SUN ON MY LOVER'S BOAT

Dissociative personality disorder, transference, projection of self to others ... a breakdown that precedes an intense onset of psychoses. This women was so sick. How had he failed to see it? How had she functioned? Obviously, in her residual periods ... Still, there had been symptoms, the erotomanic delusions, the notes, the calls ... the surveillance, the stalking!

Spinner's mind was racing. He reached for a yellowed newspaper article caught between the pages. The dateline said January, 1988. There was a picture of a smiling girl. Her hair worn long and straight, parted in the center. A locket hung at her neck. The headline read:

HIGH SCHOOL SENIOR FOUND MURDERED IN STATE PARK.

The body of a young girl apparently slain in the early morning hours as she jogged in the park ...

Spinner's hand trembled as he turned one more page. It was the last thing in the album. Only blank pages followed.

The last picture was of Anneka. She was seated at her desk in her office laughing at the camera. He remembered the picture from the school year book.

LOU WAGONER, TEACHER OF THE YEAR, HOORAY.

Spinner's autonomic responses were signaling frantically. The bottom of his forearms rippled with sensation. Terror, like spiders scuttled through his veins. He started to rise from his kneeling position but his knees had gone weak.

Anneka. Anneka was the only woman in the album still alive!

His back turned, he didn't see the half-naked figure gliding along the wall behind him.

Like a snake through the deepening shadows ... Shaved skull revolving from the turning neck.

CHAPTER 37

This is Radio KST, Coast Emergency Broadcasting System. KST will be continuously broadcasting on this emergency network. Stay tuned.

The weather service has issued a severe storm warning.

Winds over a hundred miles an hour are expected to hit the coastal regions early this evening. Right now, winds are clocked at seventy to eighty miles an hour.

Stay in your homes. Stay off the beaches and stay off the roads.

There is extreme danger from falling trees and landslides.

Keep away from windows. If the need arises, take shelter under heavy furniture.

No power outages have been reported as yet.

The following roads are blocked from fallen trees: 44th Street south of the SurfRider Motel. Anchor Street in the 800 block. Abbey Street on the bay front. There has been a landslide on Highway 101 north of . . .

* * *

ANNEKA SAT SLUMPED on the couch, glancing back and forth from the floor-to-ceiling windows in the living room to the wall of windows in the kitchen. All were shaking, lashed with rain. An occasional lightning bolt made her jump. When the thunder rolled it was a perfect accompaniment to the beating of her heart.

The storm engulfed her. She felt the air pressure pounding in her ears, making her head ache, filling her with anxiety.

"Just calm down, Anneka. Calm down."

She turned on the TV, amazed it still worked, that she still had power. She flipped from the weather channel to the Northwest news channels. They were all showing live feeds of the storm about to hit the coast. Towering waves pounded the shoreline, waves reportedly reaching heights of forty to fifty feet. The weatherman pointed to the eye of the storm. It was poised to hit dead center on New Albion.

She got up and walked to the window. The big trees swayed impossibly back and forth, caught in the wind's teeth. As she watched, a tree branch flew past and out of sight.

Stay home, stay home, stay in, stay in, warned the TV weatherman. Stay home, stay in, warned the announcer from the radio in the kitchen.

The radio crackled and spit with static, faded with the electrical interference and then sputtered back to life.

Facing a storm like this by herself was nerve-shattering.

Damn it, where was Spinner?

She was angry at him, angry and terribly worried at the same time.

FOUL WEATHER

* * *

"Sergeant Lucas here."

"This is Anneka Ericsson."

"Ms. Ericsson, are you all right? "

"Yes, I'm fine. I'm calling because I'm concerned about Dr. Hartmann. He was supposed to be here two hours ago. I was wondering if you would know of any accidents or..."

"We've got several roads blocked by trees but, so far, nobody reported as injured. They're clearing the roads as fast as they can. I'm sure he'll be along."

"It's just that he would have called. He's got a cell phone in the car."

"Maybe he left it somewhere or it needs to be charged. I wouldn't worry. We'd know if anyone was hurt. All our cars are out and the fire department's, too."

The phone crackled.

"Ms. Ericsson, are you there? Can you hear me?"

"Yes, we lost our connection there for a minute. If you should hear anything about the doctor, will you let me know, please?"

"You bet. I'll log your call."

She felt no better after speaking with the sergeant. Her stomach churned with apprehension. Spinner would have called. Something was wrong.

Then again, maybe his phone did need recharging, or maybe he was stuck on a road that hadn't been reported blocked as yet.

But maybe, oh, maybe he was lying hurt somewhere and no one knew about it, or a tree had fallen on his car and he was pinned...

Damn! Stop it, Anneka. He's probably just delayed by a blocked road like the sergeant said, and he could have left his phone at school or his office by mistake. He carried it with him all the time.

"Laverne, Shirley! C'mon, let's go upstairs. Where are you guys?"

Laverne and Shirley were in the mud room noisily gulping food out of their dog dishes and slurping at their water.

"Nothing ruins your appetites, does it? That's it. Eat every last morsel. C'mon, now, let's go upstairs. C'mon."

* * *

Anneka curled up on the bedroom chaise and drew the afghan over her. Laverne and Shirley cuddled up busily on each side and were soon dozing happily. Anneka envied them. She shivered and drew them closer, petting their silky heads, comforted by their compact warmth.

The fireplace cast long shadows into the corners of the room. Anneka looked longingly at the king-sized bed with its puffy comforter and pillows stacked a mile high. She loved sinking into all those pillows.

There hadn't been a spare minute at school all day. The stress over Spinner and the threat of the storm had combined to make her dead tired. The two glasses of wine were having an effect, too. She was incredibly weary.

Perhaps she could nap and maybe, when she woke up, Spinner would be there.

Anneka made a mental list of everything she'd need if the power failed: extra batteries, flashlights, candles. All there, in the pantry. And her gas fireplaces would keep on burning even if— She jumped slightly at a scraping sound from the kitchen. What was that? Laverne growled softly and alerted Shirley who sat up and growled, too.

Then, she heard Shameless meow from downstairs.

"Don't worry, puppies. It's just the darn cat scratching at the door to the pantry. It's his supper time. No problem."

* * *

I can get in this house you're so proud of.
I can come through the windows that are locked. I can enter through the walls. I can come through the trap door in the pantry. I can crawl under your floor.
I am with you when you go from room to room.
I am with you.

* * *

Anneka pulled the phone over and called Nogood, just to hear her voice would make her feel less spooked.

"Hello?"

There was static on the line and she could scarcely hear Nogood's voice with the wind shaking the windows so hard and the branches scraping the side of the house. Something was banging downstairs, too.

"Nogood?"

"Anneka, are you okay out there?"

"Everything's fine so far. The wind's getting really bad, though."

"Spinner's there, right?"

" No, he isn't here yet. I'm afraid he must be stuck somewhere."

"Damn it, Anneka! You should have come here while you still could. It's too late to drive it, now. Too dangerous. You'll have to stay put. What about the neighbors? Are they home?"

"No. Everyone on Breaker's Scarp left for sunnier climes. The Smythes are gone for the rest of the winter."

"Nogood, wait while I get the remote phone, will you? Something's banging like crazy downstairs."

She grabbed the remote from the table at the top of the stairs and headed down, the dogs at her heels. One of the shutters must have come unhinged.

Reaching the kitchen, she stood and stared.

The back door was swinging wide open.

At that moment, it slammed back against the wall with a bang that lifted her off the floor and sent Laverne and Shirley into a frenzy.

"Anneka, what was that!"

"It's all right. I must have left the back door open when I went out to check the trees. There, all secured and double-locked. That's the noise I heard before, I guess. I thought it was the cat, but he's still sleeping on the rocker.

"But, Nogood, I'm worried about Spinner. Could you call your friends at the fire station and ask them to be on the lookout for a '97 dark-green Jeep Cherokee?"

"Sure, but all the trucks have gone out. There's only Joe left on radio duty. Damn! I wish you'd come into town!"

"Don't worry. I'm fine. I'm just worried about Spinner, that's all."

"You're getting pretty hooked on him, aren't you?"

"Well, it's a nice feeling having somebody like Spinner around. You should try it sometime. Like Merrill Grady, he—"

"Anneka, I don't want to go out with Merrill Grady. I'd just be bored."

"You don't know that until you give him a chance. He's intelligent and he's very good-looking, sexy, even."

"Yeah, my heart's doin' the Macarena."

"You're hopeless. I've got to get off the phone in case Spinner's trying to call."

"Okay, I'll keep checking with you, Anneka. Take care."

Anneka clutched the receiver connecting her to her friend for an extra few heartbeats.

She could hear Dirty Harry squawking in the background.

"Make my day. Make my day. Bawk-Baaw-k . . ."

One more try, she thought, and dialed Spinner's house. Static cracked in her ear.

"Nelson residence."

"Mrs. Nelson, this is Anneka Ericsson. Has Dr. Hartmann been home?"

"I haven't seen him, dear. Not since he left for work this morning. I hope he's not out driving around in this."

"Did he take Ollie with him?"

"What's that? I can't hear you, dear."

"I said, did he take Ollie with him?"

"I can't hear you, could you speak a little louder?"

"DID HE TAKE OLLIE WITH HIM?"

"Oh, Ollie. Oh, my yes. He always does. That dog just sits in the car and waits for him. He's a wonder, that dog. I didn't want to rent that apartment to anyone with pets, but Dr. Hartmann assured me Ollie would be no trouble and he was right. That dog and the doctor are inseparable. I have never seen—"

"Yes, well, thanks, Mrs. Nelson. I was expecting him a couple of hours ago. So, if you should hear anything, would you let me know?"

"Of course, dear. Let me get your number. Say, again? All right, dear. I've got it. Try not to worry. That other one was calling for him too. She called three times early this afternoon. I'm getting real sick of it, I tell you. Sometimes, she calls real early or real late."

"Who's that, Mrs. Nelson. Who called?"

"That Wagon woman or Wagoneer or whatever her name is. She bothers the doctor all the time. I told him he ought to—"

"Thanks, Mrs. Nelson. Let me know if you hear anything."

"What's that? I can't hear you, dear."

"IF YOU HEAR ANYTHING, LET ME KNOW!"

The phone crackled and went dead.

Poor Spinner, Anneka thought. He had told her Lou was

pestering him. It was worse than he let on, according to the landlady.

Where *was* he, anyway?

She opened the pantry door to do a double check on emergency supplies.

Laverne and Shirley followed her in, their nails scrabbling on the hardwood floor. They were jittery. The storm was getting to them, too.

The trap door squeaked as Anneka walked over it to her emergency cache. She grabbed one of the flashlights to take upstairs, the dogs still whining around her legs. Nervous from the storm, no doubt. She had to climb over them to get out of the pantry. At the foot of the stairs, she grabbed the portable radio, too.

The dogs hadn't come. She could hear them in the mud room. Eating again, by the sound of it. She'd thought their bowls were empty. They're such piglets, she thought fondly.

"Laverne, Shirley! C'mon. We're going back upstairs."

Laverne came running but Shirley curled up on the hall rug and promptly went to sleep.

"Hey, Shirl. You silly. C'mon, sleepy-head, we're going upstairs."

The little dog wouldn't budge. Anneka picked her up and headed upstairs, Laverne trotting behind.

The calm voice on the radio was still urging, "Stay in, take shelter..."

But the voice was fading in and out. The battery-operated radio was in the bedroom though, not to worry.

She left the fireplace on so the pilot light would't have to be relighted if the electricity failed. It was amazing the power was still on. It was the worse storm Anneka had ever experienced, anywhere. She could hear the waves pounding the cliffs. The house creaked with the wind. Lightning spit like burning dry logs and thunder rumbled. One bolt split the night apart and made Anneka jump.

She was lucky to have such a solid house. She was confident it could withstand the storm. It had been built to survive earthquakes, after all.

The windows could be a problem. But so far, so good.

Anneka felt reasonably safe but she would have felt better if Spinner had been there.

Upstairs, she deposited the slumbering Shirley on the king-sized bed and Laverne jumped up after her.

She pushed the towering mound of pillows to one side and lay down, drawing the comforter up around her neck. She'd stay warm, at least.

Outside, it was completely black but inside, firelight flickered on the walls and ceiling.

Laverne and Shirley were snuggely close and already snoring softly.

Anneka felt shaky with fatigue and drowsy from the wine. She'd rest a minute...

Sleep hit like a brick.

CHAPTER 38

THE BIG DOG had waited too long for his master to return. His basic instincts stirred. He threw back his head and began to howl in concert with the wind.

* * *

Next to Anneka's house, the giant hemlock fought desperately to keep its hold, but for generations the great roots had spread in an ever-widening circle, not deep enough to cement its covenant with the earth. The tree groaned, bending tortuously with the force of the whipping wind until the rain-saturated earth gave way.

The roots began to heave, to loosen and break free.

* * *

Mourning Ann . . . she came from the cliffs at a dead run. Now one with the trees, her arms reached out through the storm. Black rain streamed down her face and into her open mouth.

"Danger," she wailed. "Come ouuuut, come ouuuuuut!"

* * *

In her sleep, Anneka felt the power surge and crackle. The bedside radio ceased to hum and the clock stopped.

She struggled in fitful dreams. Strumming wires probed at her consciousness and anxiety goose-pimpled her arms.

In her dreams, a hooded figure stood among the storm-wracked trees and called to her. It waved and beckoned wildly. Its cloak ripped in the wind like a torn wing.

Come out! Come out!

Anneka whimpered and felt a light touch of fingers on her hair.

Fingers, like insects crawling on her scalp.

CHAPTER 39

ANNEKA CAME SUDDENLY awake. It was dark. Only the fire lent a wavering light. An unnatural silence permeated the house. The furnace no longer hummed, no digital numbers glowed red in the darkness.

The power was out.

She woke from the vivid dream to the frightening reality of the storm. The gale was hitting with full force. The wind ripped at the house. The floor shook with the power of the pounding waves.

She shuddered deep in the blankets, still feeling the fingers in her hair, still hearing the mournful warning in the dream. Burrowing under the comforter, Anneka drew it over her head, felt its enveloping warmth and didn't want to ever come out.

The puppies seemed lifeless. Close to her body on each side, they slept heavily, oblivious to the storm. The three of them crammed together in one small space on the large bed, pillows piled high to one side.

Grateful for their presence, Anneka crooned softly, "Hey, puppies. You okay? I wish you'd wake up. I need your company."

She spoke out loud just to hear her voice, so small-sounding, so insignificant in the storm's din. Except for the animals, she was alone in the scariest weather she'd ever experienced. Spinner wasn't coming. Something had happened. She prayed he wasn't injured.

Anneka became aware of the discomfort in her bladder and reluctantly emerged from the warm bed, nudging the dogs to one side. She made her way to the bathroom, shivering in the darkness.

Laverne and Shirley never moved; they snored loudly in their nests under the comforter.

* * *

The bathroom was large, the commode separate in its own little room. She felt her way in the dark through the open door and sat.

Opposite the small room a large mirror hung over the bathroom vanity.

A shattering lightning bolt lit the room, so near, she clutched her ears with the staticky hurt of it.

Reflected in the mirror was a huge looming shadow, arms extended.

She jumped and felt hot urine down her leg.

Frozen in place, she stayed motionless for long minutes until another flash rent the darkness.

This time, the silhouette of the large basket of ivy hanging from her bathroom ceiling. Just the plant.

Anneka cleaned herself hurriedly, pulled up her jeans and bolted back to bed, hiding under the comforter with the dogs.

Her heart beat wildly, her good sense telling her, "It was nothing. An ivy. A hanging ivy."

Gradually, her breath began to slow. The firelight cast a glow on familiar objects. It wasn't a house of horrors, after all. Just her bedroom. Her safe and comfortable bedroom in her safe, comfortable house. Her earthquake-proof house... secure even in this wild storm.

She talked to herself. She talked to the sleeping dogs. She tried to "self-soothe" in that nightmare of a storm.

"In with the good air, Anneka. Out with the bad. In with the good air, out with the bad."

She carefully monitored the cadence of her breathing, in, out, in, out, until her heart left her ears and returned safely to her chest.

* * *

Lightning, thunder, rain, wind.

But from somewhere came the feel of something that was not the storm.

Something watchful, breathing softly, stirring on the other side of the bed.

Shameless. Kitty Shameless. He must have crawled in bed with them. Anneka reached over the pile of pillows to pet him.

Not the warm fur of a cat...

Cold flesh on a human leg.

She swept the pillows aside.

Beside her lay the naked body of Lou Wagoner, bald skull gleaming in the firelight.

Lipstick black as blood smeared on her lips and teeth like she'd bitten through a small animal.

She pursed those hideous lips, blew a kiss, and exhaled a soft

"Boo."

CHAPTER 40

SHE WAS IN the middle of a nightmarish play. The light from the gas logs lit the stage, throwing ghoulish silhouettes on the ceiling and into the corners of the room.

Anneka recoiled as the horror that was Lou Wagoner raised her arm revealing the large knife clutched in her fist.

Breathing raggedly, Lou's mouth gaped in a wide grin.

She lashed out, flicking the air with the blade, now pointing it an inch from Anneka's belly. Then she raised the knife high over her head and lunged like a matador at a bull's neck.

Anneka rolled and fell to the floor, bringing her hands up to protect her face. The cutting edge sliced her arm from wrist to elbow. Blood spurted from the wound. Shock jettisoned through her body and slapped the air from her lungs.

"Just like filleting a fish, huh, Anneka?"

Lou roared with maniacal laughter, her mouth a purple hole in the dark. She rolled back to the far side of the bed, kicking her legs in the air, her face convulsed with mirth.

Flight was necessary but flight was impossible. Anneka

was caught in a terror that sent paralysis to every limb, impaled her to the floor where she lay.

"It was you! You killed them, not Nate!"

Her voice was scarcely a croak. Her slashed arm shot fire to her fingertips and back to her elbow. She thought she'd faint from the pain.

"Ohhh, the clever Miss Marple speaks! Of course. I killed them all! It was hilarious. Everyone racing around looking for that little bastard, Nate Dupray. God, how I laughed."

"But why? Susanne and Jamie—"

Anneka gasped as Lou stabbed a pillow and slashed it through.

The pillow lay just to the side of Shirley's silky head. Both dogs still slept.

Why didn't they wake up?

"They were whores! Nate Dupray's little whores! They both showed up at inconvenient times. I was waiting for you the night I killed Susanne. She saw me. She couldn't live if I was going to kill you at the same time, now, could she?"

Anneka's head reeled from pain and the shock. She struggled to her knees.

"You murdered them for nothing!"

"Ah well, things don't always work out exactly as you plan but it all worked out beautifully in the end, didn't it? Susanne was easy. She didn't expect her history teacher to be quite so deadly. And Jamie was even easier. She was here in the cove waiting to help Nate with his drug deals. She was afraid I'd tell her dad-dy."

Lou folded a blue-veined leg over a bony knee and placed a lacy pillow behind her head. She still held the knife upright in a clenched fist. The blade was red with Anneka's blood.

"I'm only sorry I didn't get his other little whore, the one who delivered his loathsome spawn."

She stretched and and scratched at her shaved skull. It was red and irritated with little bloody nicks.

Lou seemed oblivious to the storm. She reclined on the bed paying no heed to the lightning, the ear-splitting thunder,

"I like this house, Anneka. It's real comfortable. More comfortable than your crawl space. I spent a lot of time down there, you know, listening to your life. You had a nice life. Much nicer than mine. Ah well, that's all over now..." She gave Anneka a beatific smile and stroked the sleeping cockers lovingly.

Anneka held her breath. If she hurt them... She had to get them away.

"Laverne and Shirley, come here. Come!" Impossible they should still be sleeping, Anneka thought desperately. "Come here puppies!"

Lou reached over and gathered Shirley to her scrawny naked breasts.

"I'm afraid they're not going to wake up for awhile. I've been putting sedatives in their food."

"You, you *poisoned* my dogs?"

"Anneka, Anneka, what kind of a person do you think I am? I'd never hurt a little animal. The girls and I are great friends. We've spent a lot of time together. I think I'll take them with me when I go."

She kissed the top of Shirley's lolling head.

"You're not taking them anywhere, you sick—"

"But we were talking about murdering people, Anneka, dear. Did you know butchered people bear a remarkable resemblance to meat?"

Anneka reeled with aversion to the woman's words. She felt sickness rising in her throat. She couldn't let the fear immobilize her. Needed time, time to think...

"Stephanie, you murdered Stephanie, too."

"Ah, Stephanie, that was really great fun. I tossed her off the cliff and still got back before my second period. I don't like the district to have to call a substitute for me. No, sir, I'm a dedicated professional. Course, I had to help cover all the bitch's classes."

Lou carefully placed Shirley back beside her slumbering sister. She gave them both a gentle little pat.

"But it was worth it. Oh, yes, it was worth it."

Anneka's arm was turning numb. She no longer felt intense pain but a flap of skin hung loose and blood dripped down her fingers to the floor. She was losing a lot of blood. It was hard to concentrate. The bedside table . . . it was so close . . . the gun. If she could only stall this mad woman. She felt some strength returning to her body. She might even be able to run.

"You killed Stephanie because of Spinner. Didn't you?"

"She was a damn whore, flaunting herself all over the school, thinking she could have any man she wanted, thinking she could have Spinner! You saw how she threw herself at him that day in your office. I fixed her. You should have seen what—"

"Lou, *I'm* the one who was dating Spinner and he didn't want anything to do with you!"

"Oh, he would have come around, Anneka. I had it all worked out and sure enough, he showed up tonight for those special ed papers just like I planned. I'm afraid I wasn't dressed properly, though."

Lou threw herself back on the bed again, her belly heaving with laughter, obscene amidst the pillows and the unconscious dogs.

"*Tonight? You saw Spinner tonight? Where is he? What have you done with Spinner?*"

"Don't yell at me, Anneka. My mother does enough yelling every damn day. It's enough to wake the dead."

"Your mother *is* dead, you lunatic!"

"SHE'S NOT, SHE'S NOT DEAD!"

She came at Anneka with raised fist. The blade sliced the air.

Anneka, moving in slow motion as if through water, heard it hissing past her ear. Opening her mouth to scream, she could only force out a whisper of sound.

CHAPTER 41

THEN THE SKY fell.
With one last defiant gasp, the ancient hemlock tore loose from the earth.
The noise was deafening. The tree came crashing through the ceiling with a crack like the earth had split. Shattering glass fractured and burst from the skylights. Splinters of wood and pieces of roof and plaster flew in all directions. Large chunks of the ceiling crashed just inches from Anneka's head.

A piercing scream came from the other side of the bed where a flailing Lou was barricaded by the branches of the enormous tree.

"Laverne! Shirley! No—ohhh!"

Anneka dug frantically through tree branches and leaves to unearth the sleeping cockers, miraculously unhurt. She shoved their unconscious little bodies under the bed.

"You'll be all right, puppies. Just stay there."

The gas log still burned. Its shadowy light revealed chaos and ruin.

Branches, limbs, and debris filled the room everywhere, as if a bomb had dropped from the sky.

Anneka saw any hope of reaching her revolver was gone. The bedside table was totally blocked by an immense limb, the top of the table crushed under its weight.

She peered through an opening in the branches and saw Lou, her face contorted with agony, a large piece of glass embedded in an eyelid streaming with blood.

The wounded woman was howling in pain but still attempting to tear at the limbs and branches that held her captive on the other side of the bed.

"*Come ouuuuuut! Come ouuuuuuut . . .*" Anneka heard the wind wailing through the broken skylights. She was torn by indecision. Should she stay and fight or run for her life?

Lou was thrashing about wildly, making headway in her quest to be free of the thick screen of branches and limbs. Her screams and curses joined with the howling wind.

Could she overpower a mad woman? She had a useless arm and no weapon. Anneka decided to run. Find help. Get the police.

"Forgive me, Susanne and Jamie, I can't!"

She stopped long enough to wrap a scarf around the wounded arm, grabbed shoes and a jacket from the closet and ran.

Anneka fled the horror within. Fled from the thing that liked the smell of her blood. Fled her seashaken house and raced to the shelter of the terrible storm.

Lou's hideous screams were behind her as she flew down the stairs and out into the ravening night. Through the back patio filled with the storm's debris, she sped to the edge of the steep cliff down to the cove, finding the over-grown path in the blackness easily, she had come this way so many times before.

The path was slippery with mud and running water. Anneka clung to the roots and high grass and slid halfway down the cliff on her side, frantically trying to protect her arm from the rough basalt on the sides of the hollowed-out path.

Above the wind, she could hear crashing and cursing behind her, the ravings of the insane woman as she stumbled through thick foliage and slippery grass searching for a way down.

Safety for Anneka lay on the other side of the cove, past the gazebo and up the wooden walk to the highway.

But she stopped short at the sight before her. This was not the same place as yesterday when she had sat in the gazebo watching the thin winter sunlight on the water while the surf lapped lazily at the mouth of the little cove.

This cove was filled with monster waves that roared and reached halfway up the side of the cliff, threatening to rip her from the branch where she clung. They shot stinging spray in Anneka's face and she screamed with the agony of salt water in her wounds.

Rain poured down in solid sheets and lightning flashed with ear-shattering intensity.

One mighty wave crested and began to recede. When it did, there was a break in the water and the gazebo could be seen through the storm.

She *had* to make her way across to the gazebo, then up the wooden walk to the highway.

Behind her came sounds of falling rocks. Lou was sliding and smashing her way down the steep slope, emitting hoarse guttural sounds more animal than human.

Anneka waited out the next giant wave. Watched it crest and begin to fall back. There would be only seconds. She hurled herself to the beach and began to fight through the receding wave. The undertow grabbed her, pulled her back as she fought desperately to make her way to the gazebo. The sea clutched at her legs, her body. It was too strong. She wasn't going to make it.

She was pulled back between the waves. When the next

wave came, it was with crashing force, like being slammed against a brick wall. A gigantic log shot past her face just inches away. She was propelled forward on the crest of the wave like a speck of matter through a giant straw, thrust forward by the massive wave.

She hung for a second on the pinnacle, then was hurled upward with a mighty force smashing her head against the rough cross beams supporting the underside of the gazebo roof.

She grabbed out desperately for the supporting rafters, wrapped her arms and legs around them and hung on for her life. She struggled to remain conscious, her ears ringing from the blow to her head.

She gulped in great draughts of air. Her limbs shook. She tried to relax her muscles, to breathe evenly. If the wave hadn't thrown her on top the beams, she'd have been swept out to sea.

It was a miracle.

But relief was short-lived. Another wave crashed through the gazebo threatening to tear her from her tenuous perch. It swamped the wooden structure, washed over the top. Anneka was once again under water. She felt the oxygen leave her lungs. She couldn't see, couldn't hold on. She felt herself slip from the beams.

* * *

There was a softness all around her, a curious ringing in her ears. She opened her eyes. A dark silhouette swam before her and hovered there. Long tendrils of softness spiraled and floated and entwined her. She wondered at the peacefulness of it. She surrendered.

Was she dreaming? Was she dead? Was this death, then?

A powerful force gripped her, enveloped her. It wrapped round her arm and one leg, and held her solidly in place.

FOUL WEATHER

"*Nooooooooooo, don't gooooo, don't gooooooooooo.* "
Anneka saw light.

She gasped for air and wondrously, sweet air filled her lungs.

She still clung to the beams, half drowned, retching saltwater. A tight coil of sea kelp was wrapped round her wounded arm from wrist to shoulder. It was as strong as the strongest rope, she knew.

The kelp wrapped around her arm and the beam on which she stretched. It wound, also, around one leg and secured her firmly to the rough beam.

When another wave crashed over the top of the shelter. She moved with the force of the water but she was held fast. A great gulp of air sustained her through the wave.

She got through the waves like that. Felt their rhythm, rode out their fury.

She hung there feeling the rough wood slivers in her skin, the pain of her torn arm in the water's pull. Her body ached and throbbed from the assault of the waves against the rough wooden beams.

Suddenly, the wind's pressure dropped. Circling cumulus clouds whirled above her.

She could see the night sky overhead. She could see one bright incredible star through a great maze of swirling clouds.

Light channeled down from the sky, penetrating her being, bringing her hope.

Then the gale resumed with renewed fury. The wind roared. The waves crested at incredible heights, throwing wood and seaweed, vomiting up all the detritus from the ocean's depths.

Each time a wave passed, Anneka gulped in air.
She was alive.

CHAPTER 42

NEW ALBION SHOOK with the force of the storm. Residents huddled in cold houses lit by candles and firelight and longed for sunny summer days and summer nights rich with stars.

Sirens screamed and red and blue flashing lights shone through the driving rain, casting ghostly reflections on streets surreal in the predawn dark.

Tree-services using huge crab-like cranes worked to clear streets and coastal roads of fallen trees. Police, sheriff and fire crews raced to the rescue of residents on low-lying beaches. Whole neighborhoods were evacuated as towering waves threatened to swamp their homes. Such swells had never been seen before.

> "We don't know if the house will be there when we get back. The whole front deck just tore off. My husband and I grabbed the dog, the family pictures, and took off."

Chunks of sandstone broke free of cliffs and beaches eroded with the force of the water. The coast guard used megaphones to warn off thrill seekers anxious to view the drama of the storm. A Bell Jet Ranger rocked in the wind as it inched up the rocky coast, its blades slicing through the night. Rescue squads signalled frantically to one another.

"Car nine, do you read me?"
"Affirmative."
"We got a call from a cell phone. A woman with a tree through the roof of her car on Ebbtide. She sounds hurt. Can you get over there?"
"We're not near there, but we'll swing over that way."

* * *

In the firestation, powered by emergency generators, one lone man handled the phones, dispatched the trucks and reassured citizens that help was coming.

The station was also serving as a shelter. Hot coffee and chocolate were being served along with sandwiches. Cold, wet people pressed closely together under scratchy blankets and worried mothers rocked crying babies.

Nancy George Geoffreys dispensed coffee in between urging the dispatcher to check on Anneka and Spinner who were both presumed missing.

The parrot, Dirty Harry, sat unhappily in his cage on the table next to the dispatcher. Harry was trying to avoid the dirty fingers of children poking through his cage trying to pet his ruffled feathers. At odd intervals, he let loose a squawking rampage of profanities that successfully cleared the area. Children were hastily led away by their distraught mothers.

"C'mon Joe, I know something's wrong. If Anneka were all right, she'd answer her phone. It's ringing, so it's working.

She doesn't answer her cell, either, and she'd have that activated. Can't you send a car out there?"

"Damn it, Ms. Geoffreys, would you shut that damn bird up? "

"Well, he's nervous and the kids keep pokin' at him. Hey, son, don't put your finger in there. He'll bite it right off. He will!"

"Joe, I have to know about Anneka. C'mon!"

"I don't have a car right now. They're all working accidents and blocked roads. Both roads to Spirit Cove are impassable. They'll get to it when they can."

"Lainey Dillon said Dr. Hartmann's missing, too. Have you heard anything about him?"

The harried fireman blew out air in exasperation. His broken leg in its plaster cast was itching terribly and he hated being left behind when the other guys were out on emergency runs.

"This isn't the missing person's bureau, Ms. Geoffreys! I'm doing the best I can here!"

"I think you're just getting back at me for those times I busted you for skipping first period. I'm going to have to drive out to the cove and check on Anneka myself if I can't get you guys to do it."

"Damn it, Ms. Geoffreys. I'm not a student anymore. I'm a grown man, so stop playing principal with me. You are not taking a car out in this storm. We'll find somebody. Just hold on, okay?"

"YOU'RE A BIG TURD!" shrieked Dirty Harry.

"What did that damn bird call me? I'm gonna' wring his scrawny neck!"

"Simmer down. He doesn't mean anything personal. Shut up, Harry," said Nogood.

"I'm a GR-EEEEE-NNN chicken." said Harry.

MARY ANNE LARSON

* * *

Across from Lou Wagoner's house, the curtains parted and George Lassiter peered down the street at the Jeep parked in front of the old Wagoner place. For the last few hours, the wailing of someone's dog had gotten on his nerves. That wasn't the neighbor woman's car. She must have a visitor, which was odd. Nobody ever came to that house since the old woman died. George sure avoided it. The daughter gave him the creeps. He'd been sorry when she'd come back to live with her mother. Mrs. Wagoner had been better off by herself. Sometimes, he'd hear the daughter screaming like a banshee. He thought she was a touch queer. She'd had his garden hoe for three months now. He bet he'd never see that again.

There was no candlelight reflected in the windows over there. He supposed he'd better check and make sure the fool woman was okay.

Mr. Lassiter sighed and reached into the closet where his musty old slicker hung. Damn fool woman. Damn foul weather. Now he'd have to go out in the storm. That animal was still howling. Why they'd leave a poor animal in the car this long? But she'd never had a lick of sense, that one. Damn house was falling down around her. You'd think she could at least give it a paint job. The neighborhood was going to hell. When he'd moved here all those years ago, it had been real nice. Everyone kept a respectable house, nice looking lawn. Now, huh! Nobody had respect, any pride for the neighborhood. Mr. Lassiter grumbled to himself and lowered his head against the rain.

When he reached the side of the Jeep, the dog stopped barking and looked at the man hopefully.

"Well, you're a big fellow, aincha? Are you friendly, big fellow?"

"I dunno..."

Mr. Lassiter reached out a tentative hand and tried the car door.

Ollie bounded out almost knocking the old man down, leaped up the rickety stairs and resumed barking at the door.

"Well, I dunno... should I check on her or not? If she's okay, she'll tell me to get the hell off her property, call me a nosy old fart like the last time I knocked on her door."

Ollie's frantic barking made up the old man's mind for him. The door creaked open when he turned the knob. He moved the flashlight around the hall and recoiled from the odor within.

"Gawd! Smells like cat pee in here!"

The dog barked and ran into the living room off the hall.

"Hey! Come back here, doggy."

The old man muttered but followed the big Lab into the room.

Ollie was sniffing in the far corner, whining pitifully.

"What's the matter, big fella? There ain't nothin here that I can see. Who left you out there, I wonder?"

He knelt stiffly to pet the dog's head and the flashlight illuminated a dark red spot on the floor.

"What's that? Hey, get outta there!"

Unnerved, George shined the light around the corner. A black leather briefcase lay on the floor next to a large open scrapbook spilling its contents into a puddle of blood. Something had been dragged through leaving a smeared trail that led toward a closed door. George felt the hairs prickle on the back of his neck and he felt more than the usual weakness in his knees.

"I dunno what went on in here but we're calling the police. I ain't lookin' any further. "

The dog was sniffing and scratching at the closed door. George Lassiter grabbed the frenzied Lab by the collar and pulled him back out into the rain.

293

Turning to close the door behind him, he spotted a muddy hoe leaning against the side of the porch rail.

"Damn, if that ain't my hoe! I'm takin' it."

With the tool under one arm and dragging the reluctant whining dog, the old man picked his way carefully down the stairs.

CHAPTER 43

PALE MOONLIGHT PENETRATED the torn clouds. Across the cove, Lou clung to the side of the cliff, terrified and small, barely suspended above the surging wave,

Her fear inspired the opposite in Anneka. She watched calmly as the wave receded and Lou dropped to the beach and took off. Lifting her legs high in the receding water, pumping her arms to gain momentum, she floundered toward the gazebo.

Anneka watched as Lou reached frantically for the side post of the structure. The wave, when it came, was not a strong one. Lou scrabbled onto the side and hung on.

She grinned up at Anneka.

The water's rush had carried in another visitor. A rat clung to the kelp wrapped round Anneka's torn arm, its pink paws scratched in a frenzy at some exposed flesh. With her unsecured hand Anneka grabbed it. The rodent felt soft and mushy like overripe fruit. Shuddering, she dropped it to the black water below. The rat squeaked furiously, feet churning rapidly in the undercurrent.

"Scar-ry. Brrrrr," Lou said.

Anneka stared coldly at Lou. The woman had tied a white scarf across one eye. It was red with blood. A yellow rain slicker covered her nakedness.

"That rain slicker is mine," Anneka thought. "She wants everything that belongs to me. She wants my whole life."

Behind Lou, the next wave crescendoed to a great curving wall of black water. She turned and saw it coming.

Anneka watched as Lou flailed desperately for a safer hold.

She saw Lou grab for the trailing edge of kelp hanging from the crossbeams.

"Help me, you bitch! Hand me that end!"

Lou couldn't reach the kelp alone.

It was a powerful wave. Its jaws plucked the screaming woman from the wooden post and swept her back into the sea.

"Just like the rat," Anneka said.

* * *

Anneka clung to her perch and thought of a way out. She wanted to live.

She pushed the fear that Spinner was dead from her mind. That would weaken her resolve.

The waves weren't swamping her anymore. She could probably ride them out. But she was bone cold, suffering from exposure.

If she could get over to the path . . . it was uphill. The water couldn't reach her. But the path up the wooden walk was strewn and blocked by logs. She wouldn't be able to run through them in time to escape the waves.

To the south, past the totem pole, there was a path climbing the cliff to Big Whale Cove. From there, she could possibly skirt along the edge of the big cove and get through the forest. There were no houses along the rim of the second cove, but it was just a short distance to the highway. Someone would help her.

Getting out of the gazebo would be the hard part, but she thought she could make it. At first, the saltwater had been agonizing on her torn arm, but cold water and the tight kelp had stopped the bleeding. The arm would be useless to her but she felt no pain.

Anneka began to unwind from the kelp. It had saved her, kept her from being torn from her perch. She thought of the dark soft presence in the waves and it infused her with strength.

When she was free, she eased herself along the beams to the gazebo's side.

The wave waned. She ran, stumbling... and gained the side of the hill before the next wave hit. She flung her arms around the totem pole and held on.

The totem was anchored solidly in the ground. The cove's first totem had been carved by Mourning Ann's tribe. It had long since been lost to the sea but Anneka imagined its spiritual force remained, giving her the will to hang on.

In the wake of the next wave, she struggled up the path, fighting the brush and the slick salal. Slipping and falling several times, she made the steep summit.

Big Whale Cove boiled with waves. Its wild cauldron churned with logs that catapulted through the water and slammed against the rocks. The ground shook with the force; the air echoed the thundering crash.

She stopped for a moment, taken in by the magnitude of the sight. Then she continued on the rugged path toward the highway and entered a thick canopy of trees and foliage that offered some protection from the storm. The narrow, black tunnel of a path diverged now into several paths. She followed the one along the cove, careful not to get too close to the edge, dangerous in the rain; erosion could mean a catastrophic fall to the beach below.

Here was the rope to the ladder down the steep slope. Somehow it had survived the storm and the waves. Although the wooden ladder looked tenuous, the rope itself was tied securely to the sturdy tree on the path. Anneka had frequently scaled the cliff from the beach below using that ladder.

Pausing to rest, she struggled to catch her breath. It came in ragged gasps but she was beginning to feel hope. She plowed through the heavy growth, treading cautiously on the narrow and rugged path, cringing from the swinging branches that whipped at her face. It was only a few feet now to the clearing. She pushed aside some broken branches that still clung stubbornly to the tree.

The branches parted to reveal the bloody face of a Cyclops, just inches from Anneka's.

The makeshift bandage over Lou's eye was gone.

She had pulled out the shard of glass. The eye hung loose from the socket, an oozing black hole.

Lou screamed. She raised her long arms high above her head and flapped like a raptor sighting prey.

Then a hand unsnapped a pocket, and the arm snaked into the slicker and came out with a knife. Lou stabbed at Anneka's face.

Anneka lurched to one side but she didn't run. She was finished with running.

"*WHERE'S SPINNER?* What have you done with him, you murderous piece of shit!"

Lou stabbed at the air in front of Anneka. A flash of lightning lit her face.

The night was charged with electricity. The two women circled and spun in the rain. An abhorrent parody of a dance at the edge of the sea.

Lou lunged and feinted and lunged again.

Anneka screamed with rage, lowered her head, and powered into the tall figure with all the force she could muster. She didn't feel her hanging useless arm or her battered body. She rammed into her tormentor with a fury like nothing she had ever felt before.

The momentum carried both women to the edge of the cliffs. They slipped and slid on the treacherous slope. Huge chunks of sandstone broke loose beneath the two women. They fell.

Anneka groped desperately with her good arm for the rope that hung from the tree. Lou slid downward but grabbed at the ladder. Her feet scrambled on the rungs and held. She cried out triumphantly and began to climb back up.

Anneka shot a tremendous kick at the wooden ladder and felt it give. She swung out on the rope and kicked again as hard as she could.

It gave way with a loud cra-a-a-ck, pitching crazily to one side.

Lou clutched at what was left of the ladder. It tore a huge slab of earth from the cliff's edge and plunged to the maelstrom below.

* * *

Moonlight fell on the churning water in the cove.

Anneka could hear the woman's high pitched screams, could see the face bobbing up and down with the driftwood, an extended arm, a tossing leg, something white tumbling in the mouth of the wave.

CHAPTER 44

"I DON'T THINK we should have tried to come back so soon, Martha. This storm's still too bad." Sid Hoffman struggled to see through the slanted rain bombarding the windshield. The coast road was deserted, at least as much of the road as he could see through the rain.

He hadn't wanted to leave the shelter of his daughter's tight little farmhouse just inland from New Albion. This was one time he should have stood up to Martha.

"The radio said the wind's died down and the storm's moving north," his wife fretted. "I've got to see if our house is still in one piece. Maybe the windows broke and everything's getting drenched. I think it's time we started spending our winters in the south. We're getting too old for this kind of weather. I'd like to rent a villa in Mexico, maybe Puerto Vallarta or Cancun, somewhere real warm and sunny and we could sit by the pool and just—What are you *doing* ? SID? SIDDDDD!"

The car swerved sliding sideways on the slick road and came to an abrupt halt.

"*DAMN*! Sweet Jesus! I almost hit her! She stepped right out in front of me, Martha!"

The couple stared in horror at a dark figure collapsed over the car's hood. Headlights outlined the body and profile of a woman.

"Help her, Sid! My God!"

Sid was already out of the car, lifting the half-drowned woman carefully into the back seat. "She's hurt, and half-frozen. Martha, get the hospital on the cell-phone. Tell 'em we're bringing her in."

The woman roused herself with great effort, pleading through bloodless lips, her breathing ragged, shaking violently.

"No! Call the police... Find Dr. Hartmann. He's at Lou Wagoner's house near the bayfront. She might have killed him. Please, please help him..."

* * *

"*Car nine, do you read me? Car nine.*"

"*Loud and clear. What've you got?* "

"*Damnedest thing. Got a call from old George Lassiter over on Bay View, top of the hill there? Lives next to Lou Wagoner that history teacher at the high school. George says somebody left a Jeep with a big Lab in it out in front of her house. Says he went in to check on the woman and the dog found a big puddle of blood in the living room. I need back-up. Let's check it out. Over.*"

* * *

The cop didn't much like the feel of it. Spooky place... pitch-black... haunted in the pouring rain, the windows dark and menacing.

He waited for his partner to join him on the porch. Old

Man Lassiter was already there, his hand wrapped in the collar of the whining, straining dog.

"Where's Ms. Wagoner, do you think? Have you seen her, George?"

"No, I ain't. Don't care to, neither. She's an odd one. That ain't her car though. Her car's gone."

"Jeff, I think that's the psychologist's car. The one we had the bulletin on from Joe at the fire station? They said he had his dog with him."

"Well, I'll go in first. You cover me. George, you stay out, ya hear?"

"The blood's right outside the closed door from the living room. I didn't look in there."

George's voice shook from excitement. He held tightly to the frantic Lab who was struggling to free himself from the old man's grip.

The two men held their flashlights at shoulder level and unsnapped their revolvers.

"Police! We're coming in."

Silence, but for the rain, and then a skittering scratching sound on the hardwood floor on the far side of the room.

"Shit! What was that?"

"Probably just a mouse or maybe a rat from the looks of this place. How could anybody live in this mess? Stinks in here, too."

The cop bent to peer closely at the puddle on the floor that reached to the edge of the door. "Looks like blood, all right."

"Police!"

He threw open the door and froze.

* * *

"Ms. Geoffreys! We just got a dispatch from the squad on the coast highway. They've picked up a woman and transported her to the hospital. They said its Anneka Ericsson."

"My God, Joe! I'm outta here. Call those numbers I gave you and tell them we've found her. Take care of Harry, will ya?"

"No, no! Take the bird with you! Take the bird—Ms. Geoffreys—Oh, MAN!"

The fireman's desperate cries echoed in the wailing wind from the open door.

Nogood was gone.

"BAWWWK, BAWWK! YOU GOT *SOME* BALLS! " shrieked Dirty Harry.

* * *

Spinner lay on a rusted wrought iron bed. The huge canopy hung in tattered shreds, the color gray and faded, some parts crumbling into dust. The bare mattress was lumpy, the pillows filthy and torn.

His mouth hung open. Blood from the wound on his head had saturated his beard and soaked through his white shirt. A dirty old towel lay beside his head, covered with gore, as if someone had tried to help, to stem the vital flow, then given up on the attempt, and fled. He lay against the iron headboard, seemingly lifeless, his face dead white.

The policeman who reached his side first, felt for a pulse at the side of his neck.

"I think he's still breathing. Get an ambulance fast. He's lost too much blood."

The dog seemed to fly through the air landing dead center on the bed where he began to lick his master's face, whimpering pitifully. When the policeman pulled him off, he lifted his head and began to bay, a chilling tune as old as time... lonely as the last wolf left in the forest.

* * *

"Hello, Hello? Can you hear me? Hello?"

"This is the hospital, nurses' station. May I help you?"

"Yes! This is Lainey Dillon. Do you have an Anneka Ericsson there? She would have just been admitted?"

"Yes, we do. Is this a member of the family?"

"No, she has no family here. This is a close friend. Please, how is she?"

"Well, I really shouldn't release—"

"*Please* !"

The nurse lowered her voice.

"Ms. Ericsson will be fine. She's suffering from exposure and fatigue and she was also very agitated. The doctor tranquilized her so she could rest."

"Is she hurt? Is she injured?"

The matronly nurse bent to consult the chart and answered in a kind soothing voice.

"She has a badly wounded arm and several lacerations but she's in no danger. Her condition is listed as stable. You can leave a number and we'll call you if there's any—"

"Can't we see her?"

"There's already a lady here in the lobby. It's Ms. Geoffreys from the high school? The doctor told her no visitors right now. The patient has to rest. Ms. Geoffreys was very persistent. She—"

"Yes, all right. And Spinner—Dr. Hartmann? How is he?"

"I'm sorry." The nurse's tone turned crisp. "We've had no word on Dr. Hartmann's condition. The doctors are with him now."

"Is he alive, then? Just tell me that!"

" . . . Yes, he's alive."

CHAPTER 45

STRANGE SHAPES SWIRLED and spun in Anneka's dreams. A serene and buoyant silhouette wound with sinewy kelp beckoned to her, then twisted and transformed into horror, black as night, clutching, grabbing, stabbing—

"Mourning. MOURNING!"

"Anneka. ANNEKA! It's all right. It's all right. It's me, Destry."

She woke from the dark dream to the anxious faces of her friends hovering over her bed.

A nurse, short and matronly, hurried in, followed closely by a tall man in a white coat.

"You're fine, Ms. Ericcson," soothed the doctor. "You were just dreaming."

Anneka clutched at the man's arm.

"Spinner! She may have killed him! Call the police. You've got to—"

"It's *all right*, Ms. Ericcson. Dr. Hartmann was brought in several hours ago."

Anneka struggled to sit up but the doctor gently eased her back on the pillow.

"Nurse, let's get something to calm—"

"Spinner's here! Are you sure?"

"No doubt about it," said Lainey. She was standing at the foot of the bed, worry creasing her face, tears of relief in her eyes.

"We let all your friends in because they wouldn't go away," said the doctor. "But I'll need you to stay calm. How do you feel? Does that arm hurt?"

Anneka looked at her bandaged arm. It was all coming back. The storm . . . "My dogs! They're in the house. The tree fell on us! And my cat and Ollie! Where's Ollie?"

"They're at my house," said Nogood. "They all got a ride in the firetruck. Not a scratch on any of them. I fried the dogs a couple of steaks and the cat ate a can of my finest albacore."

"Oh, thank you!" Anneka sank back on her pillows and began to cry.

"I understand you've been through quite an ordeal," said the doctor. "You're suffering from shock and exposure and you have a badly wounded arm. There was still a piece of kelp wrapped around it that helped stop your blood loss. I'm amazed you had the strength to do that in the condition you were in."

"I didn't. Mourning Ann did. She—"

"Who?"

Anneka shook her head impatiently. "Nothing. Did you find Lou Wagoner? I pushed her into Big Whale Cove. She was trying to kill me. She killed them all, you know. She was insane."

"Shhhhh. The police are going to want to talk to you, but not yet. A few more minutes with your friends, then I'm having the nurse give you a sedative." The doctor patted her hand awkwardly and left the room.

"But I have to know if Lou's really dead. She was swept away once but she washed back in because she just appeared out of the bushes on the edge of the cove and she had this knife and she wanted to kill me. She—"

Lainey was there, stroking her face. "You're safe, Anneka. Lou's *gone* . Try not to think about her now."

"I killed her, Lainey. I just pushed as *hard* as I could till the ladder broke—"

Anneka sat up and pulled Lainey toward her. Her voice rose higher. "She'd been hiding in my house! Under the trap door. And the day Susanne was killed? She was waiting for me in the mail room but I didn't go in there so she *murdered* Susanne and she wanted Spinner—"

"I'm getting the nurse. I'll be right back," said Skye and hurried from the room.

"We'll talk about it later." Lainey gently pushed Anneka back on the pillows and smoothed the hair back from her face. "After you rest, we can see Spinner."

Anneka felt a sharp prick in her good arm.

* * *

Spinner came tunneling up from the dark fighting all the way. His movements set bells ringing. Tubes hung from his arm and his head hurt. Damn, his head hurt.

And there was something he had to remember. What *was* it? Dread crawled down his arms and probed deep in his gut. A collage of pictures bounced off his memory; pictures of laughing girls, high school girls in a school annual, pictures of Anneka, by the Jeep, laughing in the early morning light—

"*ANNEKA!*"

"Dr. Hartmann, you're awake. I'll get the doctor." And the nurse rustled out in starched no-nonsense white.

* * *

"Shhhhhh! You'll wake him up."

"I want to wake him up. The doctor said we could wake him up."

"Okay, Anneka," Skye said. But we don't want to startle him. Let him wake up gradually."

They were gathered around Spinner's bed, Anneka still in her wheelchair, watching the face of the sleeping man.

"I wish he'd wake up, now. " Anneka whispered to the women clustered around Spinner's bed.

"Don't worry. The doctor said he has a concussion but he's already been conscious and talking. He remembers everything. Up till he was clobbered on the head, that is," Maggie added.

"He could have died from losing all that blood."

"But he didn't die. He's fine. Just be patient."

"She hit him over the head?"

"With a bookend. Then she dragged him into her bed and left a note saying she sure loved him a lot and she'd be right back to fix him dinner!" Skye rolled her eyes.

"Thank God, he's all right. But I want to hear him talk. C'mon Spinner, wake up, " Anneka pleaded.

"How long do you think it'll be before he's up and around? A week, maybe?" Nogood asked.

"I don't know, why?" asked Anneka.

"Cuz he said he'd watch Harry for me during spring break."

Maggie couldn't believe what she was hearing. "Good grief, Nogood! The man's concussed. He was smashed on the head by a lunatic and you want him to baby sit your damn bird!"

"Well . . . he promised. I've finally found a man with opposable thumbs who wants to take me to Mexico."

"You're unbelievable, you know that?" said Skye.

"Well, I can't take Harry to Mexico."

The man in the bed opened one eye.

"Yeah, we've still got diplomatic relations with them."

CHAPTER 46

IN NEW ALBION, the Pacific lapped at the edges of the little harbor reflecting the glow of the full moon and a million bright stars.
Feeling peaceful and serene a young child snuggled into his bedcovers and gazed through his window at the star-splashed sky. He watched as a falling star flashed across the dark indigo night and fell to earth, as bright a falling star as he had ever seen. .

* * *

It was that same brilliant sapphire night that sent Anneka slipping through her door just before dawn. She paused to drink the cool crisp air, raised the hood of her woolen cloak and then ran down the seawalk to the ocean's edge.
She was there at that precise moment the moon slipped into the sea, a perfectly round orb that sent color shimmering in a path toward the shore, a trajectory of pure gold.
A butterfly of cloth fluttered on the wet rocks, moonlight

captured in its silver threads. The reflected light caught Anneka's eye.

Curious...

Cautious of her bandaged arm, she tread carefully on the fragmented basalt to the edge of the scarp, reached out and almost grasped the bit of cloth, when a gust of wind tore it loose and sailed it out to sea. The remnant glimmered for a short time in that molten lane of light, then sank from sight.

Anneka stood perfectly still, just her cloak furled around her in the wind.

Suspended in that moment in time... a woman of the cove.

EPILOGUE

DAWN CREPT SLOWLY in from the East. The first clear rays streaked over the Coastal Range. Sunlight began to dapple the rocks, to reach into the water's black depths, where a body shifted back and forth with the movement of the waves, kelp gently covering and uncovering one unseeing wide eye.

The body did not experience the rays of sun awakening the underwater world. It could not feel the vibrations from the heavy motors of the whale-watching fleets. Could not hear the happy squeals of children sighting their first whale.

The movement from the motors churned the water vigorously and sent the body swirling more deeply into the bed of kelp, limbs twisting over and over in rhythm with the waves.

Printed in the United States
1706